# PRAISE FOR L. R. JONES

"In this devilishly twisty standalone . . . Jones reveals her characters' secrets and motives slowly, expertly ratcheting up the pace before an explosive conclusion. This white-knuckler is not to be missed."

—*Publishers Weekly* (starred review)

# THE WEDDING PARTY

## OTHER TITLES BY L. R. JONES

*You Look Beautiful Tonight*

# THE WEDDING PARTY

*a thriller*

# L. R. JONES

THOMAS & MERCER

Text copyright © 2024 by Julie Patra Publishing, Inc.

Published by Thomas & Mercer, Seattle

www.apub.com

Amazon, the Amazon logo, and Thomas & Mercer are trademarks of Amazon.com, Inc., or its affiliates.

ISBN-13: 9781662508899 (paperback)
ISBN-13: 9781662508905 (digital)

Cover design by Sarah Horgan
Cover image: © faestock / Shutterstock; © Jaroslaw Blaminsky / Arcangel

Printed in the United States of America

*Thank you to my incredible editor, Megha Parekh,
for her insight, vision, and guidance, and most of all,
for believing in me. To Louise Fury, my agent, who
stays in tune with the industry, and the ever-changing
landscape, guiding me through it all.*

# PROLOGUE

## Elsa Ward

*Franklin, Tennessee—*
*Six months ago . . .*

Moxie sticks her wet, cold nose against my cheek and whines. I grumble and eye the clock that reads 7:00 a.m., groaning at the realization that my miniature poodle and her miniature bladder have saved me from oversleeping. Although her bladder isn't the real issue here. Moxie likes her breakfast at exactly seven. I throw away the blanket, and my bones moan with protest. Why can't we retire when our body still loves us as much as we love the freedom to enjoy life?

I grab my robe, and despite Moxie's barking—she's a snarky little thing for twelve whole pounds—I head into the bathroom, where I carry out my morning must-dos. That means I pee, brush my teeth, and fret over my wrinkles and gray hair. Maybe I'll break down and get a face-lift. I am a single woman now that Daniel found himself a younger woman. Bastard.

Once I'm in the kitchen, it's not long until Moxie is scarfing down a fresh bowl of chicken and rice that I made her yesterday. I've barely had time to brew the coffee before the little white devil is yapping and running for the door. "All right, all right, Moxie, but we're going to discuss the order of things after this. Mommy gets coffee first. Everything else, after."

Together we shuffle toward the door—well, I shuffle, and Moxie bounces—and I decide I'll make today's adventure a hunt for a coffeepot with a timer. Then my coffee will be ready when I wake up. I open the door, the thick air of the morning promising a hot Tennessee day, while Moxie rushes into our yard, protected by an electric fence. I glance down to find a white box with a big red ribbon on it. *Whatever.* If Daniel thinks gifts will make me forget the thirty-year-old bimbo he was romancing, he has another thing coming. All those years together, all the trust I had for him, wasted, trashed, lost forever.

Moxie zips past me back inside the house, and I grab the box, lock up, and then walk into the kitchen. I set it on the kitchen table, fill my coffee cup, and then ensure it's well creamed before I sit down in front of the box. I don't know why I hesitate to open it. Perhaps because no matter how done I am with Daniel, we spent a lifetime together, and the betrayal between us is still ripe only a few months later.

I down a sip of caffeine and just do it. I grab the note card that reads only "Elsa Ward" on the front with nothing else and then rip away the bow. I pull off the lid and stare at what's inside. Confused by what I find, I pick it up, and the realization of what is inside hits me. I throw down the "gift" that is no gift at all and I stand up.

It's over.

My life is over.

My God. I don't even know what to do next.

———

"Joe, watch the road! Are you trying to kill us? It's that damn basketball game you're listening to."

"I am watching the road, Marianne," I bite out through clenched teeth, irritated at her nagging. We've been married five years that feel like fifty. At least we're two blocks from home, where I can occupy my man cave and escape her incessant yapping for a few hours. I didn't even like basketball until about year two, when I needed anything but her constant nagging to occupy my mind. I'd divorce her, but she'd take me to the cleaners.

"Stop!" she shouts. "Stop."

I curse at her outburst, about to vocalize my disbelief, when a puppy rushes in front of the car. I slam on the brakes. "What the hell?"

The pup sits in front of the car and I shift into park, opening the door. The minute I'm standing the pooch runs toward me and barks a warning.

Marianne is on the other side of the car. "Isn't that the blonde bimbo's dog whose packages always end up at our house?"

"Elsa," I say, grinding my teeth. Elsa is a kind woman, recently divorced and, while older than Marianne by a good ten years, still better on the eyes and ears. "Yes, it's Elsa's dog. Take the car and I'll return the dog." I scoop the pooch up, and she licks my chin.

"Fine," she says. "Take the damn dog back to her."

Marianne rounds the hood and climbs in the car. I watch her drive away and then hold Moxie up. "Good girl. You gave me a chance to see your mommy tonight." Elsa always invites me in for coffee. Maybe tonight I'll take her up on it.

I step onto her lawn and frown. The front door is open. This doesn't feel right. I set the pup down and she darts toward the porch, up the stairs, and then disappears in the door. I pull my phone from my pocket and then follow in Moxie's footsteps, my heavier body weight causing each step to moan. I enter the house and walk inside.

"Elsa!"

No answer.

I ease into the kitchen and see nothing. Maybe she's not even home and the door didn't latch. I don't know. She parks in the garage, as most of us do here in these parts. It rains too damn much, and that means hail, wind, and tornados. I decide that's what's going on, but still there's a gnawing sensation in my gut.

Unable to just walk out and shut the door until I satisfy the necessity to ensure Elsa is safe, I walk down the hallway calling her name. "Elsa! It's Joe from next door."

I grimace as the smell of copper permeates the air. I know that smell a little too well.

Blood.

I step into her bedroom and grab the wall on either side of me. Elsa is lying in the center of the bed, blood spattered all over the walls, pillows, and blankets. Survival instinct has me scanning the room, looking for an attacker, but I see no one, and I can feel the room's emptiness.

I dial 911 on speaker and hurry to her side. Her lips are blue and her eyes shut. I hold my hand over her mouth, hoping for a trickle of air.

"911. What's your emergency?"

"I need an ambulance now for what looks like a gunshot wound, but"—I scan the bed and room—"I don't see a weapon. She's breathing, but it's weak."

There's a lot of conversation and instructions that follow.

It's an hour later when I hold Moxie in my arms and watch the ambulance drive away.

But I already know that Elsa is as good as dead.

# Chapter One

## CARRIE REYNOLDS

*Denver, Colorado*
*Present day . . .*

In life, there are light moments, moments that twinkle like stars in the sky, moments that stand out even in the darkest of times, giving us joy, strength, and renewed energy. And then there are dark moments that scorch us with pain and torment and leave us desolate, struggling to move forward at all, and when we do, we're walking on eggshells, tentative, afraid of what comes next.

I've known a lot of those dark moments. The first time I felt one, I was twelve. My brother was fourteen. Neither of us saw the car coming. I don't remember much about that day.

Suddenly, he was just—*gone*.

Instead of him and me walking to school together, I walked to school alone. There were no more varsity football games to attend. No more sibling arguments over breakfast. No more video game battles. No more games of hide-and-seek.

Struggling to shake off the horrid place my mind has taken me, I finish filling the wine fridge with the new bottles I picked up on the way home. Oliver, the blessing that man is in my life, sensed I was off today when we talked on the phone and suggested wine and takeout, despite his work on some multimillion-dollar acquisition for Phoenix Technology. Of course, his father decided to retire right after we set our wedding date, which was unexpected. Once Oliver was forced to claim the reins of a multimillion-dollar company, we had to put the wedding off a year. But almost a year later, we've settled into all that is new. Almost.

Reaching back into the wine fridge, I grab a half-full bottle of riesling and pour a glass. We'll open a new bottle when Oliver arrives. I walk to the kitchen island, sit down on a stool, dig into my giant Louis Vuitton bag, and pull out a bottle of pills. Contrary to what I, a nurse, would recommend to my patients, I down my nightly cocktail of medication with my wine before tabbing through an architectural magazine, looking for ideas for the house Oliver and I want to build. After the impending wedding and holidays are past us, of course. Coming right off the holidays to dive into our wedding in January is a big undertaking.

The front door alert goes off, and I quickly slide my pill bottle back in my purse and settle the strap on my seat. Oliver rounds the corner, Mr. Tall, Dark, and Handsome, and so JFK Jr. in his navy suit and tie. Some might say I'm marrying up. Not that I'm horrid or anything. I have nice long brown hair, warm brown eyes, good skin, and a heart-shaped face, but it comes together as rather average. And it's an unsaid thing that I'll always need to lose a little weight. Meanwhile Oliver is a lean, mean muscle machine, eating whatever he wants, while I diet. It's the curse of my life. And being five foot three doesn't help. A few pounds are like pudding pads on my hips.

Oliver sets his briefcase down on the counter behind us, eyeing my wine as he does rather than kissing me. I'd prefer the latter, but we don't always get what we want in life. Don't I know that for a fact.

"Started without me, did you?" he asks, shrugging out of his jacket and settling it on the back of the stool next to mine.

"A few sips," I say, "but I bought some new bottles. Let's try one of those. And where's my takeout?"

"I ordered your favorite. Giovanni's lasagna coming up in"—he glances at the Rolex his father gave him when he took over the company last year—"fifteen minutes, I would guess," he adds.

"Perfection," I say as he kneels in front of the wine fridge and starts reviewing my purchases.

"How was work?" I ask.

"Complicated and exhausting," he says. "But that deal I told you about is coming together."

He actually didn't tell me anything about "that deal," as he calls it, except that it's worth millions for his company and is some sort of an acquisition of a smaller competitor. He's always too exhausted to dive into the nitty-gritty with me. But I've come to know that men share differently than women. They give us pieces, while we read them a book right out of our minds.

"You got that pinot I like," he says, holding up the bottle. "I approve." He pushes to his feet, grabs two glasses, fills them, and then joins me at the island, and we angle toward each other.

"Talk to me," he urges, sliding my hair behind my ear, his touch tender and attentive. "What's going on with you today?"

*Attentive* is really the word I highlight in my mind. Oliver is always attentive and present. No matter what is going on in his life or in the world, when we're together, he's engaged.

"We lost a little boy today." My voice hitches. "It was, uh"—I look away and reach for my wine—"rough." I sip and glance over at him.

"How old?" he asks.

"Twelve, Oliver," I say. "And the mother . . . as you can imagine, she was devastated. You couldn't help but feel her emotions." I ball my fist between my breasts. "Her pain just bled right from her heart and soul to ours, all of us there when it happened, and twisted around us like, like a rope choking the life out of us."

"Holy hell, I can only imagine." Oliver contemplates, sipping his wine. "Just hearing you talk about it gets to me, too. And, babe, I know this was bad timing."

He means the anniversary of my brother's death.

"I was worried about you taking that job in the ER department," he adds, taking this topic one step further, as he always does.

"It's a supervisory role," I remind him. "And a big promotion for me."

"That your parents pressured you to take," he reminds me. "I mean, I get it. Your father runs three hospitals in Houston, and your mother heads the nursing staff for the largest hospital in Texas. You're following in her footsteps, but at what mental health cost?"

"Someone has to do it and do it well."

"And you do. I know you do, and I'm proud of you. You're a hero. And I'm just some guy in a suit you helped save on a rainy night in Houston."

He'd been in town on business when his rental car had caught a rough spot on a narrow, wet road and flipped. He'd broken a rib and an arm. He could have punctured a lung. He was lucky. And so was I that night. I helped save his life, I think, but since then, he's saved me in all kinds of indiscernible ways.

"But you know," he continues, and because I know him, and I know he's about to launch into a protective bear lecture, I head for a detour.

"What *I know*," I say, "is that my mental health is just fine. Made possible by the fact that my parents are in Houston and we're in Denver, thank you, Lord. They micromanage me to the point of causing insanity." The doorbell rings, a blessed relief from the deeper conversation about my history of personal tragedy that had been sure to follow. "That will be the lasagna," I say. "And lasagna makes everything better."

"And the pinot," he says, pushing to his feet and kissing me.

He rushes away to grab the food, and I stand up and hurry about the kitchen, grabbing plates, napkins, and silverware that I set up on the island. The oversize black-and-white granite island is one of the things that sold us on this house. The house itself was Oliver's way of inviting me to live with him, and his gift to me for waiting on the wedding date.

My fingers thrum on the island, and time ticks by a bit too heavily. Curious about what might be taking so long, I head for the front door. I find Oliver resealing what looks like a big white box, a red ribbon hanging from its side.

"Oh. Did we get an early wedding gift?"

Oliver's spine stiffens slightly, and he slides the box under his arm before facing me. "A gag gift, and a bad one."

"I see. Well, I'm sure I'll laugh about it. What is it?"

"Not a chance. I'm not letting you see this."

"You're kidding, right?"

"Not at all."

"Who sent it?"

"It's from one of the groomsmen, Carrie. You'd hate him if I told you who, and I'm not doing that to us right before the wedding. Grab the food if it shows up, babe. I'm going to call and ream out a certain someone."

He doesn't wait for a reply. He walks to his right and into his office, and to my shock, he shuts the door. He never shuts the door. The card for the gift is lying on the hall table, and I pick it up and glance at the front of the envelope. It reads "Oliver Phoenix," not "Oliver and Carrie." That gift was for Oliver, and the writing is distinctively female.

My hands begin to shake and my stomach twists in knots. I walk to the office door and tentatively turn the handle. The door is locked.

# Chapter Two

I wake the next morning to cool sheets and a comfortable mattress, sighing in contentment and reaching for Oliver. And reaching yet again, stretching my hands and feet to find him with no success. I sit straight up, the sheet falling away from my naked body, my gaze scanning the dimly lit room to find I'm alone. Even the bathroom is dark. I glance at the clock—it reads 6:00 a.m., which is before our normal wake-up time. I snag my robe from the end of the bed, my body heavy from last night's bedtime activities, because what better way to get me to stop talking about that box with the red ribbon than sex, right?

My feet find my pink, fluffy slippers, and I rush forward and travel a fast path to the kitchen, which is dark, but the aroma of freshly brewed coffee teases my nostrils. I flip on the light to find the pot full and a note sitting in front of it. I snatch it up and read: *I didn't want to wake you. I have to close up this deal I'm working on. Work now, play together soon. I can't wait to call you my wife.—Love, Oliver.*

I read the note three times. Nothing about it feels right, and my mind goes back to dinner last night. I'd just pulled the food from the take-out bag when he reappeared. "Smells good," he said. "Did I tell you me and my sister had a disagreement today?"

I wanted to ignore the question and push him about the box, but Oliver and Natalie rarely fight, despite the fact that he's CEO and president of the company while she, as the oldest, is in the lesser role of VP. I couldn't just dismiss something I knew impacted Oliver negatively. So I set the box aside, with the intent of coming back to it. Instead, we ate, talked about Natalie, and then ended up in bed. The topic of the box had been firmly shoved under the sheets, so to speak.

I set the note on the counter, walk toward the front of the house, and end up at the door of Oliver's office. It's open. Of course it's open. With the exception of last night, the door is never shut, most certainly never locked. I enter the room, which is really more a den than an office. A heavy oak desk is the centerpiece, with a sitting area complete with cozy chairs and bookshelves, lined with a variety of books, to the left. I scan for the box and see nothing. I round the desk and open the credenza against the wall, with no luck in my hunt for the gag gift. Settling into the leather chair, I begin opening and shutting drawers, looking for I don't know what. Obviously, a box isn't going to be in a drawer full of hanging files. I'm just looking. For something, anything, that tells me what is going on with Oliver right now.

I find nothing.

And yet, whatever was in that box was not nothing.

It was the reason Oliver was more passionate last night, the reason he kept telling me he loved me. There was a desperation to him that, while all-consuming, was not him. The something I'm looking for has already found me. And it's trouble. I feel it in my bones.

# Chapter Three

My morning at Denver's Memorial Hospital starts with another child and another mother freaked out about her baby. The little girl has meningitis, which is not as common as most people might think and is really quite lethal. Fortunately, Dr. Mathis, one of our top pediatricians, steps in, and the little one responds to the medication and we turn her circumstances around rapidly.

Feeling harried, I step into the facility break room for coffee, and he joins me. He's a tall man, with dark hair, very TV doctor–like with his good looks. All the nurses swoon over him, but he is, of course, married. Though warm and friendly, at least with me. But then, I'm that average girl who never looks higher than her status—except once. And I'm marrying that one.

"You're good with kids," he comments, filling his cup. "You going to get pregnant and retire to raise your kids with that rich fiancé of yours?"

"I don't actually want kids," I confess. "So you're stuck with me here for a very long time."

He leans on the island next to me, appearing genuinely interested in what I have to say, perhaps a little too much. "No kids? Really? Why not, might I ask?"

My defenses bristle under his scrutiny. "You don't have kids."

"Yeah, well, that's because my wife and I barely like each other. We're divorcing."

"Oh," I say. "I, uh, didn't know."

"I'm not making it public," he says. "And I'd appreciate it if you don't."

"No. No, of course not. I'm . . . sorry?" It's a question. I never really know if divorce is a grief-type situation or one of celebration. I think it's like a medical treatment: often highly individual.

"I'm not sorry," he says. "And I see enough sick and dying kids around this place. I don't need one of my own to worry about." With that, he pushes off the counter and walks away.

I think he might have been digging around about the state of my marriage, for personal reasons, which obviously backfired on him—and me, for that matter. He's hit a nerve, one that I have nightmares about, and rather frequently.

I've always believed that if I were to have a child, that child would end up dead.

Oliver dismisses it as fear of such a great responsibility, but there's more to it than fear. And one day we'll face that truth. Until then, I don't intend to think about it.

By lunchtime, I'm ready to throw my wedding diet to the birds. Which is how I end up at Mama Mac's, where mac 'n' cheese rules, with Lana Melody, the newest nurse on our staff. But despite Lana's mere six-month tenure at the hospital, and our opposing places in life right about now—she just went through a nasty divorce, while I'm marrying my Prince Charming—we have become fast and, dare I say, close friends. A feat made easier as Erin Sterling, my other best friend, has a dislike of Oliver that has become a wedge between us. But then, Erin doesn't like men. Lana just doesn't like assholes. Her words, not mine.

"The card," I announce after telling her about the box, "was written in distinctively female script."

"And you know this how?" she asks, sipping her diet drink.

"I saw it with my own eyes. He took it or I'd show you."

"My ex wrote like a girl. No kidding." She grabs her phone and tabs through photos, adding, "I keep a copy of my divorce decree so anytime I feel sad, I can give it a look-see and I'm all cheered up. Here." She slides her phone in front of me and shows me the signature line. "Like a girl. Dr. Fenley does, too."

I scan her ex's signature and she's right. I'd call it feminine. "Okay," I say, handing back her phone. "Signature aside, why not just show me what was in the box? I'm a big girl. I can take a joke, even a bad one. And then he shut the door in my face."

"Okay," Lana says, mimicking me as she digs her fork into the center of her Mexican mac, "I see why the shut door bothered you, but"—she holds up a finger and takes a bite, swallowing before she continues—"what if it was something just really raunchy and gross? He loves you. He wants to protect you."

"What in the world could be that gross?"

She shrugs, shoving her blonde hair behind her ears and waving a fork as she says, "You know"—she stabs a cluster of pasta—"guys are universally gross together. Believe me, it's not just in Colorado. I saw it in Boston, too. Though thank God I'm back home in Denver. The men aren't that different, but the Tex-Mex is killer." She motions to her mac. "Even this has green chilies done right."

At this point, my fork is down, and I'm ignoring my mac, which I can't afford to eat anyway, while she's a waif of a woman who can eat what she wants. "Raunchy?" I ask, my voice appropriately appalled. "Like what?"

"Hmm. Well. Maybe something like topless photos of all the women they're bringing to his bachelor party. Immature, yes, but isn't that kind of what bachelor parties are supposed to be?"

"We're having a combo party in Estes Park. All the women and men will be there. You know this."

"But they're going on their way and we're going on our way midevening," she says. "There will be naked women at their event. Don't fool yourself and think otherwise. And that means nothing. It's a tradition. The last time he can see another woman's breasts. It wasn't for my ex, but my ex was an asshole. Oliver loves you. I see it in his eyes when he looks at you."

"I don't want him looking at a bunch of women's naked breasts." I bristle, uncomfortable with this idea, in what one might call an excessive way considering said tradition, but I don't care.

"Exactly," she says. "And now you see why he might have hidden the box. *To protect you.* And as he said, to keep you from hating the guy who did that." She lowers her voice conspiratorially. "Maybe one of his groomsmen has the hots for you and wants to break you up. And maybe Oliver knows."

Now she's weaving a story of pure craziness, but somehow, she's made me feel better. Almost. Mostly. I'm somewhat better.

# Chapter Four

Oliver calls me just after my return from lunch. "Sorry for sneaking out this morning."

"I was shocked to wake up without you," I say rather primly despite my efforts to sound natural.

"Babe," he says softly. "Don't be angry. This competitor we're acquiring is massive for the company. I meant to tell you more about it last night, but we got a little distracted, you know?"

My cheeks heat. "Yes. I suppose we did."

"How are things today? Better?"

"Not as bad as yesterday," I say.

"Good. Two more weeks until the bachelorette party and three months until our wedding. Almost there. And you're almost mine."

We hang up and I'm bothered by the call. I feel off with Oliver. It's a feeling that stays with me most of the afternoon and is reinforced when just one hour before my shift ends, he sends me a text: Final stretch of this race. I'm going to have to work late.

"He's having an affair," I whisper to myself, silently adding that it's really the only explanation for the box and his behavior.

# Chapter Five

My shift ends an hour after expected, and I decide I'm driving myself crazy with this affair mumbo jumbo. Oliver is not having an affair. He's working hard, which deserves my appreciation. I leave the hospital and drive to his favorite taco joint, not far from his downtown offices, and order us both food. I arrive at his building a bit after seven, and the guard, Henry, who knows me well, greets me and motions me on up.

I arrive on the twenty-fifth floor to the empty reception area of Oliver's office, which is the norm at this hour. With the lay of the land on hand, I round the desk and enter a hallway that leads to Oliver's corner office. I step inside his doorway to find Allison, his blonde bombshell of an assistant, on his side of the desk, leaning over him, staring at the MacBook screen. At the moment, there is ample cleavage present, while her ass, which is squeezed into a pencil skirt, is in the air. Thankfully Oliver's eyes are on the screen, not her.

Allison, who predates me with Oliver, says she's gay.

I don't believe her.

"I need this tighter," Oliver says. "It's wordy. Cut it back."

"Right," she says. "Of course." She straightens and her eyes land on me. "Carrie."

Oliver's gaze shoots to mine, and his expression warms. There is nothing in his reaction that holds defensiveness or resistance to my presence.

"Tell me you didn't eat already," I say. "I brought Margarita George's, enough for all."

"We didn't," Oliver says. "And I'm starving." He runs a hand through his hair. "And exhausted, with at least another two hours left to work."

"Well, let's eat, then," I offer. "And you can get back to work."

"None for me," Allison says. "I'm on a diet. Which sucks, but you know, it is what it is."

She's on a diet. *Whatever.*

She lifts the papers in her hand. "I'll get this done." She hurries around the desk, and I step out of the doorway to allow her exit. Once I'm inside the office, I shut the door. Oliver stands up, stretches, and meets me at the conference table. A few minutes later, we've fallen into a familiar place—that place that is "us"—and we're eating, laughing, and talking.

When dinner is over and he's back behind his desk, having thoroughly kissed me, I should leave, but I hesitate. I step to the opposite side of the desk. "The box is bothering me, Oliver."

"Wasted energy," he says softly. "I threw it away. We're better than raunchy jokes, and I told the bastard as much."

*Raunchy.*

There is that word again. Is it that commonly associated with bachelor parties?

Maybe it is.

"Let me get back to work," Oliver says. "That way you don't have to wake up alone tomorrow. Or save me when I fall asleep at the wheel and crash my car."

"Don't say things like that," I chide.

"Just a joke," he says. "Thank you for dinner. It was a nice break, but *go home*. I'll see you soon."

And so I do. I go home.

Alone.

I settle onto a barstool with a glass of wine again and pop another handful of pills. I have a momentary flashback to a time in my life when I'd thought everyone was more blessed than me. My mother had said, *"You only live the fairy-tale life when you decide you deserve it. You get what you give. If you expel negative energy, it comes back to you."*

Those words had changed my perspective, which changed my life.

Oliver didn't cheat on me. He's not cheating on me. And the box meant nothing.

I choose my fairy-tale life. I choose to marry my Prince Charming.

# Chapter Six

## ANDREA "ANDI" CASTLE

Drinks with a friend, with not a murder in sight. It's a novel idea, at least for me, when murder is my job and my job rules my life.

It's Saturday night, and I'm sitting at a corner table in a dimly lit, hip martini bar in downtown Denver with Lana, an old friend from college who I haven't seen in years, not since she got married and moved away. "You look great," I say, and it's the truth. She's just as blonde, petite, and pretty as I remember, with loads of personality.

"I look divorced," she complains. "I mean, thanks. I do appreciate the compliment, but Lord help me, I'm thirty-two and a divorcée. How screwed up is that?" She presses her hands to her face. "And I'm sunburned. I had winter skin in Boston. Now I'm back to getting sun all the time. My skin is angry." She eyes me. "You look beautiful, Andi. Or should I say, FBI Agent Andrea Castle, badass profiler? Kind of like Jaclyn Smith from the original *Charlie's Angels*. Murder does a girl right, eh?"

I laugh. "I don't think any of Charlie's Angels were profilers, and how do you even know that version of the Angels? I think they're your mother's age now, but thank you for the compliment. Aside from the divorce, how was Boston?"

"Cold, but pretty. And they have ticks."

"*We* have ticks. This is Colorado."

"I've never seen a tick here in my life. And no matter what, they're worse there. Those bastards will suck your blood almost as quickly as my ex-husband did my bank account."

A remark that reminds me that Lana comes from a family retail empire and lots of money, but she rarely shows it or talks about it, mostly because her father is hard on her. She's helping save lives, but from what she told me, he doesn't approve of her career choices one little bit.

Lana waves at the waiter and points to her nearly empty glass. "Another chocolate martini," she calls out, and immediately turns her attention back to me. "He dipped his stick, and now I have to *pay him*. It's ridiculous." She holds up a hand. "I need to talk about something else. This is still raw."

"I can tell. I get it," I add. "I have a few of those topics. So, let's try this. Are you still a nurse?"

"Yes. I love nursing, but I've spent six long months in the ER right now, which is not my favorite. I'm hoping to get back to pediatrics."

"I've heard the ER is brutal."

"That's an understatement. It's a bloody, violent nightmare. And the doctors are assholes and you can't even blame them. They're under pressure. They are the life or death of everyone who walks through the door. But the death is just too much for me. I don't know how you do it. Murder is what you do. It's *your zone*."

"It's necessary," I say. "Just as the ER is to saving lives."

She sips her martini and studies me. "You just caught some big serial killer, right? That creep who killed people with spider poison?"

I down most of my martini and now I'm the one flagging the waiter for another. "And here we are, riding this conversation right into *my* taboo topic," I say. "But yes. The Spider Man, the press called him. And after weeks now, they're still obsessed with me and him. He might as well be the ex-husband who just won't go away."

"Well, then, Jesus help us both," Lana says. "No talking about assholes. The whole lot of them." She shifts the topic. "Is your father still a badass?"

Good grief, she still has a crush on my father. But then, so does everyone I know who's ever met him since I was a teenager, including the men, even if it's just a manly-man crush. "I thought we weren't talking about assholes?"

"Oh, come on. Your pops is a legend, not an asshole. A badass single father and widower." She holds up a hand. "Sorry. I don't mean to downplay your mom's car accident."

"I was ten." I sip my martini. "I'm not that sensitive, not about her, but my father is another story." Which is the truth. I've learned how to compartmentalize the death of my mother and the reactions of others to her passing. My father can't be compartmentalized. He's too in my face and everyone else's.

Apparently unable or unwilling to catch a hint, Lana wiggles an eyebrow. "Did he remarry?"

"Do *not* even think about dating him."

"That's a no," she says, smiling coyly. There is nothing about Lana that is coy.

"For all his faults, that man loved my mother. I don't think anyone will ever win his heart again."

She grins. "I'm not really worried about his heart."

"Okay, that's enough," I warn. "Stop now. He's *my father.*"

The waiter sets Lana's chocolate martini on the table and takes her empty glass. I accept my new drink as well with a thank-you to the waiter.

"And I'll remind you that he rides all the Frank Castle / Punisher comparisons to the point of unhealthy," I add. "Like he's his own Marvel character. You don't want that in your life. He's just Eddie Castle, a PI who got kicked off the force for use of force. That's not badass."

"Isn't he still contracted by the Denver PD?"

"To do all the dirty work?" I ask. "Yes."

"And didn't he get kicked off the force for beating up a guy who raped a woman?"

"Yes," I say. "What's your point?"

"Well, they didn't want to kick him off. They were pressured. And he's kind of a badass."

"You weren't there that day," I say tightly, telling her what I've never shared with anyone. "I was."

"You were there when he beat that guy up? No way. I thought that was back when you were in high school."

"It was," I confirm. "He'd picked me up from school when his case blew up. He took me with him." I sip my martini, thinking back to that day, when I'd gotten worried about him and sneaked out of the car. I'd watched him beat the guy to a pulp. And then I'd watched him get cuffed and put in the back of a patrol car. Being my father's daughter is exactly why I let the FBI recruit me out of college. It was my path. Not my father's.

Except the Spider Man case threatened to prove that I'm just like him.

"A change of subject is obviously needed," Lana says, drawing me back into the moment. "So here we go. On to another topic. I'll lead. While I'm on dating sites meeting losers and feeling awkward, tell me something good about your love life."

"Funny thing about hunting serial killers—it scares men off." I leave off the part about me having an on-again, off-again thing with my boss, which is as inappropriate as it sounds. We're on a special task force that operates outside the normal constraints of the bureau. And now, I think, I'm just making excuses for my behavior. Good Lord, maybe I'm more my father's daughter than I realized.

"I hate to say it," Lana teases, "but I can kind of see why. I'm honestly not sure why I'm your friend." She sips her martini. "I guess because I'd date just about anyone now, even a serial killer."

"If you ever do date a serial killer, at least I have handcuffs you can borrow."

We both start laughing, chatting a bit before she says, "This is fun. I needed this girls' night out, and I forgot how much we click, but we do. We really do. Therefore," she adds dramatically, "I have a proposition for you."

"Oh no," I say. "Please tell me this is not like that time you convinced me to go to that frat party."

"That frat party was fun."

"You aren't the one who was locked in a bathroom filled with sweaty guy socks for an hour as a joke," I say. "You were off making out with some guy and didn't even know. I think I decided that night to join law enforcement, with plans to arrest everyone who did that to me."

"So, see. You can thank me. That night defined your career. And it's not a frat party, but—"

"Oh God," I say, sipping my drink. "Any sentence with a 'but' from you is not good."

"That's a character attack. How dare you?" she chides in mock offense, before she adds, "I'm going to a party in Estes Park next weekend—it's this combo bachelor/bachelorette party. Weird, I know, but whatever. I've become fast friends with the bride—she's helped me adjust to working in the ER. I have to go, but I'm socially awkward these days. The post-divorce 'find myself' progress is going rather slowly. I could sure use some support. Please come with me."

"You are not even a little socially awkward. No party for me."

She doesn't give up. "It's at that hotel where Stephen King wrote *The Shining*. It's supposed to be haunted, which is kind of cool."

"The last thing I need is some killer I put away coming back to haunt me at some spooky hotel. No, thank you."

"Screw the ghosts. We'll eat, drink, and shop. It'll be fun."

"The bride doesn't know me."

"The bride is supersweet and easygoing. She told me to bring a friend if it made me more comfortable. If you coming along with me convinces me to go, she'll be thrilled."

"No party for me," I say, and this time I firmly change the subject. "Tell me what's going on with your family. How are they?"

She sighs dramatically. "I'm going to ask again," she promises, but she lets the subject die, at least for now. She moves on to tell me a bit about her family's retail empire, which she has boycotted because of her parents' controlling nature. I sympathize. I didn't exactly boycott the family business like she did, but I've boycotted the control my father has over my life.

When our girls' night wraps up, I head to the bathroom, and I'm still in the hallway by the bar when my phone buzzes with a text message from Aiden, my on-again, off-again relationship and boss: How are drinks with your friend?

I stop walking and reply: I was socially acceptable. I didn't talk about murder for once. Well, not in my customary graphic detail.

Miracles do happen, he responds. How about I come over and bring tacos?

On most nights I'd likely say yes, but something about the whole forbidden nature of our relationship feels kind of dirty right now. I reply: Rain check.

I don't offer an explanation. And he won't push me for one, but I have a sense lately that might change. I'm not sure what to do with that, and I don't want to think about it right now.

I head on into the bathroom, and while I'm at the sink washing my hands, a midthirties woman, brunette like myself, primps her hair and glances in the mirror at me. "You're Andrea Castle, right?"

*Hello, reporter,* I think. "And I'm obviously going to need another drink, because what comes next is either Spider Man or Eddie Castle," I say dryly.

"Spider Man," she states. "Can I just steal a moment?"

"Do you know who my father is?"

"I do. Why?"

"Ask him about Spider Man. I'm certain he'll have more to offer than me."

"What can he tell me?"

"Probably how pretty or obnoxious you are, depending on his mood."

With that, I leave the bathroom.

My father hates reporters. No matter what he does, they never hate him. And she's pretty. He'll thank me for the referral. The two of them will be a match made in heaven.

Once I'm at the table where Lana waits, I snap up my coat, thankful we've already paid the bill. "There's a reporter here," I say. "It's time to leave."

Her eyes go wide. "Oh no. Okay." She grabs her coat and purse and we head for the door, exiting the bar. Once we're on the sidewalk, we both huddle into our coats with the damp cold of an October night. Colorado is an odd fellow in late October, often warm in the day and quite chilly at night.

We cut right toward the parking lot and Lana asks, "You sure you don't want to escape to Estes Park with me?" We pause at the hoods of our side-by-side vehicles.

After weeks of being stalked by the media, I've had enough. I turn to face her. "You know what?" I say. "I *will* go. I'm off for two more weeks. Maybe if they can't find me, the press will move the heck on, and I can go back to work in peace."

She grins. "Perfect. It'll be fun."

We chat through the travel arrangements and a few minutes later, I climb into my car and crank up the heat. I don't know about the fun Lana has predicted, but she's right. I need a break, and not from my job or the press. From the me that only I know, which is a little too like my father. I need to get my head back on straight.

# Chapter Seven

I don't know how to talk to people if it's not about dead bodies, murder, and alibis. I just don't. I don't pretend otherwise. That's why Aiden and I get along. After years in law enforcement, he's like me. Translation: he has no social skills. Date night to us is takeout and a murder file. In other words, why, why, *why* did I agree to attend a party of *any kind*, let alone one in another city that ensures I'll have to travel with a friend I haven't seen in years? My resistance and second thoughts are so extreme that I don't start packing until thirty minutes before Lana will be at my house.

At present, I'm staring into my closet, wondering which of my numerous dresses fit and don't fit since I've worn none of them in far too long. The idea of dressing up is not such a bad thing. I like dresses. I like being a woman. And truth be told, it's been a long time since I was a woman, not just an FBI agent. And I'm certainly not worried the dresses will soften me up and hurt my job or backbone. There's no reason I can't be a woman and do my job and do it well. I'm actually thinking that maybe, just maybe, I need to be a bit more human right about now. Which, I remind myself, is why I need this weekend.

The doorbell rings and I grimace. Lana's early and I'm not even close to done packing. I abandon my hunt for dresses and race down the stairs, but I don't fling the door open as many would, not when I know all too well how many monsters who look like average men and women walk this earth. Instead, I pause, glance through the blinds covering a small window at the right of the door, and find Carson Whitlock standing on my porch. Whit, as I call him, and not to his liking, worked the Spider Man case with me. I have a love-hate relationship with him for about a hundred reasons, which he'll probably make me list before he leaves.

He has a short memory.

I do not.

I open the door to bring him into view. He's a big, broad, fit man with dark hair and a goatee speckled with a hint of gray.

"What are you doing here?" I demand.

"Don't hate me," he says, holding up two cups. "I brought Starbucks. White mocha. Your favorite," he singsongs.

"I can't be bribed."

"This is Starbucks. Yes, you can."

He'd be right any other time. But not this time. Not after he went all Eddie Castle on Spider Man by beating the shit out of him, and kept on beating him, even after he was unconscious. He made me lie for him and say we found him that way. Okay, he didn't make me. I did it on my own, and too easily.

When I don't move, he says, "I fucked up, Castle, but he killed six people, and one of them was a kid. The kid got to me. Let me come in."

I hesitate, but damn it, we were friends. I think we still are, but I just don't know. And he has saved my life, and vice versa, more than once. I take the cup. "Only because you have coffee." I sip the warm, sweet beverage, which hits the spot oh so well. "And I have to pack for a trip, so follow me to the bedroom." I turn and start walking, leaving him to shut the door.

I'm back in the bedroom when he catches up. "Where you headed?" he says, leaning on the doorframe.

"Estes Park," I say, walking into the bathroom and grabbing several items before returning to the bed and my bag. "A bachelor/bachelorette combo party, whatever that means. A friend convinced me to go."

"Hell yeah. Sounds fun. I'll go with you. Lots of drinking and stumbling back to the hotel room and shit. I'm in."

I give him a side-eye. "You're not going with me."

"Whatever. I've got a case anyway. That's why I'm here. To get you to profile this asshole for me."

"How do you have a case?" I challenge, straightening to study him. "We're on forced leave. Remember?"

"How can I not remember that stupid counselor asking me all about my feelings, like I'd let Spider Man get in my head."

"He did get in your head."

"And yours. I'm cleared to go back to work anyway. I don't know why they're making me take off two more weeks. You cleared?"

"Yeah, I'm cleared," I say, and just like him, I had to do the whole feelings thing with the counselor. "And yes, I have to take off two more weeks." I get back to the real topic at hand. "How do you have a case?" I repeat.

"About that," he says in that tight, thin-lipped way he speaks when he knows I won't like what he has to say. "It's a side gig. Contract job."

I lower my chin and pin him in a stare. "My father," I accuse, because he worships him. All of law enforcement worships him. "You're working for my father."

"Yes, but—"

"Are you kidding me right now? Acting like my father is what almost got us both fired."

"I need to work, Castle. You might not need to work, you might want to luxuriate in Estes Park, but I need to work. When I don't work, I drink, I fuck around. I get in trouble." He motions to his head. "I get in my own head too much, and I lose my mind."

I draw in a breath and let it out. I've only worked with him for two years, but he's got ten years of this job on me, and I've seen how he gets in his head and it ends no place good. But I also know what's going on here. My father has been trying to get me to work with him for pretty much my entire career. "You aren't roping me into working for my father, and yes, you can tell him I said that. You don't need me to profile for you."

"It's a big case."

"They all are," I remind him.

"But this PI stuff actually pays big, and we don't have rules."

"Which might be why my father was hired to help, but it'll also be why you get fired."

"Or I quit and work for your father."

"There's a smart decision," I say dryly.

"What if I said we have three people dead and a potential serial killer?"

"I'd say don't get killed before I get back to work and can do it myself."

"Come on, Castle."

"Stop calling me that," I snap.

"You call me Whit. I call you Castle. *Castle.*"

The doorbell rings again. "That's my friend." I glance at my watch. "Crap. I'm late. Go entertain her, but don't flirt with her," I warn because he's the biggest flirt I've ever known. "Lana is her name, but not your game." I shoo him away.

He gives me a two-finger salute. "Yes, Agent Castle." He disappears into the hallway.

I start tossing things into my bag, no longer taking my normal care and time in all things that require preparation. Exactly seven minutes later, I'm lugging my bag down the stairs while Lana laughs at whatever Whit is saying to her. I leave my bag at the bottom of the stairs and head into the living room, where I find Lana batting her blue eyes at Whit.

"No," I say. "He's off limits. Believe me, I'm doing you a favor." I step between her and Whit, facing him. "Go home."

"What about my case?"

"No," I say. "And tell my father I know he took a bottle of my cherry wine the last time he was over. I want it back. They aren't making it anymore."

He stares down at me and smirks. "All right. I'll email the file to you." With that, he turns and heads for the door. I wait until he exits the house, and I turn to find Lana all wide-eyed and smiles.

"He's interesting," she says. "And I do like a man with muscles."

"Oh, please. The man barely showers. Believe me, I know. I've done plenty of stakeouts with him." I grab my bag. "Estes Park, here we come," I say, and funny how a visit from Whit, which might as well have been my father, has me looking forward to the future, and a weekend, just one weekend, without a murder to solve. And yet, as we load into Lana's BMW for that murder-free weekend, I'm thinking about the case Whit is working on. I'm thinking about murder.

# Chapter Eight

I once read that control freaks don't love heights. I've never considered myself a control freak, no matter what anyone else claims. This trip aims to prove me wrong.

Apparently, the town of under six thousand is at a ridiculously high altitude, and our path to the hotel is up and around a narrow, icy road with a drop-off on the passenger side—my side. In other words, Lana is driving, which I agree to but I also quickly change my mind.

I don't trust anyone this much with my life. "Stop," I order, about a fourth of the way up the snowy mountain. "I have to drive."

"I'm fine," she says. "This doesn't bother me at all."

*Okay,* I think. *Whatever.* "It bothers me."

She laughs. "You don't trust my driving?"

"To be frank, no."

"I'm insulted!"

"I can live with that. Now pull over. Get out. And let me drive."

She's laughing as we switch seats and I end up behind the wheel. In control.

Maybe I am a control freak.

Finally, near dusk, we arrive at the Stanley Hotel, a big white mansion of a place, nestled beside the towering mountaintops.

"By the way," Lana says, "I'm assigned to a haunted room. Hopefully, you won't be saving me from any nasty ghosts. This one is supposed to be a cowboy that stands at the end of the bed and stares at you."

I tilt my head to study her, looking for the insanity beneath the surface. "You paid to sleep in a room with a Peeping Tom? Really? Please tell me the appeal of this."

"It's not my idea. It's the bride's. She insisted all her girls—I guess I'm one of her girls now—have the full haunted experience. You can't say no to the bride."

"Oh yes I can." And to prove that point, once we're at the check-in desk, I quickly go to work snagging a room that isn't a fabled haunted one. "I need a room that has never seen a ghost. Ever. And I mean *never*."

The hotel staff of three behind the counter all laugh. I'm not laughing. They haven't seen real monsters. I have. Seeing a dead guy walking is not fun for me. In fact, the idea of a perfect weekend is me not seeing anyone dead at all.

"Lana!"

At the sound of Lana's name, she and I both turn to find a pretty brunette racing toward us, and considering her T-shirt says BRIDE, my exceptional investigative skills tell me that she's the bride. Or rather, bride-to-be, technically. Lana is embraced by "the bride," who then casts me a smile. "You must be Andrea Castle."

"Andi," I amend. "Call me Andi."

"The FBI agent," she adds. "I've never met a real FBI agent." She offers me her hand. "I'm Carrie Reynolds, which of course you figured out by now. But it seems I'm kind of starstruck and excited."

I shake her hand and clarify what I must have misheard. "By me?"

"Of course by you. You're a real-life FBI agent." She holds up her hands. "Talk about girl power and all that stuff."

I wave that off. "Believe me, law enforcement is a bunch of tedious work. I'm about as exciting as a *Golden Girls* rerun and a peanut butter sandwich, minus the jelly."

She laughs. "That's funny, but us true crime buffs see things a little differently. My God, watching those shows makes you appreciate our law enforcement. And my God, there are so many dumb people killing other people and thinking they can get away with it. I'm sure you hope for the smart ones to at least feel challenged."

"If only they were all dumb," I say, and with a shift back to her, I add, "Congratulations on your upcoming wedding."

"Thank you," she says. "It's exciting. It's not until the new year, but we thought the Halloween party would be fun for the bridal party."

"It's a unique twist for sure," I agree.

"What's really fun is you being here." Carrie turns to the clerks. "Give her 217"—she glances at me—"the room Stephen King stayed in when he wrote *The Shining*." She turns back to the clerks. "She's an FBI agent. Maybe she can figure out the secrets of that room."

"Oh no," I say, and now I'm holding up my hands. "I'll take a regular room. Save the scary stuff for your real guests."

"Nonsense," she replies. "You are a real guest. I insist. This will be loads of wonderful."

Lana gives me a look and says, "What the bride wants, the bride gets."

"That's me." Carrie grins. "Give me my thirty seconds of fame and authority. It's the last you'll see of it." Someone calls her name, and she waves before she says, "Gotta run. Drinks at eight in the bar, both of you. Don't be late."

She hurries away, and I grimace at Lana but say nothing. I turn to face the hotel counter, and a clerk slides a key in front of me. "Enjoy room 217. It's one of our most in-demand rooms."

*Of course it is,* I think.

Of course it is.

# Chapter Nine

## Carrie

I decide I need to start drinking rather quickly or I'll end up confronting each and every one of the groomsmen about who sent that box and what was inside.

Oliver's closest friends, all members of his cigar club, are gathered at the building adjacent to the Stanley, known as the Lodge, for drinks. Once I've coordinated the weekend events with the hotel staff, I head in that direction to update Oliver on a few details about tomorrow night's big party and events. The Lodge resembles a giant old-fashioned house. When I arrive, I find Josh, the best man, and Cade, a groomsman, on the porch beside a large white banister, sipping whisky and chatting.

Both men smile at me, and Josh waves me forward. Returning their smiles, I hurry up the wide steps, feeling blessed to quite like Josh and Cade, since they are, in fact, Oliver's closest friends. At thirty-four, Josh is Oliver's age and especially kind. He's often in our company and seems oblivious to his young Leonardo DiCaprio–ish good looks and massive success as a corporate attorney at Phoenix Technology. Cade is nice enough as well, though a bit older, in his forties, and while not as good-looking, he sports an excess of arrogance. But then, aren't all surgeons arrogant? My exposure says, oh yes, they are.

"Seen any ghosts yet?" I ask, completing my climb to join them.

"The ghosts of whisky past," Josh indicates. "We're about a bottle in so far."

"Which is by design," Cade adds. "It's our way of being so damn mellow the ghosts won't feel threatened."

I snort. "Mellow? That's not what I've heard about you two and whisky. There was that arm-wrestling incident."

Josh laughs. "Oliver actually arm-wrestled the CEO of one of the largest banks in the country. And at a high-end cigar bar, no less."

"At your prodding," I remind him. "That could have gone badly. He could have made an enemy."

"And yet, he didn't," Josh reminds me. "Now he's investing in Oliver in all kinds of ways left and right."

"He's got a point," Cade says.

"Speaking of Oliver," I say, "where is he?"

"No idea," Cade replies. "He was here and then just kind of disappeared."

I eye Josh, who replies with, "What he said."

"He went to his room to work," Nick Ross, another groomsman, the CFO of some security company, calls out from a seat on the porch.

My fingers curl into my palm. Oliver promised me no work this weekend. Josh must read my reaction, offering me his version of comfort, his voice low and for my ears only, and Cade's as he's right here with us. "This deal he's trying to close will set your kids up for life," he says. "He's looking out for your future."

I have two thoughts. One: it seems odd to me that Josh doesn't know that Oliver and I don't want kids. Oliver and Josh are like brothers. And two: yes, Oliver wants to take care of me, but it's unlike him to leave guests unattended. He's not himself right now. He hasn't been ever since that box arrived.

"I'm going to check on him," I say. "Don't forget the ghost tour tonight at ten." With that, I turn away from the guys and begin tracking a path back to the main hotel. And I do so confused. Oliver and I already celebrated the success of his new acquisition over a week ago.

# Chapter Ten

Oliver and I are in room 407, which is said to be haunted by a lord of some sort who used to own land here where the property sits. Apparently, he still feels he has a claim to ownership and likes to move things around and frustrate those staying in the room. I doubt we'll actually have anything crazy happen to us in our room, or the hotel in general, but it would be nice to just be with Oliver and find the fun in all of this. There is a rich history here at this hotel, and Oliver loves history. I need to find out what's going on with him once and for all and, if it's really work stress, help him free himself from the responsibility.

I slide my keycard and open the door to find Oliver sitting at the desk, busy at work on his MacBook. "Hey," I say, entering the room with a bottle of whisky that one of his buddies handed me downstairs. "Look what I have. Compliments of Trevor."

Trevor is yet another member of Oliver's cigar club and some sort of cable TV exec. Apparently, cigars and whisky go together, though I wouldn't know or pretend to understand. That's Oliver's thing. I don't particularly like either.

"That's an expensive bottle," Oliver says, shutting his MacBook and joining me in the center of the room to inspect its label. He's in jeans and a polo shirt today, looking as handsome as he does in a suit, but no more relaxed. His shoulders are stiff, his energy tight. His hair is mussed up as if he's been running his fingers through it.

"I'll pour you a much-needed glass," I offer.

"Great." He runs fingers through his hair, adding to its disarray. "I do need it, actually."

This admission offers me hope that he'll really talk to me about whatever he's struggling with. Our room isn't fancy. The price to be in a haunted room was to give up luxury, but the fun is worth it, though our space is limited. So are the room's resources—thus, I'm forced to grab a glass from the bathroom that I fill with ice and whisky. When I return to the main room, Oliver's by the window, looking out at the mountains, and while his MacBook remains, for some reason I notice there was a file on the desk that isn't there any longer. I have no idea why this stands out to me or why it bothers me.

I step to Oliver's side and offer him the glass. "Thanks, babe," he says, leaning in and giving me a peck on the mouth. "Did all of your ladies get in just fine?"

"They did. Lana brought an old friend. Would you believe we have a real FBI agent at our party?"

"No shit," he says. "That's interesting." His surprise turns to a grimace. "Are we sure she's a friend of Lana's? I mean, how well do you even know Lana?"

I blink. "What? Why are you even asking that?"

He sips his whisky. "It's just a little odd to suddenly have an FBI agent in attendance."

I turn to face him, suddenly concerned his stress is over something bigger than a box. "Do we have something to hide? What don't I know?"

"No," he says quickly. "Of course not. But I have no idea what any of our guests might be into."

"Surely we're aligned with friends that are as honest as we are? Which brings me back to, What don't I know, Oliver?"

"Nothing, babe. It just feels off to me."

Unsettled, I say, "If anyone on your crew of friends crossed the law, and brought it to our event, I'm going to be upset, furious even. So if you know something about someone, get them out of here."

"I don't," he says. "But I'm certainly going to gauge reactions over drinks tonight. If I get a read on a problem, I'll handle it." He cups my face and steps closer. "You know I'll always protect you, right?"

"I told you, I don't need—"

"Protection. I know. But you have it anyway." His hands slide away from my face and he glances at his watch. "It's six thirty. We need to be downstairs for those drinks by eight. I need to work until then."

"I thought we'd celebrated this deal being closed."

"We did. But as is normal, verbal agreements can turn into disagreements when the contract is produced for execution."

"And that's what's happened?" I push.

"Paperwork is my hell right now. I'm just working through the legalities of the issues."

*That's not really an answer,* I think, but I just want him to finish what he has to finish. "Is this going to consume you all weekend?"

"I'm close to getting this handled," he promises me. "I just need another hour."

"Okay. I'm going to shower and change for tonight."

I leave him to his work and head into the bathroom, but everything about the exchange bothers me. Why is he worried about the FBI agent at our party? And what was that whole "I'll protect you" declaration? He's still not right. And I go back to what I keep going back to. That box. He's not been right since he got that box.

# Chapter Eleven

## DETECTIVE BOONE

*Franklin, Tennessee*
*Six months ago . . .*

"Detective Boone, you want to see this."

I'm standing over Elsa Ward—staring at the placement of the gun next to the body, with alarms going off—when that shout-out occurs.

I lift a hand with confirmation but keep my eyes focused on that weapon. I don't need anyone to tell me the placement is off. Elsa didn't kill herself. I step away from the body and find Nathan, one of the lead forensics guys, waiting on me. I follow him to the kitchen table, where there's a red gift box with a ribbon draped off the side. There's also a stack of papers placed haphazardly inside.

I'm already gloved up and I grab them, giving them a gander, and what's inside is not a pretty picture of Elsa's morality. The documents indicate that she works in accounting for a local who she's been stealing from for years. A card outside the envelope reads: *I know. You're over.*

I tap the table and think about the gun placement, forming a working hypothesis. Someone wanted us to believe Elsa killed herself over these documents. The question is: Who? And why? I'd assume revenge over the stolen money, but the biggest rule of detective work is never assume. The suicide is smoke and mirrors. That means everything about the first look at this crime could be smoke and mirrors, which may have been the killer's intent.

I eye the dog bed by the table and then the front door as David, the first responding officer, walks in. "Where's the dog?"

"Neighbors got the dog," he says. "Apparently, they found it on the road and knew something was wrong. She never leaves that dog's side."

*And yet, she did,* I think.

This is not a killer who understands the art of details.

# Chapter Twelve

## ANDI

I end up in the hotel bar with Lana before heading to my room. During the short outing, Whit sends me three text messages. In between ignoring him and chatting with Lana, I down most of a burger and a few fries.

"What did you think of Carrie?" Lana asks. "A little starstruck, eh?"

"People get weird about law enforcement," I say. "They either fear us, hate us, or idolize us."

"I don't fear, hate, or idolize you," she says. "Maybe it's because I knew you before you had a badge."

"Or maybe you're confident in who and what you are, and therefore who and what I am doesn't faze you at all."

"You don't think Carrie's confident in who she is?" she asks, sipping her soda. For now, we've avoided alcohol. After all, we do have drinks with everyone later.

As for Carrie, the answer that I keep to myself is no, she is not confident in who she is. It's in her mannerisms, and most certainly her awkward obsession with my job. But one thing a fellow profiler told me during my training is to avoid playing FBI agent in social situations. It never leads anyplace good. I take that advice now and simply say, "I'm speaking generically. I don't make it a habit of profiling people during social events."

Which is not a lie. I don't engage in many social events; therefore nothing related to such events can be called habits. Lana laughs. "Okay, that's bullshit. And we both know that I'm *not* confident. I just got divorced. I'm that desperate chick who needs someone to tell me I'm beautiful."

"Well, you *are* beautiful," I say.

"Thank you," she replies. "But I really need to hear that from a hot man right now."

"You don't need to hear that from a man. You are defined by no man. Just by yourself."

"You're right. You're so very right."

"And for the record, there's a difference between an inborn insecurity and a situational insecurity. And don't ask me to explain that." I flag down the waitress. "I need to go unpack and get settled, and so do you."

"Yes, me too," she agrees. "And a fifteen-minute nap will do the body right."

A few minutes later, I'm in the elevator alone when my phone buzzes with yet another text message from Whit: It's not for me. It's for the tormented families of the victims.

Whit knows how to push my buttons.

I finally make it to my haunted room, where a former housekeeper for the hotel is supposed to be present and gainfully employed as a ghost. Elizabeth, the staff tells me, likes to tidy up, and she often wedges herself between unwed couples. She's quite traditional and old-fashioned. Not that I believe she exists, but the premise of Elizabeth works for me. I like tidy, and me and anyone but Aiden, who isn't here, is a no-go. And even Aiden is questionable right now.

"Hi, Elizabeth," I call out before setting my purse on the bed and removing my MacBook. With it in hand, I walk to the desk against the wall, settle into the chair, and power it to life.

I download the confidential file Whit has sent me and start looking over the case. After a few minutes of reading, I'm baffled by the crimes. A billionaire heiress and a teacher seem to have committed suicide, hanging themselves within twenty-four hours of each other, but the facts don't add up. One of the victims is blonde and forty-five. The other is brunette and twenty-five.

And still, the police won't connect the cases, which is why the family of the wealthy victim hired my father. I want to resist involvement because of that, but damn it, I'm intrigued. I remind myself that my father is capable, and neither Whit nor I should be working right now. We could both end up with longer leaves. And yet, what do I do?

I get to work on a profile of the killer.

It seems I just don't know how to leave murder out of the weekend.

# Chapter Thirteen

My uniform of a blazer and dress pants is officially off-limits this week-end. Therefore, when I meet Lana outside the bar at eight, I do so dressed in a pair of nice jeans, ankle boots, and a turquoise blouse.

"Any ghostly encounters?" Lana asks, looking all hip and pretty in her own version of nice jeans and a red blouse.

"Not a one," I say. "Did you really think I would?"

She casts amused eyes on me. "You're not a believer, I see," she accuses.

"I believe in monsters," I reply. "Not ghosts."

"Unfortunately," she says dryly, "working in the ER these days, I do as well. No ghostly encounters for me, either. And with my luck, if I do see that cowboy they say haunts my room, he'll look like my ex." I laugh and she grimaces. "On that note," she adds, "I need a Godiva martini."

I laugh again. "I'm in," I say, and allow her to lead the way.

The next thing I know, I'm at a table full of women, including the groom's sister, Natalie Phoenix, a striking brunette who ends up one seat over and across from me.

Carrie, the bride-to-be, is directly in front of me, which all but ensures I'll need a martini just to answer all of her questions about being in the FBI. Of course, Lana is beside me, as is a quiet redhead named Tabitha. Another woman sits next to Carrie, but I'm not introduced to her, which is fine by me. I spend my life tracking names and details about everyone I come in contact with. Despite having spent the last hour working on a profile, I really am trying to turn that part of my brain off.

Chatter begins, lots of hospital jokes floating about. "Am I the only one who isn't a nurse?" I discreetly ask Lana.

"You and Natalie are the outliers. She works for Phoenix Technology, which is owned by Carrie's fiancé, Oliver. The company does something in the oil industry that I don't pretend to understand."

My gaze lifts, and I find Natalie whispering something to Carrie. Displeasure flickers on Carrie's heart-shaped face, and she reaches for her drink without comment. She and Natalie are far from sisterly.

The gossip and girl talk continue, with lots of chatter about Denver's own Dr. McDreamy at the hospital, and I'm officially out of my element. Lord help me, this is not where I belong.

And yet, suddenly all eyes are on me as Natalie asks, "What exactly do you do for the FBI, Andrea?"

Of course, this was inevitable. I'm the new and shiny thing in the room. Hopefully, a few well-chosen answers and I'll be old news. "I'm a profiler," I say. "Which is basically a bunch of tedious paperwork."

She doesn't let it go there, pushing me for more. "What type of criminals do you profile?"

It's an interesting question since most people assume I only profile killers. "It depends on the need at the time."

"I googled you," Carrie chimes in. "You just caught a serial killer. The *Spider Man*." There are murmurs around the table because, of course, this group is from Colorado. They've all heard of the Spider Man. "God," Carrie adds, "how do you sleep at night, hunting criminals like that man?"

"Bad subject," Lana says immediately. "As you can imagine, Andi wants to escape that world this weekend. Besides," she argues, "tonight is about you, Carrie. How are the wedding plans coming?"

*Thank you, Lana, for the diversion,* I think, but it doesn't work. Natalie remains focused on me. "I read a profiler helped with that Dirty John case when that man was scamming women. They did a special on him on Netflix."

"That was so good," Carrie says, and the woman next to her chimes in with more of the same. "Did you watch it?" she asks me.

"I read about the case but didn't watch the show," I say. "I've been a little preoccupied until this weekend."

Carrie seems to have a light bulb turn on in her brain. "Oh, right. The Spider Man case."

I don't comment on the Spider Man, but I do glance at Natalie. "And yes, a profiler was most likely involved at some stage of the investigation of Dirty John, as the case is being called. Sometimes it's not about identifying a suspect as much as understanding what makes him or her tick."

"Interesting," Natalie comments, sipping her martini. "Then you do it all. Con artists, bank robbers, killers, and even white-collar crime?"

"That's exactly right," I say, and it's right then that the waitress brings another round of drinks. Turns out the hotel's Godiva martini is a perfect way to drink and not feel like you're drinking. Which could be good or bad. I'll be stopping at two.

I've just taken a sip of my newly poured drink, when Natalie bluntly adds, "I'm a little shocked you came to the party, Andi, or really, I should say, *Agent Castle.* You don't even know the bride."

At that moment, the woman next to Carrie chokes on her drink. Carrie herself shifts uncomfortably in her seat. The next thing I know, Carrie's margarita tumbles over. The *extra-large* margarita she's been sipping is all over me before I know what's happened. I set my drink down and I'm on my feet wiping my blouse, with Lana standing beside me helping.

"It's so damn cold," I murmur, shivering and tossing icy slush from my shirt.

Lana steps in front of me, pressing napkins to the mess all over me. "Natalie's a bitch," she whispers. "Ignore her."

"I'm not that sensitive," I assure her, because it's true. After years in law enforcement, I've been belittled, spat at, cursed at, stabbed twice, and even shot at more than once. "But," I add, "I do think it's time I call it a night."

"We have the ghost tour with the guys here in half an hour. You have to come. Don't make me do this alone," she pleads. "Not with Natalie here. I think we *all* need FBI protection from her."

I'd laugh and agree if I weren't a sticky mess.

Carrie chooses that moment to appear by my side with a stack of napkins in hand. "I'm so sorry. I'm really, really sorry." She offers me the napkins. "You have to be freezing."

I pat down my wet blouse. "It's okay. Believe me, I've experienced worse."

"Oh," she says, her eyes going wide. "Of course you have. You're an FBI agent."

I suddenly wish we had told people I'm a schoolteacher. "I need to go change."

"And you'll come back?" Lana asks urgently.

Mentally I resist, but she really is remarkably insecure right now, so I concede. "Yes," I agree. "I'll be back."

"I'm sorry again," Carrie coos. "I feel *horrible*."

I dismiss her worries. "Accidents happen." I glance at Lana. "I'll be back as quickly as possible."

"You want me to come with you?" she offers, almost eagerly, so much so I wonder why she's here at all.

"No need," I tell her. "Drink. Have fun."

On that note, I hurry away and waste no time dumping the napkins on an empty serving tray set up by the bar exit. I enter the hotel lobby and rush up the red carpeted steps, and it's not long before I'm on the second floor. Once I'm in my room, I say, "Hello, Elizabeth. I'm a mess. You won't approve," and then head to the bathroom.

Perhaps it's crazy to talk to a nonexistent ghost, but probably less so than making a living by hunting real-life monsters.

Once I've changed into a black, lacy top and hung my wet blouse on the bathroom towel rack, I am halfway to the door when I pause just a moment. My mind replays the drink incident as I do with so many crime scenes and witness interviews. I focus on Natalie confronting me about being at the party, and the more I think about it, the odder it becomes. Her confrontation and my presence. She's defensive with me, but also correct. I don't know the bride or the bride's family. But neither of these things is what is really bothering me. Carrie's reaction to the exchange is what's bothering me. I'm back to replaying those moments at the table. Carrie had shifted awkwardly, but right now I'm focused on the incident when she "accidentally" knocked her drink over on me.

There'd been a desperate look on her face at Natalie's comment, a look that I'd been analyzing when her hand hit that glass and the icy-cold liquid soaked my blouse and skin.

I think about the look she wore and the lift of her hand. I think Carrie knocked that drink over on purpose, but with what endgame? To get rid of me or shut up Natalie?

Or perhaps, I think, both.

# Chapter Fourteen

I'm still in my room rather than returning to the party, but not for long.

I'm not a person to be driven off. Furthermore, the more someone wants me gone because I'm a member of law enforcement—which is what Natalie's confrontation indicates to me—the more I feel as if I need to be irritatingly present. If those things weren't enough to convince me to return to the party, the fact that I'm Lana's emotional support right now does. Divorce sucks. I've never lived it personally, but law enforcement tends to feed the demise of marriages, so I've been highly exposed to the drama and pain of those breakups.

I exit my room only to pause at the sight of a man to my left at the end of the hall, pacing back and forth.

As is just natural for me, I size him up. He's a fit man, midthirties with dark hair. Tall. Over six feet, by my estimate, and wearing jeans, a polo shirt, and a whole lot of tension in his shoulders. I tell myself I'm not on duty and I need to ignore the man and the situation, but as I start to turn right toward the stairs, I find myself pausing. There is no real time off in law enforcement. There's a sworn oath to protect and serve that I take seriously. And the bottom line here is that something bristles uncomfortably inside me at the idea of walking away from this man.

I walk toward him. He's oddly unaware of my approach, and when I am all but on top of him, he jolts. "Holy hell," he grunts. "You scared me."

"I noticed," I say. "Sorry about that."

"Am I blocking your room?"

Considering he's in front of the last door in the hallway and it's the only door he's blocking, I wonder, *Which room is his room?* "Actually, no," I say. "You seemed out of sorts. I wanted to see if I can help."

"I locked myself out of my room," he explains. "I'm waiting impatiently for rescue."

His room that he thought was my room? Obviously, I was bristling for a reason. "Is the front desk bringing you another key?" I ask.

"No, I'm expecting a business call any moment, and I can't do anything until it's over."

"I can go for you," I offer. "What room are you in?"

"No need," he says quickly. "But thank you. I really can't risk the aid arriving while I'm bumping heads with a client."

He's jittery, moving his fingers at his sides, but a work challenge while locked out of his hotel room could certainly explain his state of mind right now. I just want to know which room is his. Perhaps he's standing at the end of the hallway to stay out of the walkway. It's a semireasonable possibility.

Deciding that's likely, I concede my position. "All right, then," I say. "I hope the meeting goes well." I back away from him and then start walking. Still the bristling sensation inside me just won't let go, but I have no grounds to take action at all.

I force myself to leave the man behind.

———

My return to the table of women in the bar comes with a pleasant surprise. Natalie is gone and two other women, both nurses and quite welcoming, are present. It's almost as if Natalie left when I left. That strikes me as interesting. Another thing that's interesting is how much more fun the table seems to be having with Natalie gone, Carrie included.

At present, everyone is comparing ghost stories. "No ghostly cowboy staring at me from the foot of my bed as promised," Lana says. "Not that I've really been in the bed so far." She snorts. "Actually, I've not done a lot in bed lately." Everyone laughs and she adds, "I'd rather have a real-life cowboy anyway."

"At least a ghost won't ask for commitment," one of the women, whom I now know as Bianca, offers. Bianca, I've learned, works in the ER with Lana and Carrie. She's proudly Hispanic and undeniably beautiful, with a big dose of kindness.

"Sounds like an eternal commitment to me," Lana replies. "And no, thank you. I didn't make it five years with the last man."

Everyone laughs and Carrie says, "Some Lord Dunraven, who used to own land where the hotel sits, is supposed to live in my room, but it's been silent as well. We'll see if that lasts."

"Me and Bianca are in 418, where children are supposed to laugh and play," another woman, Sally, offers. Sally sports a dark bob and glasses, giving off a distinctly schoolteacher vibe. "Since I work in pre-natal care, I'm all in on that, but we've seen and heard nothing."

"Wrong," Bianca says. "Footsteps. We heard footsteps."

"It's a hotel," Sally argues. "Of course we heard footsteps."

Bianca spurts out something in fast Spanish and then says, "We heard footsteps where there is no upper level above us. There's an overhang. It's insane."

Carrie looks at me. "What about you? How is Stephen King's room?"

"I'm not sure what inspired him to write *The Shining* in that room," I say, sipping my martini, feeling the most relaxed I've been since we arrived. "It's quiet, and the ghost that is supposedly in the room is a sweet, tidy housekeeper. If she shows up and cleans up, I can't really go wrong."

Laughter erupts around the table, and Carrie glances at her watch. "Oh, it's time for the tour. Let's go, ladies." She waves at the table. "Drinks are paid for."

Everyone murmurs our appreciation as the group makes its way into the lobby before being directed to a special room where the tour will begin. We end up in a small theater-type room, where we all claim random seats. The women have only just settled in when a group of about ten men joins us, and Lana starts pointing out groomsmen and random friends of the groom.

"There's the groom," she says, pointing as Carrie greets a tall, familiar man. The man from the hallway by my room.

My mind travels back to the talk about haunted rooms. Carrie said specifically that she and Oliver are in a room on the fourth floor. Oliver was on my floor, the second floor. Of course, there are explanations. He could have been meeting his sister, who left the bar before I returned. He could have been meeting a friend or business associate who is also a friend and arrived at the room sooner than they did.

There are many reasons he could have been there.

But none of those reasons fit his mood when I found him in the hallway. None of those reasons feel right.

# Chapter Fifteen

Our tour guide gives a little speech that includes a short clip from Stephen King's *The Shining* before we are off to see the ghosts. We start at the concert hall, where we're told that one of the property ghosts can sometimes be heard playing the piano, while another tells you to "get out." There are other random little happenings, like orbs floating about, or so they say. None of those things happen to us, but as the tour guide turns out the light and has us stare into some mirror and hunt for orbs, the hair on the back of my neck stands on end. It's a little freaky. Especially since the lights come back on and Oliver is standing in front of me.

I actually jolt, and he laughs. "Sorry. My turn to say that I didn't mean to scare you. We met in the hallway earlier, right?"

"We did," I say. "You were a little distressed."

"Yes," he chuckles. "I suppose I was. I'm here to focus on fun, and my wife-to-be and a work situation have been haunting me instead of the ghosts of the Stanley Hotel."

"Because there are no ghosts," I whisper conspiratorially.

"And now you've gone and angered the ghosts," he warns. "They will *most certainly* visit you tonight."

"Hmm. You could be right. But at least I can go home and say the ghost stories are real. And I do have my gun, though I doubt it works on ghosts."

"Right," he says, waving a finger. "You're the FBI agent I heard about, then, right?"

As if he didn't know this already, I think, but I perform well and groan. "The FBI agent wishing she told everyone she was a schoolteacher. I'm trying to escape that world right now."

"Really?" he asks. "Why is that?"

"I have a big case that's in the news, and it just won't go away. Lana and I went to school together. She suggested I join you guys out here to get away from it all. I hope that's not a problem."

"Not at all," he says. "The more the merrier. I'd say we feel safer for your presence, but I'm not sure you have authority over the ghostly realm. And on another note, no wonder you were checking on me. It's your nature to be suspicious."

"I prefer 'protective and helpful.'"

His eyes gleam just a bit, as if there is more to this conversation than what's on the surface. I'm ready to find out what, but I never get the chance. Carrie chooses that moment to appear and link her arm with Oliver's. "I see you two met finally," she says. "I was telling Oliver we have an FBI agent in the house."

"Don't you mean schoolteacher?" Oliver asks, eyeing Carrie and adding, "She's incognito, hiding from the press."

"Oh, right," Carrie replies and grins at me. "From now on, you are *not* an FBI agent. Because as much as I'm all about your job, honestly, you scare everyone more than the ghosts in this place."

"I get the fear thing a lot," I say, not at all surprised by her accurate assessment. Law enforcement stirs a mix of comfort and anxiety in people. There's no way around it.

Lana appears by my side. "No ghosts or orbs. It's kind of anticlimactic. At least we could have gotten a ghost playing the piano for us, but no. Nothing." She sighs. "No single men lining up to date me. No ghosts lining up to entertain me."

We all laugh and Carrie snags Oliver's hand. "Let's go look for ghosts and hot men to entertain Lana."

"Can I meet the one who looks like Leonardo DiCaprio?" Lana asks. "The man, not the ghost. I have no idea what a ghost looks like, but I'm sure it's no Leo."

Everyone laughs some more, and the three of them, no doubt expecting me to follow, are on the move. But I don't follow. I hang back and do so with two thoughts: Carrie and Oliver seem to be a happy couple, and Oliver doesn't seem to be uncomfortable with me at all after what happened upstairs. But looks can be deceiving.

My impression of the couple is simple. I feel as if I'm working on a box puzzle, and one of the pieces that should work with the others just doesn't quite fit. But their relationship is none of my business.

# Chapter Sixteen

The next stop on the tour is the underground caves, used ages ago by staff to move around beneath the hotel. Ripe with quartz and limestone, they are said to attract ghostly spirits. Right now, I'm pretty ready to go to my room and finish that profile I worked up for Whit's case, but Lana won't hear of it. She's been promised an intro to Josh, the best man and Leo look-alike, but she's nervous. I'm her safety net, but I'm done after this part of the tour.

The cavern is as expected—a small, tight space with a low ceiling and lots of rock formations. We pile in, and I briefly meet a few of the men here at the party, because how can I not? We're squeezed into tunnels like sardines.

We're deep in the caverns when the tour guide turns off all the lights. Once again, we're hunting for orbs. Once again, there is nothing. There are whispers and flickers of random flashlights. Then more darkness, more nothingness.

That is, until someone screams bloody murder, quite literally, as in letting out a bloodcurdling scream. At this point, I can only assume the woman has caused bleeding in at least a handful of eardrums.

Lights come on, and I'm already pushing through the crowd toward the scream, my hand in my purse on my weapon, which I don't pull, not yet. I can hear a woman speaking panicked, muffled Spanish, and as I clear the crowd, I find Bianca in a corner with Carrie next to her.

"Someone . . ." Bianca says as I step in front of her, "someone touched my hair and whispered in my ear."

My hand slides away from my purse. She thinks a ghost touched her, and that is so not in my wheelhouse. Call the Ghostbusters, not the FBI, for this kind of playdate. We do monsters, not ghosts. Furthermore, I'm not the warm and fuzzy kind of gal. I leave the delivery of comfort and creating a sense of well-being to Carrie and the tour guide, who is now by Bianca's side as well. For my part, I make a beeline for the door. Once I've cleared the caverns and stepped into the lobby, I hear, "Is the FBI agent scared of the dark?"

I pause at the unfamiliar mocking voice, turning to find a dark-haired man in khakis and a button-down leaning on the wall. He's tall. Fit. Attractive enough, I guess, in someone's book, if not mine, and despite the severeness of his features. At Lana's insistence, she had given me a rundown on every human, and supposed ghost, attending the party, so I know him to be a groomsman named Cade Winston.

"The FBI agent is not scared of the dark," I guarantee. "Are *you*?"

He laughs, the voice as sharp as his nose. "I'm not. I'm a surgeon, and I had a call related to a patient, though I do admit I'm less entertained by the ghostly premise of the tour than others present."

"Yes," I agree. "I deal with enough monsters without adding ghosts to the picture." I prepare to depart. "Have a good night."

"Can I buy you a drink?" he asks.

I don't even consider the offer. "I actually have some work to do, but thank you. I'm sure I'll see you tomorrow night at the big party."

"You will," he says. "I'll look for you."

I give him a nod and turn away. What I don't tell him is that I won't look for him.

Surgeons, ER doctors, and even members of law enforcement save lives, or they should, but a select few possess a God complex that I can spot a mile away. This man is one of those few. And that's a little too like the Spider Man and my father to suit me right now.

# Chapter Seventeen

## CARRIE

When the tour is over, Oliver and I end up in the hotel bar with a group of friends. We drink, laugh, and have a great time. And yet, just beneath his surface, Oliver is still on edge, not all here, not himself, which is unexpected. He's assured me that he's wrapped up his business problems and done so with a big bow on top. But because he's edgy, I'm edgy. On the bright side, Lana and Josh are getting along marvelously.

I nudge Oliver, who's in deep conversation with his groomsman Nick, and I lift a finger toward the corner where Lana and Josh sit at a private table, an intimate tilt of their bodies toward one another. I saw Lana and Brody flirting earlier, but I doubt there will be a fight over her. It wouldn't be the first time those two had swapped the same woman. Oliver tries to protect "his boys," but I work in an ER. Getting to the truth is half the battle we face in emergency medicine. I've learned to see what isn't obvious to most. Josh is the right choice for Lana. Not that I'd ever explain why, and if Josh keeps doing what he's doing, my silence won't matter.

Oliver glances in their direction and grimaces, apparently not as pleased with the pairing as I am. "They're both amazing people," I say.

"And our friends," he points out. "Once they get naked together and end badly, they'll avoid each other and maybe us."

"Or *maybe*," I offer, "they'll fall in love and get married."

He runs a finger over my jawline. "Always the romantic. I love that about you."

I catch his hand. "Stop being a pessimist. Give them a chance."

"You say that now, but soon it will be 'Oliver! Cleanup on aisle eight.'"

"Oh shit," Trevor says, tapping the table in front of Oliver. "There's talk of Edelman coming back to football. And guess where?"

"Who cares?" Oliver replies. "Brady retired. They were better together."

From there, they launch into football talk that includes someone named Mahomes.

And just like that, the topic of friends falling in love with friends is over.

At the other end of the table, Bianca and Sally are in an intense conversation about wallpaper, leaving me trapped between wallpaper and football. I decide this is a good time to hunt down my drink the waitress seems to have forgotten.

I walk to the bar and lean on the counter, my back to our group. The bartender is quick to attend to my needs, and soon I have a martini in front of me. This one is pineapple, a drink I noticed Andi chose earlier. It caught my interest, but then, everything about her intrigues me. I wasn't joking when I told her I'm a true crime buff. It's actually an obsession that sometimes drives Oliver a little crazy. *"Are you planning my future murder?"* he once asked me.

It was a horrible joke and we fought afterward, but the flowers he got me to make up were beautiful. Lilacs. I adore lilacs, while my mother says they remind her of death, which is silly. She's going to freak out when she sees the lilacs at my wedding. On that note, I reach into my purse, discreetly grab my bottle of pills, and pop my cocktail of drugs, which I down with my martini.

"Does your doctor know you're taking those with alcohol?"

I glance up to find Cade standing next to me. The truth is that I've never really liked Cade much. He's arrogant, with a bit of a God complex, and therefore I've never understood what a humble, kind man like Oliver sees in him.

"My doctor," I say, "doesn't care what I take my vitamins with as long as I take them. In fact," I add, "I believe he'd be quite impressed that I took them while on vacation."

He smirks and motions to the bartender. "Whisky sour, and give me the top-shelf booze, whatever you recommend." The bartender gives a nod and walks away.

Cade leans on the bar and eyes me. "Good little bride-to-be, taking her vitamins."

"Back to this?" I say. "You're obsessed with my vitamins, aren't you."

"More like entertained. Oliver won't even take an aspirin for a headache, and you're a cocktail-and-pills kind of gal. But opposites attract, right?"

"We're hardly opposites," I say, boldly sipping my drink. I will not be made to feel anything I'm doing is wrong. I grew up doubting myself, and my marriage is a celebration of believing in myself. That's what Oliver has done for me. Taught me to believe in myself. "Shouldn't you be with the men, chatting about football and guy stuff?" I challenge.

"My mother is a rather formal, proper woman," he replies. "She taught me the bride-to-be is always the star of the party." The bartender sets Cade's drink down, and he gives him his room number before eyeing me. "Congratulations, Carrie. You are Oliver's perfect bride."

He picks up his glass and walks away.

His words feel like a compliment. And yet somehow, they're flavored with a bit of that sour in his whisky sour, and I don't know what to make of it. I wonder if *he's* the one who sent that box.

Suddenly Oliver and Josh are on either side of me. "Hey, baby," Oliver says, kissing me and then sipping from my glass.

"Thanks for the intro to Lana," Josh adds. "I like her."

"You better like her enough to be good to her," I chide. "If you mess with her—"

"I'm not that guy," he says quickly. "You know I'm not *that guy*."

"Say all guys before they become *that guy*," I point out.

"True," he concedes. "But I'm really *not* that guy."

"Hey, hey, hey! The life of the party is officially here."

At the sound of Brody Matthews's voice, my gaze jerks to Oliver's. "How is he here?" I demand.

He eyes Josh and arches a brow.

"I might have mentioned the party," Josh replies. "But it's time to mend fences. He's a good friend. You know he's a good friend, Oliver."

"He was a good friend, Carrie," Oliver argues.

"*Was,*" I emphasize.

"Hey, hey, hey," Brody says again. "I'm here. Right here behind you."

Oliver's jaw sets stubbornly. "I'll handle this and meet you in the room later."

He turns and faces Brody. Josh has already done the same. I don't turn. I reach for my martini and down it, a rush of vodka numbing my senses, and I like it that way. Brody is the good-time guy who lures everyone into trying new things. Sometimes to their own demise. In Oliver's case, one of those times was a bet that cost him fifty grand. And that's just one of Brody's sins in my book.

He's not the kind of friend a married man needs. He's not the kind of friend a good man needs, either, and Oliver is a good man.

I do not approve, but this weekend is not the time to push that issue. Brody is here. I'm not going to make him leave. I'm not going to make a scene. But my God, I'm glad I found pineapple martinis. Because Oliver isn't the only one with a past with Brody. I have one, too.

# Chapter Eighteen

## ANDI

The one full day Lana and I will be in Estes Park, we spend checking out the cute little town.

We stroll the streets, browsing stores and eating at a local restaurant. Turns out she and Josh have been flirting. I try to remind her she's rebounding, but like most rebounders, she feels this does not apply to her. They're both divorced, which according to her washes away the rebound effect.

"Who caused the divorce? Him or her?"

"Not sure," she replies flippantly. "He's an attorney at Oliver's firm, and his ex-wife is in accounting. Maybe working together got to them."

"That's weird and sounds like a future love-triangle murder. Be careful. And why is he at the wedding and she is not?"

She shrugs. "Carrie must not like her."

———

Our girls' day is cut short when Lana and Josh decide to meet for drinks.

All this wedding stuff is making me crazy, and I need a drink, too. I settle for a coffee, which is why I swing by the hotel lobby coffee shop. I'm waiting on my white mocha to be made when my gaze catches on a table deep in the attached restaurant. Oliver is sitting in a booth facing me and seems to be arguing with whoever is across from him. That person—I can't even tell if it's a man or woman—is sitting with their back to the coffee shop. My order is called and I pick up my cup, only to have one sip reveal my drink is wrong.

Once the barista is remaking my beverage, I glance toward Oliver again. He's gone, and I don't know where he went. The person who was with him is still in the booth. I don't know why I need to know who that person is, but I do. My coffee order is up again, and this time, I grab it and keep my eyes on the table.

That's when a woman stands up and walks toward an exit on the opposite side of the restaurant, which is how I'm now sure Oliver left. I thank the barista, stick a tip in the jar, and then walk back into the lobby, hurrying to the elevators in hope of catching a glimpse of this woman. I don't find her.

But from what I did see in the restaurant, her build and frame were smaller than Carrie's. She's not Carrie, and I don't think she's Oliver's sister. I frown and punch the elevator call button. Or was she? Maybe, but I don't think so, which means what? Is she part of Carrie's wedding party? Why would Oliver be fighting with a member of the wedding party?

The elevator doors open and I step inside the car, chiding myself as I do. Clearly, I don't understand the words *time off*. I'm not on duty right now, per my boss. I'm not happy about it, either, but unlike Whit and my father, I follow the rules.

Oliver's life is Oliver's life.

His business is not my business.

# Chapter Nineteen

Dressing for success means carrying a gun on me, even to a party, though my little going-out purse doesn't want to shut. In my book, this is a real problem, but while the gun won't fit in my purse, on a positive note, I fit into the little black dress I'm wearing. There's a knock on my door, and I do my whole cautious door routine and then open up to find Lana standing there, also in a little black dress. Hers looks better on her than mine does on me, but whatever. I guarantee I handle a gun better than her, and besides, I don't have divorce tormenting me like she does. I decide that she deserves to look better. "I'm almost ready," I tell her, waving her into the room.

I'm quickly back to trying to force the gun into my purse. "What are you doing?" Lana asks, joining me, watching what I'm doing.

"If it fits, it ships," I say. "I need to make it fit."

"It's not going to fit, and if it does, you'll shoot someone trying to get your lipstick. Just leave it. I mean, why do you need a gun? And frankly, I'd rather you not have one while drinking."

"Good point," I say, but I mentally resist leaving my weapon behind, and self-analytical as I am, I question my actions this weekend. Perhaps I didn't have Lana tell everyone I was a schoolteacher because my badge and gun are my security blankets. I don't think I even know who I am without them. That's what Aiden insists, though I'm not so sure.

Whatever the case, I'm just going downstairs to a party. I won't need to shoot anyone. Decision made, I place the gun in the hotel safe and lock it. "I'm ready," I announce.

A few minutes later, Lana and I enter an intimate banquet hall, which is just large enough for the thirty to forty guests. The overall feel and look are exactly what one might expect from a hotel-hosted event: tables, waiters, and people everywhere. The women are in dresses, the men in suits. Apparently, the idea of loosening your tie and partying hard for a bachelor party is lost on this group.

"When exactly do the men and women split up?" I ask, suspecting some of that tie loosening will happen soon, when the booze does the job of relaxing the formality in the air as well.

"After announcements," she says. "I know it's weird to do this together, but it's kind of cool, too." Lana grabs two glasses of champagne from a tray. By the time we're sipping and sitting at a table, Josh is by her side. I'm the outsider, but I don't mind. That's kind of my life. I spy a chocolate fountain and decide this night is better already. I head in that direction, and I'm stuffing my face with a chocolate croissant when I hear, "You're Lana's friend, right?"

I rotate right to find a tall man with brown, tamed, slicked-back curly hair and chiseled features standing beside me in what appears to be eager anticipation for my reply. "Otherwise known as Andi," I say when I manage to swallow.

"I'm Trevor," he offers. "One of the groomsmen."

He's in a gray suit with a burgundy tie, worth a good $5,000. Which I know because every case I work on leads to all kinds of random facts, like the way to tell what suit costs what price, that will live in my head forever. In other words, Trevor is a corporate type, able to navigate social scenes. Meanwhile, I'm not quite sure what to say to him, since

I'm not asking where he was last night when the crime took place. There is no crime. And I'm not interrogating him.

Reluctantly, I set my croissant on a plate and the plate on the table. *Soon,* I promise myself as I ignore the vast selection of chocolate items.

Trevor rambles a good five minutes about his CEO job, his father's connection to Oliver's father, and the cigar club again but lands fairly quickly on, "I heard you catch killers."

Here we go *again.*

It's a little curious how obsessed these people are with my job, almost as if they want to convince me they are the good guys who would never commit a crime. Only those people don't exist. Everyone has a line, and everyone has something that will make them cross it. "Something like that," I reply.

"*How* do you do it? It's one thing to watch a horror movie, but to study real-life crime scenes, to see real-life brutality, has to be the making of nightmares."

"Not really," I say. "I'm used to it. Once you've walked through puddles of blood and studied rigor mortis for the time of death, you get numb to it all."

He pales and makes an excuse, before leaving quite abruptly. Obviously my social skills are rusty, but I don't know why they ask if they don't want the answer.

"If your plan was to scare him off, it worked."

I turn to find a man with wavy light-brown hair standing next to me. He's tall. Fit. Good-looking and inappropriately dressed in jeans and a tan leather jacket. "And yet here you stand," I say.

"I worked the ER department in my residency," he says. "You can't scare me off with talk of blood and rigor mortis, but you can try."

"You're a doctor," I assume. "You must work with Carrie."

"Oh, hell no," he says. "Emergency medicine is a shit show on a stick. I got out years ago."

"You're not that old," I say. "Maybe thirty-five?"

"Thirty-nine. I opened a medical clinic a couple of years back. It's all cosmetic fluff and stuff, and I love it. People pay a fortune to fix a wrinkle, and even better, they don't die on you. They cheer you on." He points at his own face. "And I won't ever age. I have all the fancy face creams and Botox I could ever want at my fingertips."

"Well, you don't look your age," I agree, sipping my champagne as my gaze just happens to find Carrie a few feet away from us. She's standing with Bianca and shooting daggers in my companion's direction. I glance over at him. "Are you a friend of Oliver's or Carrie's?"

He glances at Carrie and then me, a smirk on his face. "That's a complicated question and answer," he says, downing the whisky in his hand and setting his glass on a waiter's tray as he passes. "Brody Matthews, by the way," he says, introducing himself. "And you're Andrea Castle. Everyone is talking about you, so I listened."

Carrie breaks from Bianca and heads our way. She's in a fire engine–red dress, with an excess of cleavage, but this is her naughty night, so more power to her. Her gaze is focused on Brody, and her anger is palpable. She stops in front of him, ignoring me in the process.

"Go home, Brody," she demands. "Go home."

"I'm the good-time boy you need tonight," he argues.

"Your version of a good time doesn't work for me."

"Not what you said in the past," he replies dryly. "But I'm sure you don't want to get into that tonight, now do you?"

She glares at him. "Go home." And with that, she turns on her heel and leaves.

"She doesn't really hate me," Brody says, amusement lacing his voice. He glances over at me. "It's all an act. But I am the one who shows up and brings the topless girls. I'm not sure she likes that much."

"Topless girls?" I query.

"It's a bachelor party whether she likes it or not," he replies. "'Party' being the operative word."

There's an announcement at the front of the room, where a stage is set up. Oliver and Carrie are now in the center of said stage, a microphone shared between them in Oliver's hand. "The amazing hotel staff is handing out shots of one of my favorite whiskies," he announces. "Once everyone has a glass, we'll toast to friends, fun, and the future, before the men will head over to the next building for that fun." The men break out in cheers.

Carrie grabs the microphone. "And the women stay right here for all of our fun."

The women give their best cheers as well.

A waiter appears and offers me and Brody our shots of whisky. We both accept. Brody downs his. I offer him mine. "I'm not a big drinker."

"Never let it be said that I turned down a beautiful woman who could arrest me," he says, winking and downing my shot as well. "And on that note, I'm going to see the groom-to-be and piss off Carrie. It'll be fun." He sets the second glass down and fades into the crowd, leaving me baffled and a bit intrigued.

Obviously, Carrie didn't approve the guest list or Brody wouldn't be here. And interestingly, based on her anger and the exchange she had with Brody, in which he made an intimate past seem apparent, why in the world would Oliver want him here?

Something doesn't add up.

# Chapter Twenty

There are a total of twelve women at the party. There should be thirteen, but Lana is missing, which tells me she's off somewhere with Josh. *Someone* is getting told she's beautiful tonight, I'll bet, and hey, good for her. I'm fine on my own. I'm simply not a person who needs a companion by my side at all times. That isn't how my career allows me to operate.

However, me and eleven other women watching four dancing men strip on the stage isn't my cup of tea. I don't stick around to see just how naked they get. I came here for Lana and the escape. Lana is not here. Now I'm leaving. I can escape by myself.

I head back to my room and change into leggings and a tank top before settling in under the blankets with room service that includes a chocolate brownie and ice cream. It's pretty much heaven on a plate. Afterward, I dive into the profile I've been working on for Whit. Two hours later, he calls me before I can call him. "How's the party?" he asks.

"There are naked guys everywhere," I say. "And yet I'm still in my room working on your profile."

"Thank God I didn't go with you," he declares. "I do not want to see that shit."

I laugh at the fierceness of his rejection. "The men have their own party next door in the adjoining building. I'm sure it would have been more to your taste."

"And yet, I wasn't invited," he replies dryly.

"Nope," I concur. "You were not. But there is good news. Lana has already moved on from you."

"I can fix that," he declares arrogantly.

I roll my eyes and snort. "In your dreams. I'm working on your case. That has to be good enough for you right now."

"Yeah," he says. "About that."

"Typically, serial killers want attention," I say, diving right into the details. "They don't hide behind suicides."

"But there's not one but two victims," he argues.

"You said three before."

"I might have exaggerated to get your attention."

"Of course you did," I say, "because you already know three is the definition of a serial killer, and even then, it's not always in the same context as a perp who stalks unlimited victims and kills them. You know that."

"All right," he concedes. "So not a serial killer."

"I didn't say that, though that's not where my head is at on this, no," I confirm.

"What about revenge killings?"

"Likely," I agree, "but it could also be the killer hiding from something the victims could have exposed. Any leads?"

"Maybe. Why don't you meet me at your father's office to look at the file when you get back into the city?"

"I'm not—"

"Oh, come on. He's your pops."

"He's trouble," I remind him. "Don't be trouble with him. Once you go down that path—"

"I thought I already did?" he challenges.

"You did," I assure him. "And took me with you, and if you don't see that, then maybe I'm pulling you in the wrong direction. Maybe you belong with my father."

"Maybe I do."

"All right," I say. "I guess I know where we stand, then."

"Whatever that means," he grunts. "Are you going to look at the case or what?"

"I already did, and I told you what I found."

"All right," he says now. "We'll be expecting you at the office next week." He hangs up.

I grimace. "I'm not going to my father's office. The end."

I grab the TV remote, but the TV won't come on. I consider calling for help, but instead, I end up looking at the case again. Because I'm bored, I tell myself. And yet, I keep writing notes and I begrudgingly admit being back at work, on any case, is exactly what I need.

Hours later, my eyes are weary when I flip off the light to try to rest, but for the first time since the Spider Man case closed, there is no part of my mind hung up with anything but sleep.

I drift into a heavy slumber that ends when pounding on my door jolts me into a sitting position. "Andi! Andi!" At Lana's frantic voice, I throw away the covers and race toward the door, expecting a tipsy, heartbroken friend.

Caution be damned, I throw open the door to find her tear-streaked face. "We need you," she sobs. "Oliver's dead and Carrie is missing."

# Chapter Twenty-One

I'm stunned by this revelation. *Oliver's dead?*

"Are you sure?" I ask urgently, already back in the room, expecting her to follow.

"Very. I saw . . . I *saw him*, Andi." She sobs. "He's dead. He's in his room, covered in blood."

"Did someone call emergency services?"

I'm at my bedside now, where the clock reads 7:00 a.m.

"Yes," she says, now at the foot of my bed, hugging herself, still dressed from last night, mascara streaking her cheeks. "They're on their way."

I pull my holster on, since leggings don't exactly have a place to shove my weapon. Once I've removed my gun from the safe and secured it, I slide my badge around my neck and slip on my sneakers. I don't bother to pull a sweatshirt over my tank top. There's no time.

"407, right?" I confirm.

"Yes. Room 407, but Carrie isn't there," she repeats. "No one knows where she is right now. I'm afraid she's dead, too. I'm afraid. *God, Andi.* How can this be happening?"

*407,* I think, and I'm in room 217, which means I have two floors to travel. "Stay here until I know the scene is secure," I instruct.

She rejects that idea. "I'm a nurse and probably the only member of the medical profession here that hasn't been drinking. What if you need me to help Carrie?"

She's right. Everyone else was likely up partying until a few hours ago. "Fine," I say tightly, and I need more information. "Stay close and behind me." I shove my phone in my waistband.

I'm already moving, grabbing a small hip purse where I keep crime scene supplies from my bag—yes, I brought it on vacation—before exiting my room with Lana keeping pace. My mind is racing, checking off a list of priorities, with my one main concern confirming Oliver isn't in need of life support and then securing the hotel as well as the safety of the guests.

"How did you end up in their room?" I ask as we rush up the stairs.

"I was returning to mine when the maid backed out of the room, mumbling under her breath and shaking all over."

"From where?"

She blinks. "What?"

"Where were you coming from?"

"At that moment, hunting down coffee I did not find."

"Why was the maid in the room this early?"

"I have no idea," she says. "I finally calmed her down enough to realize Oliver was hurt. That's when I panicked, told her to call 911, and I went into the room to offer aid. I didn't want to touch anything, but I did touch him, Andi. I checked his vitals. I'm scared right now."

"You had to offer aid," I say. "As long as your prints confirm that was your intent, you're fine."

She hugs herself. "I was in her room before I came and got you in your room," she reiterates. "I went into her room, Andi." Her arms drop and she swipes at the air. "I went into Carrie's room."

Panic and shock have her talking in circles, which is not uncommon during a personal crisis. "You're fine," I say, unable to do more to comfort her, not when I'm scanning for danger.

Once we reach the fourth floor, I hold up a hand to stay Lana's position until I clear our path. She nods and I ease around the corner to find clusters of people, some familiar faces included, gathered in the hallway.

I holster my weapon so as to not create panic, motion for Lana to follow, and step into the crowd's view. "FBI!" I call out, holding up my badge. "Everyone, go back to your rooms now and do not leave until you're interviewed." There are people who move away and others who linger. "Now!" I demand again. "If you stay, I'll assume you need to be considered a suspect."

That scatters the crowd.

A fiftysomething man in a suit and tie approaches me. "Special Agent Andrea Castle, I'm Neal Smith, the hotel manager. What can I do?"

"Make sure the locals get here quickly. Secure the hotel, and that means your staff as well. I assume you have security?"

"I do," he confirms. "I have them at the front door."

"Perfect. Lock down completely for everyone's safety."

I leave him where he stands, and with my weapon back in hand, I enter the room. Oliver is on the bed, on his back, naked to the waist, stab wounds in his chest in excess. It's obvious that he's not only dead, but based on the condition of the body, that he's been dead for a couple of hours. His missing shirt and unzipped pants seem to indicate he was either in the middle of a sexual act when he was killed or simply undressing.

It would be easy to assume Carrie was present during either of those actions.

I clear the bathroom, the closet, and under the bed before harnessing my weapon and reaching inside my bag to pull out one latex glove. I pull it onto my right hand and check for a pulse that I know I won't find, and I don't. The EMS crew bursts into the room, and I identify myself with my badge. "Deceased," I say. "We're going to need the ME."

Two techs move in to confirm my analysis, and it's time for me to find Carrie. I scoffed at my obsession with something being wrong here this weekend. I should have listened to my instincts. Now the future groom is dead and the bride who will never be is missing.

# Chapter Twenty-Two

I step out of the room and toss my gloves in the trash can now set up by the door, to find a tall, thin young buck of a police officer about to enter. "Special Agent Castle," I say, quickly introducing myself. "I'm staying in the hotel. The occupant is deceased. EMS is confirming and calling in the ME."

"Officer Michaels," he introduces himself, and I swear there is fuzz on his lip—that's how new he is to this job. "And the ME is out of Fort Collins," he adds, "which is more than an hour away."

*Of course,* I think. It appears this hotel and tiny town really are the perfect place to commit a murder, sans the mistake of doing so when there is an FBI agent present. If I believed this was planned, I'd say Lana screwed up someone's perfect murder. But some murders don't need to be profiled. This was an act of emotional rage, expressive violence, which translates to the murder communicating an emotion like love, hate, jealousy, and so on. Whoever killed Oliver knew him. Statistically there's a 38 percent chance it was the spouse. As one of my instructors at the academy said, love breeds murder.

"The second occupant of the room is missing," I say, getting back to business and Officer Michaels. "We need manpower and to organize a search and start interviews. And, as I instructed the manager, we need the hotel fully secured."

"Right." He fumbles for his radio. "I'll call the chief. We don't have much available manpower, only eight officers and two detectives, but we'll get what we can out here."

In other words, this is a shit show. "Get me what you can now," I say, pulling my phone from my pocket. I start walking toward the stairs, dialing Aiden as I do.

I step around the corner, out of view, as he answers. "Why are you up so early?"

*Exactly,* I think. *Why* am *I up so early?* "Murder, of course," I say. "What else is there? The groom was stabbed to death, and I'm dealing with a police department of about fifteen. Add to that, I've had no coffee, which really sucks right now." I stop in front of the main stairwell, which connects all floors of the hotel.

"Holy hell," he murmurs. "How does murder follow you? What do you know?"

"Aside from a gut feeling something was wrong all weekend? The bride-to-be is missing, which means running or dead."

"Most likely running," he says. "Keep me posted. I'll run support. Obviously, you're no longer on leave."

I'd celebrate that news, but Officer Michaels rounds the corner. "Oh good," he breathes out. "There you are. Chief Wilhite wants to talk to you." He shoves a phone at me.

"Gotta run," I tell Aiden and disconnect.

I accept the cellphone and say, "Chief Wilhite, Special Agent Andrea Castle. Let me start by saying I'm not trying to step on toes here. I just happened to be present at the hotel when the crime took place."

"We're glad to have you," he replies, his voice a low rumble of sincerity. "We don't have the resources needed."

"Then I need to let you know that the victim was here for a combo bachelorette/bachelor party. One of the bride's friends brought me along to get me out of town, but I don't know anyone else beyond brief meetings."

"I bet you needed that. I know who you are. You caught the Spider Man. I checked you out the minute I heard you were on-site. And no, you don't need to comment. Bottom line: you don't have a conflict of interest, but I appreciate you making sure I know as much." He moves on. "I've called in backup from Fort Collins, but I'm happy to accept your aid and leadership if that's how you see this."

"We can talk about how this plays out," I say. "But considering our obvious suspects are all from Denver, where I live and work, it's logical for me to be involved in some way, shape, or form."

"Agreed. I have eight officers and two detectives on the way to you now," he says. "I'll be there shortly as well. I hear we have a missing bride?"

"Bride-to-be," I say as my gaze catches on what look like roped-off stairs leading to an attic with blood on the wall. "Chief, let me call you back. I might have something." I hang up and hand the phone to Officer Michaels, walking toward the stairs, gloving up as I do. Once I'm at the barrier, Michaels is beside me and I point to the blood on the wall.

"Oh shit," he says, at the commotion behind us.

I glance over my shoulder to find police piling up the steps. "I've got this," Michaels says, turning to greet them. I pull my weapon, then step over the barrier and onto narrow steps, starting a path upward. The wood is old, creaking beneath my weight. The paint on the walls is even older. The climb, however, is short. Once I'm at the top landing, there's a door cracked open with an unlatched padlock hanging from the handle. I step inside, weapon in front of me, and scan the room. At first, I find no one, but there's a sob and I turn quickly to find Carrie sitting in the corner, naked and covered in blood.

# Chapter Twenty-Three

I rush toward Carrie, into the small space with a steepled ceiling and wooden walls. My first priority is to assess the blood all over her as hers or Oliver's.

"What happened?" I ask urgently, kneeling in front of her. "Are you hurt?"

She blinks up at me. "I know you. Don't I know you?"

Her brown eyes are dull, glazed with what appears to be a drug and/or booze high. "Agent Castle," I say, no "Andi" to this introduction. This is business. The party is over. "Are you hurt?" I repeat.

She hugs herself, trembling all over.

"I'm cold. I'm confused. I don't know what's wrong." Her gaze catches on her stained arm and she gasps, pushing to her feet, surveying the blood on her body with disbelief before panting out, "Oh God, oh God, oh God. What is happening? What is happening?!" She screams out louder, *"Where am I? What is happening?!"*

"Agent Castle!" comes a loud shout.

At Michaels's voice, I call out, "Get me a blanket and an EMS team," and I immediately refocus on Carrie, who is now frantically searching her body, I assume for the source of the blood.

"Are you hurt?" I demand more firmly this time. "I need to know if you're hurt."

"How can I not be?" She holds out her arms, oblivious to her state of undress, at least at the moment, seemingly and convincingly truly baffled. "Look at the blood. *Look at the blood.*" She squats and covers her head with her hands. "What is happening?"

I kneel in front of her again. "Are you hurt? Where is the blood coming from?"

"I don't know," she sobs, tears pouring down her cheeks now.

"Do you feel pain?"

"No," she whispers. "I can't find any place that hurts."

*Because it's not her blood,* I think, but that isn't my conclusion to make. It needs to be hers. I need her to tell me this story.

"Agent Castle?" Michaels calls out from the top of the stairs.

"I'm going to get you a blanket," I tell Carrie. "I need you to just stay put until I can have the EMS team look at you. Okay?"

"Yes," she agrees, her voice cracking. "Yes, okay."

I stand up and meet Officer Michaels at the stairs, where EMS stands behind him. I grab the blanket in his hand, then whisper, "Make sure no one tells her Oliver is dead. No one tells her anything. She tells us." Once he gives me his silent agreement, I add, "I'm going to let you communicate that to the team, and cover her up before you send EMS in."

With that, I turn away from him, my plan in play.

# Chapter Twenty-Four

## CARRIE

Still trembling, I clutch the blanket the FBI agent wraps around me. Andi. Andi Castle. That's her name. I don't know why I had such a hard time recognizing her. I just *can't* clear my head. She kneels in front of me again.

"I'm having EMS come up now that you're covered," she says, in control in a way that I am not. I need to get a grip on myself.

She starts to move away, and I catch her arm. "Where are we?" I ask, the small room with wooden walls and ceilings like a prison I can't escape. "And why am I naked and covered in blood?"

"We're in the hotel attic, and as for how you got here or why you're covered in blood, you tell me."

"I don't know," I say. I'm not clearheaded enough to read her tone, but I'm defensive enough to jerk my hand back from her arm, and louder now—a shout, in fact—I repeat my words. *"I don't know!"*

As if I haven't just shouted at her, she calmly studies me for a few long, sharp beats, and then she stands up. Just stands up. No words. No answers. No questions. A moment later, there's a male EMS tech checking my vitals. And then *he's* asking me questions. "Where do you hurt?" he asks, followed by at least ten more queries.

"I don't know!" I yell at him, frustrated, scared. I'm scared, really scared. "I don't know," I whisper again. And then: "But I have to be hurt. The blood—and I'm dizzy." I lower my head, trying to will away the spinning of the tiny room.

The man stands up, and I don't really even know what he looks like or how old he is. I can't seem to focus. I can't focus and I start to panic. I need help. I need help. Now. "Help!" I call out. "Agent Castle! Agent!"

"I'm here," she says, and I blink her into focus, where she now kneels in front of me again.

"What is happening?" I ask, feeling as if I will never get an answer. I need to know *what is happening* to me.

"We need to get you to the hospital," she says. "I have a hotel robe on the way to give you better coverage. Can you walk?"

"Yes. I think so. I just want to go back to my room. I want to take a shower."

"You don't remember anything about what happened?" she presses.

"No. *Nothing.* I swear to you."

"What's the last thing you *do* remember?"

I shut my eyes and reach through the darkness, but I can't seem to latch on to anything, whispering the few things that come to mind: "The party. Dancers. Drinks." My voice trails off as I try to go further, but it's blank. I blink and open my eyes, fixing them on her face, letting her see the truth in them. "I'm just blank after that. And I feel weird but not drunk."

"Which is why we need to go to the hospital." The EMS tech appears above her and hands her the robe, which she then offers to me. "Put this on," she instructs, "and then let's go get this over with so you can rest."

"Do we have to?" I ask weakly.

"We do," she confirms.

There's an authority in her voice, and my parents taught me to respect the law. When an FBI agent tells you that you have to do something, you do it. I slide my arms into the robe, and as I try to stand, she catches my arm to steady my wobbly legs. Two EMS techs step forward, and they take over. At the top of the stairs, one of them moves forward ahead of me. He's a young man with red hair. He's handsome. I don't know how I make any such assessment at this moment, but I think I just need something to think about other than the blood all over my body.

Why is there blood all over my body?

"I can't carry you," he says. "It's too narrow."

*Too bad,* I think. *I'd really like to be carried right now.*

"Walk to me," he encourages, "and I'll catch you if you stumble."

Aware that I really have no other option, I wobble forward, images flashing in my head. Me. Oliver. Me. Oliver. God, where is Oliver? Why have I not worried about Oliver until now? Is he lost somewhere, too? Somehow, I manage to reach the tech without making this worse and falling.

Once we reach the hotel hallway, my gaze shifts toward our room, and there are emergency crews there. Oliver. *Oliver.* "Oliver!" I scream. Adrenaline rushes through me and I jerk away from the EMS tech, who's just caught my arm, and I start running toward the room.

There are shouts of "Stop!" but I don't stop. *Oliver.* God, where is Oliver? I think one of the shouts for me to stop is from Agent Castle, but respect be damned, I don't care. Shoot me if she wants to shoot me, but I'm going to find Oliver. My heart is racing and blood rushes in my ears. I have to get to Oliver, and I'm almost there when an officer steps between me and the room door, latching on to my arms.

"Let go!" I shout. "Let go! I need to see Oliver. I need to know he's okay." I shove at him, punch at him.

"Stop, Carrie!" Agent Castle shouts. "Stop fighting him and turn around and talk to me. Right now."

There's a snap to her voice, and mixed with the familiarity, I stop fighting. My head spins and tears spill from my eyes, my chin lifting in a plea toward the dark-haired man holding me captive. "I just want to go into my room."

"Let her go," Agent Castle instructs. "And you, Carrie, turn around and face me," she repeats.

The officer lets me go and I face Agent Castle, standing in front of her in a hotel robe and bare feet. Even my feet are naked. How? How is that possible? "Can I please just see my fiancé?" I whisper. *Please.*

"We'll walk in calmly together, but let me clear the room first." She motions to the officer.

He nods and enters the room.

"Why does he have to clear the room?" I ask urgently. "Is Oliver okay?"

"I'll let you see for yourself." She glances over my shoulder, at the officer who has returned, and then back at me. "We're clear," she explains. "Let's go inside. I'll go first." She motions to the officer who was holding me. "Please stand guard at the door." The officer inclines his chin.

The space around me seems to spin. I realize then that I'm not crying anymore. I'm quiet inside, but everything is just so black. I don't understand anything right now. Agent Castle steps into the room. I stand my ground in the hallway, in sudden resistance of what I will find inside that room—squeezing my eyes, the sensation of terror overcoming me at what I am about to see. *Oliver.* Something is wrong with Oliver.

I force my eyes open, and that's when someone or something plows into me, knocking my breath from my chest.

"You killed him! Monster!" I'm on the ground by the time I realize it's Oliver's sister shouting at me. Natalie is my attacker.

"Natalie," I whisper in a plea as she grabs my hair and starts smashing my head on the ground. "Stop," I try to shout, but the words become whispers lost in the pain of her hitting my head on the floor. "Stop."

Then suddenly she is gone—and not of her own free will. She's yanked off me, and I roll to my side. She's gone, but her words are not. *You killed him.* She thinks Oliver is dead. My head is throbbing and spinning, but I claw my way to my feet as Agent Castle and the officer work to subdue Natalie. I have to know Oliver is okay and I stumble into the room, catching my hand on the doorway and then launching forward.

It's then that I bring the room and bed into view and find Oliver on the mattress, bloody, and oh God, cold. I'm an ER nurse. I know what dead looks like. He's *dead*. No. No. *No.* I start screaming, and screaming, and screaming from the depths of my soul.

# Chapter Twenty-Five

## ANDI

Carrie goes from screaming to a sprint across the room that ends with her flat on top of Oliver's body. I shout for assistance, and there is a scramble to pull her off that includes me and an elbow in the face that may or may not have come from Carrie. There are four of us in this dogpile.

I watch as the EMS team sedates her and rolls her away on a stretcher. The fact that Carrie screamed bloody murder when she found Oliver dead on the bed might convince some people that she's innocent of his murder. In my mind, the fact she also flung herself on top of him and therefore contaminated the forensics makes me hard-pressed to believe that was an accident.

Allowing her into the room was a misstep, a rookie mistake someone as seasoned as myself should not have made. Just like Whit shouldn't have beaten up a suspect in the name of good, even a bad guy like that dude. Bad decisions let bad people get away with murder. In the end, though, the serial killer nicknamed Spider Man by the press didn't get away. I made sure of it. Oliver's killer won't, either.

———

I've just established calm at the scene when Detective Seth Edwards arrives. He's a tall man, with a belly and a shiny bald head and crinkles by his eyes that age him to at least forty. He's also as cooperative and submissive as the chief. "I hear the sister lost her shit. That's pretty rough."

"Yeah, well, sometimes those who act out the most have the most to hide."

"In other words, you think she's the killer," he assumes.

"I don't assume anything about anyone ever. I want to hear the story the people and the evidence tell me."

"What can I do?"

"I'm going to talk to the sister." I give him my cellphone number. "Call me when the ME arrives if I'm not back by then. And do we have another detective coming?"

"Yeah. Danny York. Good guy. Transferred in from Denver. He's a big-city guy with lots of experience. He'll be here in a few."

*Lots of experience is good,* I think. And with that knowledge, I leave him and the soon-to-arrive Detective York to the organization of the interviews, including the staff and dancers.

It's time to let Natalie express herself to me, and not by beating someone's head against the floor. She has been taken to her room under the threat of arrest, and I head there now. Turns out Natalie is not in a supposedly "haunted" room, but she is on my floor, in the room Oliver was standing outside when I met him.

Unlike Detective Edwards, I've learned a few things by growing up around law enforcement and living the job firsthand myself for a decade. If a person beats your head against the floor, they didn't just suddenly become capable of such violence. They always had it in them. I'm not discounting how guilty Carrie looks, but I'm not assuming her guilt, either. Natalie has shown a propensity for violence, and violence directed at Carrie. Therefore, I conclude that maybe Natalie isn't mad at Carrie for killing Oliver. Maybe she's mad at her for not dying with him.

# Chapter Twenty-Six

Under normal circumstances, I wouldn't have allowed Natalie to go to her room without supervision, but the hotel's locked down and manpower isn't exactly plentiful. I knock on her door, and she answers immediately, tears streaking her cheeks. One thing I noticed during the attack is that she's in a black velvet sweat suit, not her dress from the prior evening, but then it *is* morning. Unless she slept over in another room, as Lana presumably did with Josh, why would she be in her dress?

I lift my badge. "Agent Andi Castle. Can I come in?"

She cackles. "I might be crazy right now, but I'm not an idiot. I remember who you are. And I know who your father is."

In other words, she's researched me. In my experience, you only do that when you need ammunition. And you only need ammunition because you fear my badge. Which is interesting considering her brother is now dead.

"Eddie Castle," she says. "Fired from the police department."

"And hired at a hundred times the pay," I reply, cringing as I repeat my father's own words. "I learned the law from a man who never lets the bad guy get away. Which should be comforting right now." She hasn't moved to allow me to enter. "Can I come in?" I repeat.

Still, she hesitates, but with obvious reluctance, she backs up and disappears into the room. I follow, allowing the door to shut behind me.

Natalie is standing at the window with her back to me. The bathroom is to my left and I step inside, scanning for signs of blood or a weapon, finding nothing but fancy bottles of skin cream. When I return to the main room, Natalie hasn't moved. She's still at that window. Her back is still my welcome.

Like my daddy before me, I'm not deterred.

I pull the chair out from the desk and face her before sitting down. I could be delicate with Natalie, but then she'd run over me. And I get the sense that's exactly where she wants this to go. She's going to be disappointed. Especially since she's likely set to benefit financially from Oliver's death. I start by putting her on the defensive. "I'm sure you're aware that Carrie could press charges, at which time I'll be forced to take you into custody."

She whirls on me. "Do you think I care?" The tears gone but the mascara stain not. "I haven't called my parents yet. That's what I'm thinking about. They're what I'm thinking about."

"And the loss of your beloved brother, I'm sure."

"I'm not even going to justify that remark with a reply. What do you need from me? You know who killed him. Arrest her. Question her. *Charge her.*"

"Why do you assume Carrie is the killer and not another victim?"

"How can you assume anything else?" she asks incredulously, arms flying in the air, bare, clean arms with no scratches or marks. "She's covered in his blood," she all but yells.

"Circumstantial," I state.

Her tone lowers to contempt. "Please tell me that you're not that stupid."

I just stare at her and *keep* staring at her.

She glances upward and then at me, looking more obligated than remorseful as she adds, "I guess calling an FBI agent stupid is actually the definition of 'stupid.'"

"Unless you're rich and powerful and above the law, I suppose," I reply, wondering if that's the way her family operates.

"I never said I was above the law."

"Are you?"

"Of course not."

"And Oliver?"

"Are you questioning my dead brother's character?"

"I'm just trying to understand who I'm dealing with."

Her eyes cut as they meet mine. "I don't like the tone of this conversation."

"I'm simply trying to give you what you want: closure. That is what you want, correct?"

"I think you're a bully like your father."

Usually, I reject any comparison to my father. I don't today. "He's not a bully," I say instead. "He's more a convincing negotiator." I leave out the part that usually involves my father's fist or his big-ass Smith & Wesson—officially named "the Governor," though some might think it better named "the Intimidator." Or maybe that is just my father.

"I don't know what that means." She hugs herself in a defensive move.

"Don't you?" I challenge.

"I don't like games, Agent Castle." She drops her arms and waves me forward. "Charge her and stop harassing me."

"Conducting an investigation is not harassment," I state, not even a little intimidated. After all, she's not holding the Governor, and piles of cash have never really struck fear in my heart. "It's, in fact," I continue, "the only way I can charge Carrie. I have to show the DA that I've done a complete and thorough investigation."

"Fine," she says tightly, leaning on the windowsill, hands pressed to either side of her. "What do you need from me?"

"Hypothetically," I say, "you could have reacted to the impossibility of Carrie being the killer." She starts to open her mouth and I hold up a hand. "But instead," I continue when she bites back her reply, "you responded to the certainty of her as the killer. Why? And don't tell me she was covered in blood. Go beyond that, to your core feelings about Carrie."

"There were things about her that bothered me."

"Okay," I accept, "so let's explore that, but start from the beginning. When did you meet Carrie?"

"Two years ago, but supposedly they'd been dating a year at that point." Her voice lifts again. "Why would my brother hide his girlfriend of *a year* from me or our parents?"

"Did he introduce prior girlfriends?" I ask.

"No," she concedes, "but no one ever lasted with Oliver before her. And she was the woman he proposed to."

"Why do you think he did that?"

"Why did he pick her to propose to or why didn't anyone last?"

"Both," I say.

"I don't know in either case, but neither of them talked about her family. They're in Houston. That's all we know."

Natalie's shoulders have relaxed slightly, as if talking about Carrie rather than herself is a more comfortable place.

"That's it?" I press. "Nothing more?"

"Her father is some sort of medical administrator for hospitals, and her mother's a nurse."

"She followed in their steps, then."

"It would appear," she agrees, because we're all about assumptions right now, it seems.

"You never asked?"

"We barely saw her"—her tone lifts defensively—"and when we did, they were very good at talking about Oliver, not Carrie. And not from a lack of effort. Oliver always took over the conversation and changed the topic."

"Why would he do that?" I ask.

"I have no idea," she states. "That's the point."

"Did your parents expect him to marry for status?"

"Absolutely not."

"Did your parents find his avoidance odd?"

"Absolutely, yes."

"Did they, or you for that matter, have her investigated?"

"Of course not. We might be snobs, but we're not heathens, Agent Castle." Her mouth twists. "I'm not sure you can say the same of your family, now can you?"

This feels like her version of a bait and switch, but I have no interest in the switch. I'm not big on games. They require patience that I don't possess. I blame my father, and his need for justice before the system has time to work, for that flaw in my character. Of course, he'd claim I blame him for everything. Maybe I do. Maybe I don't. Whatever the case, Natalie baiting me reads like a desperate need to take attention off herself.

My question is *why*.

What is she afraid of?

# Chapter Twenty-Seven

I don't know what Natalie Phoenix expects from me at this point. I suspect anger or defensiveness. What she gets is a comparison to my father. "You'd like my father," I declare. "You have a lot in common."

"I highly doubt that."

"He got fired for beating someone up," I state. "I just watched you beat someone up."

"She killed my brother."

"The guy my father beat up raped a child. See the comparison? Justification equals, well, justification, right?" Her eyes brim with disapproval, but I continue to push. "Doesn't it seem strange to you that a nurse, who is by definition a caregiver, would violently murder the man of her dreams?"

"There have been nurses who killed people. In fact, didn't I read about a serial killer nurse? The Angel of Death, I think, they called her?"

She's right, of course. Interesting topic for her to read about. "Him," I amend on that particular case from the '90s. "Orville Lynn Majors. He killed upwards of one hundred people. Are you telling me you suspect she was killing patients?"

"I have no idea," she says, sounding exasperated, "but I think you should look into it. Carrie is clearly a killer. Who knows how many she might have hurt?"

Natalie's wrong on at least one point. Nothing is clear to me at all right now. I've learned the hard way what looks obvious is often what someone wants me to see, not what I should see. I keep pressing forward. "What was Carrie's personality like?" I ask.

"Quiet. Kind."

"Kind?" I ask. "You just called her a killer and now you reference her as kind?"

"Too kind. Too quiet. I never trusted her. My brother is a wealthy man."

"Yes. About that," I say. "Who inherits on his death?"

She bristles, the tension locking up her shoulders again. "I have my own inheritance, if that's what you're asking. I don't need his. I assume she inherits Oliver's."

"Okay. But if she doesn't, would it be you?"

"It would go back to my parents, and they'd decide."

"So you do inherit," I confirm.

"I don't know," she insists. "But good Lord, I'm willing to donate it all to charity if that makes you shut up about me."

She's snappy, which reads defensive to me. "What about the company?" I ask, still pushing. "Wasn't he CEO?"

"Yes," she says, nervously wetting her lips.

"And you are?"

"VP," she says tightly.

"Or is it now CEO?"

"What are you trying to say?"

"Just making an observation."

"We're done," she says, her voice steely now. "You have no heart. I just lost my brother. I'm grieving and innocent, but obviously innocent people now need attorneys."

"You attacked a woman this morning, a violent act that followed a violent act. I have no option—"

"But to be a bitch?" she challenges.

"True," I state. "It's your fastest way to being cleared."

"Like I said. You're being a bitch."

"You say potato, I say pot-tat-oh." It's one of my father's favorite sayings, and the truth is, with people like Natalie, I don't mind channeling him one little bit. I learned from seeing him go too far when to stop. Which is pretty easy to do, considering he doesn't stop.

Ever.

"Are we done?" she asks, her tone a whip meant to cut.

My phone buzzes with a text message and I glance down, reading the alert I've received. "The medical examiner is here anyway." I stand up and offer her my card.

She doesn't reach for it. I set it on the desk. "Were you at the party last night?" I ask, not quite done with her.

"I don't do that kind of party," she states primly.

"Not even the early portion of the party, when we were all together?"

"No," she states. "I didn't attend the party."

"Then why did you come here this weekend at all?" I ask.

"To support my brother."

"Huh," I say.

She scowls. "What does that mean?"

I ignore her question and ask my own. "What did you do instead?"

"I got room service and stayed in. I had work to do."

"Then how did you know what was going on?" I ask.

"I was going to the gym. I left my room and found a crowd."

"Perfect," I say. "The hotel cameras should support your alibi. I'll get you marked off the list of suspects so you can at least get that monkey off your back."

"Alibi. I don't need a fucking alibi. You know who killed Oliver."

"It's procedure. Did your brother own a knife?"

"God, no. He was *not* that guy."

"What kind of guy is that?"

"I don't know. The kind of guy who owned a knife. A biker or hunter or outdoorsy type, I guess. Oliver liked to ski. That's about the only outdoor activity he liked. He didn't like bugs or the heat."

"Did he own a gun?" I ask.

"Yes. And so do I. For protection."

"Were either of you ever threatened?"

"Not directly, no, but we're rich, Agent Castle. We're targets."

"By anyone specific?" I query.

"Oh, good grief," she says, throwing her hands up in frustration. "You really don't understand the rich, do you? From assholes and bastards and, of course, pretty little witches who want our money. Correction: pretty little witches that pretend to be pretty little innocent girls who don't want our money. Like *Carrie*."

She's direct. I give her that. "Thanks for your time." I start to turn, letting her believe I'm about to leave, but I face her again. "Oliver was outside your door the night we all arrived, pacing and agitated. Why was that?"

"He was outside my door pacing?"

"He was."

"And you know this how?"

"My room is on this floor," I state. "I spoke to him."

"That must have been when I was at the bar. He texted me and said we needed to talk," she replies. "He said it was urgent, but when I arrived, he was gone. I sent him a text and he didn't reply."

"When was that?" I ask.

She pulls her phone from her pocket and checks the message and then surprises me by handing it over. I read the short text exchange that confirms what she's told me.

I return her phone to her. "Any idea what he wanted to talk about?"

"None."

"He was working this weekend when I ran into him. He appeared stressed, urgent even. Was he closing a big deal or managing a major problem?"

"Nothing I know of," she states. "We closed up a huge acquisition a week ago. He should have been in celebration mode."

*But he wasn't,* I think. Quite the opposite. Something doesn't add up.

"Do you own a knife?"

"What? No. No knife."

"Okay," I say.

"Okay?" she asks. "What does 'okay' mean?"

"'Okay' means 'okay.' I'll be in touch," I tell her, and this time I offer her my back to exit the room, but I find it's not a comfortable feeling.

# Chapter Twenty-Eight

The medical examiner is a gray-haired, soft-spoken man named Carl who is already inspecting the body when I arrive.

"Special Agent Andrea Castle," I greet him, indicating my badge. "What do you have for me?"

He straightens from his inspection of the body and inspects me. "I have to say, despite two decades at the busy Fort Collins Medical Examiner's Office, somehow this is my first time working with the FBI."

"That's a good thing, not a bad thing," I say. "Talk to me. What do we have?"

"I just arrived, but on first inspection, a fit of rage," he says, pressing his dark-rimmed glasses up his nose. "In excess of fifty stab wounds, but many of those wounds are superficial." He indicates the stomach. "This is the wound I suspect, on limited inspection, of course, killed him. It hit a vital artery. From a humane standpoint, one can hope it came early and he didn't feel the rest."

"Do we have a murder weapon?"

"We don't, but I believe it's some sort of hunting knife."

Somehow, I have a hard time seeing Oliver as a hunter, and his sister confirmed he wasn't, but sometimes people surprise not just me but those in their inner circle. "What else?" I ask, a firm believer in all information coming to me as organically as possible, at least initially.

"I believe the attacker was female, as the depth of the wounds are shallow, indicating a lack of strength to penetrate the tissue. I'll solidify that conclusion with further examination, and, of course, the forensics team will do their thing, but I've been doing this a long time. I'm not wrong."

Meaning forensics will test, and re-create the crime scene and, yes, the force at which the stab wounds were delivered. A strong, confident, experienced ME, backed by the same quality on the forensics side, can equal a conviction. But the defense will press the prosecution and try to disprove their data.

Which is why I can't ask too many questions. "Couldn't it simply be a smaller or weaker man and that the person was riding emotional adrenaline that wore off, weakening the impact?"

"Based on what I see here, that's a stretch. Again, I need to get back to the lab to confirm any initial thoughts. Right now, I'm offering a hypothesis I will test."

"Hmm," I say, in a noncommittal reply by intent. Everyone I've met at this event is highly intelligent; a number of them have medical training. Do I lean toward a female killer? Yes. Can I rule out someone educated enough to manipulate the stab wounds to appear female? No. But in the heat of the moment, it's also highly unlikely. And this was a heat of the moment killing. Although . . . if the killer was smart enough to fake one thing, they could fake another.

"Don't assume the cause of death," I say. "Make sure he wasn't already dead before the stabbing."

His spine straightens. "I'm thorough. That's why I said nothing is certain until I get in the lab."

I eye the blood all over the white comforter. "Was the attacker on top of him when they stabbed him, straddling him, perhaps?"

"He wasn't in the bed for the entire attack," he replies, indicating Oliver's legs hanging off the mattress. He walks to the end of the bed, where there is a large amount of blood on the skirt of the comforter. "I believe he was standing with his back to the bed when he was stabbed in the stomach. There's blood on his hands in excess, which indicates he most likely covered the wound and fell back on the mattress, thus the blood on the skirt. He was all but dead at that point, but the attacker didn't stop there."

"That's when someone would have climbed on top of him," I say, "pushed him backwards, and kept stabbing."

"Yes," he agrees simply.

"If that person was naked, where would the blood be located to support such a theory? Inner thighs?"

"Oh yes, and frankly," he adds, "the crotch. The attacker would have sat on his belly, which was the location of his mortal wound."

I'm mentally replaying the moment I allowed Carrie into the room and she flung herself on top of Oliver. She'd ensured she'd be wearing his blood, but she hadn't straddled him, not in the aftermath of the crime. If her inner thighs are stained, then there will be no escaping guilt, I think. "Helpful information," I say. "I'll let you work while I look around."

I pull my phone from my purse and call the hospital, chatting with a doctor to ensure proper photos and documentation are done. Not that I don't trust the staff at the hospital to do their jobs, but this is a small town, and they won't have an excess of experience to guide their efforts.

After I disconnect, I grab latex gloves from my bag. "Any sign of a phone?"

"I haven't looked."

He checks Oliver's left pocket. I check the right. We both survey the bed and blankets. "I'll keep looking," I say when we both come up dry.

Carl nods and I leave him to his work.

I walk to the opposite side of the bed, looking for the weapon, a cellphone, and the clothes Carrie might have been wearing during the attack, but there is no luck on any of these items. I check all drawers, under the bed, between the mattresses, behind the curtains, and inside a desk but come up empty.

Inside the bathroom, I hit the jackpot. Carrie's clothes are on the floor. She clearly undressed in this room. Perhaps she did so before she joined Oliver in the bedroom. Logically, it would seem she grabbed the knife from inside the bathroom and perhaps appeared naked in front of him to seduce him. He expected sex and instead came the blade. It's a picture easily painted, and yet it feels off. Why run away to nowhere but the attic? And why in the world do so naked?

Still pondering those questions, I spy two purses hanging on a towel rack. One is a large Louis Vuitton bag and the other is a petite Gucci evening purse. Homing in on the evening bag, I inspect the contents to find only a lipstick, powder, and travel hair spray inside. The Louis is more fully equipped, with a full-size wallet, a cosmetic bag, more hair spray, and a bottle of unlabeled pills. I open the bottle and find several different drugs inside. I stick the medication in a baggie I have with me and store it in my field bag. It's going with me to the hospital. The doctors need to know what is in Carrie's system, and so do I.

I search the documents in her wallet, but there's nothing that stands out. There's no knife or blood in the bathroom. Oliver's and Carrie's cellphones remain sight unseen. I grab my phone and call Lana, who I lost somewhere in the blood and confusion as I was swept into the crime scene. She answers on the first ring.

"Oh my God, Andi," she gushes. "What the hell is going on?"

"We'll talk later," I promise. "Right now, I need to know if you have Carrie's or Oliver's cellphone number."

"I have Carrie's, and I can get Oliver's."

"Text them both to me. I'll call you later." I hang up and Lana sends me Carrie's number right away. I dial it, walking around the bathroom and then the room, listening for the ring. There is nothing. Another text from Lana produces Oliver's number. Again, I dial it, but there is no ringing to follow.

I find the missing phones more than a little interesting. Carrie wasn't exactly hiding them when we found her naked and bloody.

# Chapter Twenty-Nine

Detective Edwards joins me in the room, and I send him off to the attic to look for the missing cellphones as well as order appropriate warrants. I stay behind, examining the crime scene, my quest to understand what the blood patterns might tell me about the struggle that occurred in the last moments of Oliver's life. Unfortunately, the carpet is a dark burgundy with flowers that create visual challenges. I've given up on my efforts with the blood when the forensics team finally shows up. I chat with them on the basics of the crime scene and bottle of medication before stepping into the hallway.

There I'm greeted by detective number two, Detective York, a man I'd age to sixty, with gray hair and a potbelly, who gets right to the point. "I know your father. Don't tell him I said hi. He's trouble, and I'm near retirement. Are you going to be trouble?"

"Only for the bad guy."

He smirks. "I'm not sure how I feel about that answer." But he also moves on, updating me on the search for the weapon he has well underway. We both agree: we need to know who in this group carries a knife and/or hunts. It's at least a logical place to start.

"I get the idea the wifey-to-be's a real delicate creature, not a violent bone in her body." Sarcasm laces his tone.

"Her words are as gentle as her actions," I assure him.

"Maybe the ghost of some asshole of old residing here in the hotel made her do it."

"I'm fairly certain every ghost in this place is afraid of her," I assure him. "I'd suggest staying away from her if you want to protect that retirement you're pining after."

Detective Edwards reappears and announces, "No sign of Oliver's or Carrie's phones in the attic. And yes, of course, before you ask, I pinged them."

"So where the hell are the phones?" York asks.

"Beats me," Edwards replies. "But I have a hard time believing a bloody, naked woman was running around and hiding those phones so well that we can't find them."

So do I.

It's time for me to head to the hospital and have a one-on-one with Carrie.

# Chapter Thirty

I arrive at the hospital and find Carrie's room guarded by one of the police officers who escorted her there. The doctor in charge is Roberto Mendez, a Hispanic man with a goatee and kind brown eyes, who is quick to meet me in an empty room just down from the closed door of Carrie's.

"How is she, Doctor?" I ask.

"Ms. Reynolds has a concussion," he says, shoving his hands inside his white coat. "She's quite dazed and confused. We've done blood tests and we're sending her in for a CAT scan as soon as the tech is free."

"Did she arrive high or drugged?"

"She believes she was drugged at the party."

He didn't exactly answer my question, but I go where he's leading. For now. "And she makes this assessment why?"

"Because she can't remember anything," he replies. "She has hours that have disappeared."

"Is she right? Was she drugged?"

"I can't give you a solid answer. Her rapid toxicology test shows no illicit drugs or anything worth noting, but as I'm sure you know, there's an excess of synthetic drugs now that don't show up on toxicology tests."

I reach in my bag and hand him the baggie with the pill bottle. "These are the drugs I found in her bag. There are numerous different pills in there."

Dr. Mendez opens the bottle and pours the pills in his hand, glancing at the number etched on the side of one of them. "This is an anti-anxiety medication. It would potentially mix very badly with any illicit drug she took willingly or unwillingly."

"Could it create violent behavior?"

"I can't say for sure. I don't know what combination of drugs, if any, we're dealing with, but hallucinations could be possible with the wrong cocktail of drugs. Certainly, when Ms. Reynolds is able to communicate her medications to me, I can offer more."

I swing back to my prior question in a slightly different way. "And to you, the hallucinations make her capable of violence?"

"Hypothetically, if you believe you're being attacked, you would certainly protect yourself. If you believe you're in danger, you'd certainly try to end the source of danger."

*Interesting,* I think. It's almost as if he knows she's guilty and he's launched her defense for her.

"What about injuries?" I ask. "Was any of the blood hers or was it all the victim's?"

"She has a large cut across her belly that would have bled quite a lot, but the excess of blood is not hers."

I'm surprised by the news of a wound on her belly, but I guess I shouldn't be. Her skin was a blanket of blood. "Is the injury self-inflicted?"

"Hard to say," he comments yet again, noncommittal on every point, it seems. "I'm not an expert in such things. I just sew them up."

"What about any defensive marks on her arms?" I ask.

"None," he says, and again defending her, he adds, "but that means nothing. I spent some time working in a high-end Aspen drug rehab facility years back. When a person is on drugs, that person isn't living in reality. Therefore, the reactions aren't what we'd expect. Believe me, I've seen things. The person could see Prince Charming in the same person one minute and some sort of demon the next."

"But we don't actually know she was on drugs, correct?" I ask, going by his own assessment in this very conversation.

"Based on her physical and medical condition, we can make the reasonable assumption she was."

"Can that be faked?"

"Not easily," he replies, "but I have to go on record here and say that Ms. Reynolds's head injury complicates her evaluation. She has a concussion. Is the dilation of her eyes created by that injury or drugs? Or both? That is yet to be established."

"Let's talk about the blood all over her body. I assume the photos I requested were taken before she was cleaned up?"

"They were. They're being logged into our system and then they'll be available for your review."

"Did you examine her prior to her cleanup?"

"I did," he confirms.

"Was there blood on her inner thighs that might suggest she straddled the victim?"

"There was not."

It's not the answer I expect, and it's not an answer that clears Carrie of guilt, but it certainly doesn't work against her, either. "Can I talk to her?"

"As I mentioned, she's headed in for a CAT scan. I won't allow her to talk to you until I've had a chance to evaluate it and her more completely for purely safety reasons."

"How long do you think that will be?"

"A few hours."

A frustrating answer that I'm forced to accept. "I'll be nearby," I say, handing Mendez my card. "Call me if anything changes, or if you need me for any reason at all. I do need to point out that no matter what the circumstances, a man is dead—violently murdered, in fact—and she's our top suspect in our custody. Handle her with caution."

"She's cuffed to the bed," he says dryly and rather shortly. "I did assume as much." His lips press together. "I should get back to the medical portion of this equation."

"Of course," I say. "I didn't mean to keep you."

Mendez turns on his heel, intent on walking away, but I call out, "One more question."

The doctor pauses and turns to face me.

"How personal is the addiction thing to you?"

He bristles. "If you're asking if I'm a former addict, I am, which allows me the unique ability to root my opinions both on experience and science."

"But it also could skew your opinions," I say. "Or at least, that's what the prosecution would say."

His expression tightens. "We're done here."

He walks away, with long, swift strides. I've hit a nerve or maybe ten.

# Chapter Thirty-One

## CARRIE

I blink awake as a man with dark hair and eyes leans over me.

"Hello?" I whisper, because nothing else comes to me. My mind is foggy, my body heavy.

He smiles. "Hello."

"Who are you?" I ask.

His dark brows form a thick line. "You don't remember?"

I can feel my own brow furrow in response, and I'm acutely aware of a stinging sensation in my belly. I moan and shift, only to have the man warn, "Easy. Don't move too much. You have fresh stitches."

I blink away the shadows, and a haze that desperately works to consume me. "Stitches?"

"You don't remember?" he repeats.

"No," I whisper, not even sure I know what I'm saying no to, but I say it again. "No."

"Try. What do you remember?"

My lashes lower and lift again, relieved to find an answer in my mind. "You're a doctor. And I'm in the hospital."

"Exactly. Good, you're starting to remember things. What else can you remember?"

Suddenly I'm back in time, naked and cold, in a strange place with wooden walls, staring at the blood on my hands. More memories punch at my mind, but they won't fully develop. My body begins to tremble with the effort, a warning that whatever lurks in the shadows of my memory will hurt me. "I don't want to remember," I whisper, desperate to stop what is forming in my mind. "I don't want to remember!" I shout, sitting up, my belly burning, but I don't care. My head hurts even worse. It throbs with the memory of blood all over the bed. I jerk at my arm and I'm trapped. I'm trapped and I have to get away. Suddenly, there is screaming, loud screaming. The doctor is by my side.

"Calm down," he orders. "You need to calm down. Nurse! Nurse!"

It's me that's screaming, I realize, and I can't stop. "No!" I yell. "No! No! No!" The bloody images in my mind become Oliver. Oliver is covered in blood. Pain rips through me, and I'm screaming again. "Oliverrrrrrr! Oliverrrrr! No! No! Oliver!"

A needle is jabbed in my arm, and there is a burn there as well before exhaustion overtakes me. I ease back on the mattress, my lashes heavy, and my eyes lift to the doorway, where I find a familiar face. The FBI agent. I know her. "You," I whisper. "You."

She appears by my side and kneels.

The doctor yells at her. "Not now, Agent Castle."

"Agent Castle," I whisper, and this time her name stirs something inside me, an emotion I cannot pinpoint.

"Tell me what happened, Carrie," she orders softly.

The emotion is anger. I'm angry with her. "Why didn't you save him?" I hiss, but my lashes lower, the drugged, heavy feeling overtaking me. The world goes dark.

# Chapter Thirty-Two

## Andi

Two nurses crowd me out of the room and slam the door. The police officer is quick to offer aid, but I wave him off. "Don't let her out of your sight," I order. "Even when she's taken for testing."

Dr. Mendez exits the room and motions me to wait. "I have limits, Agent Castle. And they all revolve around my patients. Patients have rights."

"Her fiancé was stabbed at least fifty times. He's dead. I'm the only one who can fight for his rights, and for him that means nothing more than justice. That's all there is left. And that's why your 'patient' is cuffed to the bed. So she won't stab you to death as well."

"I have a sworn oath to save lives. I don't get to pick and choose which ones. They choose me when they come in the door. Surely you can understand that?"

"I do," I say. "But I also know that murders that aren't solved in the early hours and days of the investigation don't get solved."

"When the test is done, Agent Castle." And on that note, Mendez turns and walks back inside Carrie's room, shutting the door.

My cellphone rings and I snag it from my pocket to find Lana calling. Carrie is her friend, and I answer with, "How are you?"

"Are you coming back over?"

"I'm on my way now."

"I need to tell you something about Carrie and Oliver, just you. Something I think could be important."

Conversations about murder are better accessed in person, where I can read the other person, which is why I say, "I'll be right there," and disconnect without asking details.

Lana is the last person I'd expect to have something to offer in this investigation.

But at this point, nothing should surprise me.

# Chapter Thirty-Three

Once I walk back into the hotel, I'll no doubt be bombarded with people, questions, and problems. Therefore, for everyone's safety and mine, I need to caffeinate and freshen up. I stop at a store and grab a toothbrush and toothpaste and head into their bathroom, where I brush my teeth and wash my face, and then leave with a bad cup of necessary coffee. And as expected, the minute I enter the hotel, I have hotel staff and law enforcement cornering me.

Upon my return to the fourth floor, York is immediately standing in front of me. "Bad news," he announces.

I brace myself with a long swallow of coffee as he adds, "There are no cameras on the room floors. There are no cameras by the emergency exits on any level."

"Of course not," I say dryly.

"There's a bright side. Working cameras do exist in the main hotel and stairwell, as well as the exterior of the building."

"Which tells us what?" I ask, looking for the good news.

"We know Natalie Phoenix went to her floor at about ten," he says, but that tidbit of good is doused in bad as he continues with, "Now, did she leave after that? We can't know because the emergency stairwell is a blind spot."

"What about Oliver and Carrie? When did they head to their room?"

"That's where there's another problem. A ton of people from both sides of the party ended up in the hotel bar. Maybe some of those people used the emergency stairwells to return to their rooms. Apparently, the main staircase is haunted, and there was an incident that freaked people out."

"Incident?"

"Word is that someone said a ghost touched their hair and that someone started screaming. It freaked out all the drunk people."

*Which sounds fishy to me,* I think. Almost as if "someone" wanted to ensure there was a reason to use the emergency stairs. But then again, those stairs and the underground tunnels, where Bianca had a similar issue, are known for these strange encounters. If you believe in such things, which I might or might not. "Find out who that someone was and talk to them," I say.

"On it," York confirms. "As for who left the bar and when, we're going to have to compare interviews to video footage in an effort to validate stories."

"What about Carrie's and Oliver's phones? Or the murder weapon?"

"We found hers. It was dead and in her coat pocket in the hotel room. The damn thing didn't ping at all. Which, of course, seems to indicate that despite her party being in this building, she left at some point."

"Did we power up the phone?"

"We did and gave it an unofficial look since we don't have the warrant yet. She exchanged a few messages with random friends yesterday, a few with Oliver that seem like lovey-dovey bullshit, if you ask me, and then nothing once the party started."

"And Oliver?"

"We haven't found his phone. The Fort Collins tech team is working on the call logs and records."

"Obviously you've got this under control," I say. "Run with it and update me. I also need security run on everyone in the hotel. Do you have the manpower to make that happen?"

"I can collect all the data from the hotel, but it's a lot of people."

"Gather the list. I'll text you with the contact on my team that can handle it." We both whip out our phones, and I connect him with Aiden. When I've gotten him the needed information, I add, "The killer likely straddled Oliver to stab him. There was no blood on Carrie's inner thighs. So either she cleaned up or she didn't kill him. Keep an eye out for discarded clothing."

"Do you really think she's innocent?" he asks.

"It's dangerous to assume anything this early. It taints the entire way you look at the investigation. I'm going to talk to Lana Melody, who I know personally. She's a friend of Carrie's and says she has something to tell me I need to know."

York's brow shoots up. "Really? I'm intrigued. Need a sidekick?"

"Reconsider that offer," I say, good-naturedly. "I'm a Castle, remember?"

He grunts. "Right. I'll stand down."

"Good plan," I say, and by that, I mean for him and me. After Whit, I'm done with sidekicks, at least for a while. "Divide and conquer and all that wonderful stuff," I add, stepping around him as I head toward room 428.

There quickly, I've managed one knock on the door when Lana yanks it open. Her eyes are bloodshot and swollen. She's changed into leggings and a black sweater, and her face is now bare. "I can't believe this has really happened," she says, backing up and letting me in the room. "But thank God I convinced you to come."

I follow her into the small room, and she motions to the bed. "That's our only chance of sitting."

"Works for me," I say, sipping my coffee. "Anything that lets me relax and caffeinate for at least ten seconds without interruption. A shower would be nice, too, but I have a feeling that isn't happening until bedtime."

We settle onto the end of the bed and angle toward each other, me sipping my coffee, Lana hugging herself and looking tormented. "Talk to me," I say, setting the cup on the floor. "What's bothering you?"

"She loved him passionately," she says instantly. "And she's never been anything but kind and nice to me and everyone around her."

"But," I prod, pushing for what is obviously there.

"I don't want to make her look guilty. That's not what my intent is here."

"I don't assume anyone's guilt," I say. "Tell me."

She scowls, clearly not happy with that answer. "How can you not assume her guilt? I saw her. She was covered in blood."

"I've seen a number of innocent people covered in blood. They find their loved one and immediately try to revive them. That gets messy."

"Is that what she did?" she asks hopefully.

"I can't relay details on an active investigation. I'm simply assuring you that I never assume guilt. Talk to me," I urge.

"God. I hate this, but I know I have to tell you. A few weeks back, late one evening while Carrie and Oliver waited on a food delivery, Oliver received another delivery, a gift."

"What kind of gift?"

"A big box with a red ribbon on it. It was addressed to only him. The handwriting appeared female. Apparently, he opened it and shut it without showing Carrie what was inside. He told her it was a bad gag gift from a groomsman."

"Which groomsman?"

"That's just it. He refused to tell her which one. He said he didn't want her to hate that friend of his. He then went into his office, shut the door, and didn't come out for a while."

"Which wasn't normal for him?"

"No. Not at all. And she went to check on him and the door was locked. She was worried Oliver was cheating on her, which to me seems a natural fear. But that man adored her. He would never have cheated. It was in his eyes every time he looked at her."

"Was there any other reason she thought he might be cheating?"

"She said that after that box showed up, he didn't act the same. He was withdrawn and unsettled in some way. So much so that one night when he was working late, she surprised him at the office."

"She thought he wouldn't be there?"

"Or that he would be doing something he shouldn't," she replies. "His secretary is apparently gay, but also very attractive."

"And?" I query. "What happened when she got there?"

"He was thrilled to see her and to sit and have dinner with her before he finished his work."

"How often did he work late?"

"His dad retired earlier than expected, so I think that put him in a tough spot. He suddenly had to take over the company. That's why they put the wedding off last year."

"They put the wedding off?" I ask, which sounds like trouble in paradise to me.

"Yes. She was upset, but he bought her a house to make up for it."

My phone buzzes and I look down to find a message from York: Carrie's family is headed into town.

In other words, Carrie will lawyer up soon and I need to talk to her now, not later.

I sigh and eye Lana. "Anything else?"

"One night when I was with Carrie, there was this news story about a young boy getting hit by a car. It was horrible. She started crying and wouldn't talk to me."

"That's extreme."

119

"It was," she agrees. "I told Oliver. He pulled me aside and told me that when they were kids—Carrie and her brother—they were riding bikes and he fell into traffic. He died."

"Oh Jesus," I say, a distinct pinch in my chest that has everything to do with my mother's own car accident.

"Yeah, I know," Lana says. "It's horrible. And Oliver told me not to bring it up to her or her parents. I got the impression on some level they blame her? I don't know. He was weird about it, and I'm just sharing the gut feeling I had. It may not be true at all."

"Why did they blame her?"

"I don't know. Maybe it's natural to blame the surviving child? I've seen spouses blame each other over the death of a child. I think that's what makes me read some blame into what Oliver said. I've seen blame thrown around a lot in the ER and even in pediatrics."

*That's all true,* I think. I have seen similar reactions to tragedy myself. I make a mental note to check out the details of the accident and go for closure. "Anything else?" I ask again.

"No. That's it. I hope it helps."

"Thank you for telling me. It does." I stand up. "I'll check in with you later today." I head for the door.

"God," she whispers from behind me, and then: "Andi, wait."

When I turn, she's standing, fingers wringing together. "There's more, but, Andi, I swear I don't think she did this. She loved him."

"Tell me," I urge.

"She said she never saw the box after the delivery came to the house. She said he got rid of the box, the ribbon, and the card."

"But?"

"I saw a red ribbon in her work locker."

In other words, Carrie found the box. After which, she went from talking to Lana to keeping her mouth shut. I'm officially intrigued. What was in that box?

# Chapter Thirty-Four

## CARRIE

I blink awake again, staring at the ceiling, a throb in my head as I try to remember where I am. And thank God, my memory returns quickly. I'm in the hospital. Or maybe not. Maybe I don't want to remember and with good reason. I'm alone. *Forever.* Because Oliver is *dead.* I squeeze my eyes shut and reject the very idea.

No.

No.

*No.*

"Carrie."

My lashes lift again, my gaze following the voice, to bring the pretty brunette leaning over me into view. "Andi," I say. "Or is it Agent Castle now?"

"What do you want to call me?"

"Andi. That sounds more like my friend. And since no one else is here, I kind of need a friend right now."

"Then call me Andi," she says. "Glad to see you were able to sleep a bit."

"It's the only time I don't have to face the truth."

"And what truth is that?" she asks.

"He's gone. Oliver is gone," I say, my voice cracking, a pinch in my chest that grows stronger by the moment.

"I know this is difficult, and the doctor tells me you're suffering from a concussion on top of everything else."

"That's what I'm told," I reply, thankful Dr. Mendez is compassionate and gentle.

Andi pulls a chair up next to me. "Do you know how that happened?"

My mind flashes to Natalie holding my head and slamming it against the floor, and I cut my gaze.

"Carrie?" Andi presses.

I blink her back into view. "She attacked me. Natalie attacked me. I remember."

"What else do you remember?"

"You finding me in the attic." I lower my gaze and add, "The blood." I press my hands to my face and swallow the bile in my throat, panting out a breath.

"Tell me about the blood," she urges.

My hands find the blanket and my fingers ball around the top sheet, anger flaring inside me. "What do you want to hear?" I demand. "You saw it."

"I saw it all over *you*."

Defensiveness replaces anger. "Yes, well, I have stitches for a reason."

"And what is that reason?"

"I was cut in the belly," I whisper.

"How?"

"I don't know," I repeat. The words seem to be my answer to everything, and that frustrates no one as much as it does me.

"All of that blood wasn't yours," she reminds me.

"I know," I say hoarsely. "Believe me, *I know*. Being covered in the blood of the man you love is not a pleasant thing."

"How did you end up naked and in the attic, Carrie?"

My eyes meet hers, and those dreaded words follow. "I don't know. I've tried to remember."

"What's the last thing you do remember?"

"The attic," I repeat. "You finding me in the attic." I can't offer her more. I don't know more, and the very act of not knowing is defeating.

"Before that," she pushes.

"The party." I swallow hard, my mind returning to the hotel, to the room full of smiling faces, the music, the scent of Oliver's cologne. "I remember Oliver kissing me before he left for his bachelor party."

"What else?" she presses.

What else, I think, and I truly try to remember—what *else*?

There's a flicker in my mind of me fighting with Bianca, and I seize on that piece of knowledge. "I was angry with Bianca for lining up the male dancers. I didn't know they were attending the party. Or performing. I felt it was a betrayal of Oliver's trust."

"What did Bianca say?"

"I'm not clear on that yet—I think Lana calmed me down. Yes. Lana told me just to let it go and enjoy myself."

"Did Oliver have dancers at his party?"

"I doubt it," I say. "I hope not," I add. "I wouldn't want to think that the last woman he saw naked was someone other than me." I press my hands to my face. "God. I can't believe I even had that thought." I drop my hands. "He's dead. God, *he's dead*. How can that even be? We were *happy*. We were *getting married*. He was everything, *everything* I ever wanted." The room spins, and that anger I felt moments before returns hard and fast, seething inside me.

"You," I hiss. "You were supposed to protect him. Why didn't you save him, Agent Castle? Why didn't you save him?!"

A nurse bursts into the room and Andi holds up a hand, speaking to me. "How would I save him?" she replies, now at the end of the bed, staring at me, demanding of me. "I wasn't there, but *you* were."

"I wasn't there," I bluster. "I didn't kill him. I *loved* him."

"And yet you were in an attic."

"Agent Castle!" the doctor demands, entering the room. *"Stop."*

"I was hiding!" I scream at her. "I was hiding! I was afraid!"

"Hiding from *who*?" she demands. "Afraid of *what*?"

"I don't know!" I shout. "What part of that do you not understand?! *I don't know.*" There's a piercing sensation in my skull. "Oh God," I groan, grabbing my head.

"Enough, Agent Castle!" the doctor shouts. "Enough." He steps between me and her and pushes her toward the door.

"No," I whisper, wanting to call her back, but the pain turns into a hum in my ears. I can't fight through the noise, but I want to tell the doctor to let Andi stay. I didn't mean to shout at her. I need her. I need help. But the noise and the pain. It's too much.

I scream with the force of it, and a needle is stuck in my arm.

The pain fades and so does the room.

# Chapter Thirty-Five

## ANDI

By the time I'm back at the hotel, it's a madhouse of press.

Because why in the world wouldn't I want to talk to a bunch of reporters? My father calls the press bloodsucking idiots, usually to their faces. Though I often complain about his rudeness, after the past month, I swear the press would suck my blood and have me for dinner if given the opportunity.

Fortunately, with York in retirement mode, he's not only silenced the team and hotel staff, he knows every way to avoid anything that resembles trouble. He sneaks me in a side door.

"You're a hero," I tell him as he leads me into the service hallway.

"For now," he says. "Once the hotel is out of lockdown, all bets are off." He motions me forward, and we end up in a conference room he's smartly set up as ground zero. "The rest of the Phoenix family should arrive in a couple of hours," he says as I note a row of detectives around the table, all absorbed in work. "They've rented a private house."

"I'll go to them," I offer. "*We* can go to them."

He gives a nod and introduces me to the team, excusing himself to answer a call, and leaving me to direct the team.

I don't waste a lot of time on pleasantries, and quickly get right to what is important. I introduce the box with the red ribbon to the team, have them dig through the National Crime Information Center database for connected cases, and post our own in case we get a hit on a connection. It's a long shot, of course, considering this seems to be a localized crime of a personal nature, but we all thought the first Spider Man murder was a one-off. Had we just looked beyond the crime at hand, had we immediately searched and listed our crime in the NCIC system, we would have known better. We might have gotten further faster. We might have saved at least one life.

Once I'm sure that task is in hand, I step into a private room and dial Aiden. "How's it looking?" he asks.

"Problematic," I say. "I have press everywhere. One of the witnesses, a friend of the suspect, Carrie, says Oliver received a box with a ribbon. She thought he was cheating."

"Jealousy," he says. "The oldest motive in the book. I'm assuming you need a warrant for their home?"

"And their places of work."

"I'll get the team on it. What else?"

"She has a cut on her belly. She says she ran to hide. I can charge her, and that's what Oliver's wealthy family will press for."

"But you're afraid it will be premature?"

"I'm not sure she did it."

"You're kidding me. She was covered in his blood."

"And sliced open in the belly."

"You think someone else did it?"

"The defense will ask that question. I have to ask it, too, though there are a few weird things that don't add up."

"Such as?"

"It seems she would have had to straddle him to stab him, but there's no blood between her legs. Not unless she cleaned up, and I don't know if I will find evidence to prove that."

"The defense will use it against you."

"I know. Believe me, I know."

"Any other suspects?"

"The sister attacked Carrie, which could be nothing more than the obvious: she believes Carrie killed her brother. It felt a bit like a show she was putting on. And she vibes weird to me, and I never ignore my gut feeling. I don't think she's a good person."

"I'll get a couple investigators out digging into the immediate family of Carrie and Oliver and the guests at the party."

"Everyone at the hotel needs a quick look. I know it's a lot, but there could be someone here with a connection to the party that I don't know has a connection."

"Agreed."

"And Carrie and Oliver. I need everything there is to know about them."

"Agreed again."

We end with a plan for the investigators and a promise that Aiden will expedite my security checks, warrants, and DNA tests the best he can. The labs are not known for speed. But if I let Carrie go, and she did kill Oliver with a motive of jealousy, she might not be done killing.

In my mind, I need to know who sent that box. I also need to know what was inside, but who sent it leads me to the answer as well.

There's no easy way to do that.

It goes back to basic investigative work. While I believe there are details that must be discovered here on-site, I also believe the missing pieces of the puzzle are back in Denver.

Therefore, the entire goal for the next few hours is for me to use our resources, which include a mix of twenty detectives and officers, to do initial interviews, confirm alibis, log contact information, and clear the hotel. Once I have the team at work, I pull York aside and fill him in on the box.

"Huh," he says. "What the hell was in that box, and what does it have to do with murder?"

"Exactly," I say. "What was in the box? But play this coy," I add. "Don't tell anyone it exists, but let's see if we can get someone to bring it up."

"Agreed," he says. "I'll talk to the team."

"Actually," I say, "I'll talk to the main wedding party myself. Lana has only known Carrie six months, and she told her about the box. Let's see who else she told. I'll start with people who I assume to be closest to Carrie: her bridesmaids."

# Chapter Thirty-Six

Turns out the bridesmaids include Bianca, Sally, and Tabitha, the three women I met at drinks. And as one might expect under these circumstances, they've all gathered together in one room—room 418, where the ghostly children play and Sally and Bianca are sharing. I head in that direction without offering them a heads-up and knock on the door. Sally is quick to answer. She's smaller than I first assessed, barely five feet, her dark bob cut in a perfect match to her jawline. And today, her bright-blue eyes are bloodshot.

"Hi," she says softly. "Agent . . . I'm sorry, I only remember your first name."

"Agent Castle," I say.

"Agent Castle," she repeats. "Please come in."

She backs farther into the room, allowing me space to enter. I pause and step into the bathroom and look around, finding nothing of consequence before joining the three women in the main room. They're all sitting on the edge of the bed, side by side, Bianca in the center, almost as if they've created a police lineup. All of them are in leggings and big shirts, makeup streaked on their faces.

I pull up the desk chair and sit down. "Is he really dead?" Sally asks, shoving her hair behind her ears.

I give a slow incline of my chin. "I'm sorry to report that yes, he is."

The three of them look at each other, and Bianca seems to speak for them all. "You don't think she did it, right?"

"Do you?" I ask, and that's all it takes to set them on fire.

The lot of them all launch into a jumbled chatter of voices, but one message cuts through it all: Carrie would never hurt Oliver. "I'm telling you," Bianca finishes for them, rambling in Spanish about demons before she adds, "if Carrie hurt him, it's this hotel. Someone, or something, touched me down in those tunnels. This place is haunted."

"She wouldn't do this," Sally adds. "She's the most kind and patient person I know, even under extreme pressure."

"Agreed," Tabitha chimes in. "In two years in the ER with her, I've never seen her lose her cool, and I've seen her have plenty of reasons to do so. I don't believe she'd hurt him." She shakes her head in rejection. "No. There's more to this story."

"We did find her naked and covered in blood," I supply, confirming what they probably already know.

"Was it her blood or his?" Sally queries. "Because she probably freaked out and tried to save him. When I worked ER way back when, we saw that all the time."

"Very true," Tabitha agrees. "Very true. And she adored him endlessly. I can't imagine how she'd react to finding him injured and dying or, Lord forbid, dead." She presses her hand to her belly. "I can barely even say the words."

"Tell me how you all know Carrie?"

"We all work together," Bianca says. "She joined the ER about two years ago, and she and I were instant friends. We all were."

"But you're the closest to her?" I ask.

"We're all close," she reiterates. "That's why there isn't a maid of honor. She called us all family."

"Lana's part of the group now, too, right?"

"Lana is kind of a loner," Tabitha says. "She doesn't like the ER. She resists becoming a part of our group."

"But you're friends?" I ask.

"Of course," Bianca confirms. "Lana is hilarious and loads of fun. She just can't handle the blood and death. It's not her thing."

*And yet Carrie told her about the box,* I think, but I ask, "Had Carrie and Oliver been fighting lately?"

They all murmur quick replies that amount to a denial of any strife between the future married couple. No one brings up the box, but once we're back in Denver and one-on-one, that may change.

"I understand Carrie was upset over the male dancers?" I ask.

"She was worried about betraying Oliver," Bianca says. "But she got over it. She had fun."

"Was she angry about Oliver being around female dancers?"

"Angry?" Bianca asks. "That's not Carrie's thing. She doesn't get angry. She didn't like the idea of the dancers, but she knew Oliver wouldn't cheat on her."

*She doesn't get angry,* I repeat in my mind. That is, of course, disingenuous. Everyone gets angry. To say that they do not is a lie. The question is, Who's lying? Carrie's friends to protect her? Or has Carrie lied to her friends about who, and what, she is?

"When was the last time any of you saw Carrie?" I ask the group.

"She was at the bar with us," Sally says. "She left when we left."

"Which was when?" I press.

"Around two thirty," Tabitha interjects. "I remember looking at the clock. I saw some horror movie where two o'clock was when a demon came out to taunt people. I was spooked by that idea and the hotel in general and came back here to stay with Bianca and Sally."

"Was Oliver with Carrie when she left?" I ask.

"No," Bianca supplies. "He was still at his party."

"Okay," I say. "And just so you're not sideswiped," I add, "we'll likely talk to all of you one-on-one once we get back to Denver. For now, before I leave, is there anything any of you think I need to know now?"

"I know it looks bad," Bianca says, "but I also know she didn't do this."

The other women murmur their agreement, and I stand up. "Thank you, ladies. We're hoping to get you all out of here soon." I start to turn and change my mind. I glance between them and divulge what I have not to this point. "She was naked, covered in his blood, and in the attic. If there's anything I need to know, tell me now."

Bianca stands. "Naked? In an attic? I don't understand. I thought she was in her room?" She holds up her hands. "That's insane. She's shy, extremely modest. I mean, to the point of ridiculous sometimes."

"I agree," Sally adds. "She wouldn't run around the hotel naked, not unless she was terrified for her life, and even then, it's hard to imagine."

"She had to be running from someone," Tabitha suggests. "Running for her life." Her hand smacks over her mouth before she pulls back her fingers and says, "Oh my God. Poor Carrie. What really happened last night?"

"That is the question," I say. "I'll be in touch, ladies."

I head for the door, and the word *running* sticks in my mind.

Carrie claimed that she was running as well, but she couldn't tell me from who or what. But as I step into the hallway, I don't believe the answer is in the minds of the women I just left. I think it's in that box.

# Chapter Thirty-Seven

While the women gathered in a hotel room, I'm told that the men, with York's approval, have gathered in the bar. Booze does tend to make tongues waggle. And who am I to sideline free will? I head in that direction.

I arrive at the bar to find the group huddled around a table, a collection of beer bottles evident. I'm standing in the doorway, observing them, when York shoots me a cheat sheet on each groomsman that includes age and career. The list includes Josh, Cade, Trevor, and a guy named Nick. Brody is on my list, but he's not in the bar. Which is interesting considering Carrie doesn't like Brody, at least by his own admission. I'm not sure if that somehow connects to his absence at present, but it sits wrong. And when something sits wrong, it's worth a mental note.

Another outlander, Josh is alone at the end of the bar, a whisky glass in front of him, his jaw clenched, pain radiating from him. Something tells me he was coaxed out of his room by the sweet numbing effect of whisky, not by his friends, even if they believe differently. I step to the end of the table, and the other three men go silent for a few beats.

"Agent," Cade greets me, holding up his beer.

"How's everyone holding up?" I ask.

"Like absolute shit," Trevor states. "I can't believe he's dead. I can't believe she killed him."

"I'm definitely inspired to stay single," Nick says, shoving thick-rimmed glasses up his nose. He's kind of a Clark Kent geeky sort, obviously smart or he wouldn't be the CFO of a large security company.

"Says the only guy at the table seeing someone," Trevor comments, the Rolex on his wrist a flashy number, but then, I get the impression he's a flashy kind of guy. His hair is neatly slicked back, his nails manicured, the ring on his right hand expensive. Even now, his T-shirt is pressed, though his jawline is shadowed.

"Yeah, well, maybe Sharon's a little too perfect. Like Carrie."

"What does that mean?" I ask. "Too perfect?"

"Carrie is Mary freaking Poppins," Nick says. "She was like everyone's mother, sister, and best friend. Sharon loves her. The only reason she's not here this weekend is that her sister went into labor."

"No one is that perfect," Cade says. "I told Oliver that about ten times. He didn't like hearing it. She changed him."

"He means he wasn't all about the guys anymore," Trevor says, "and Cade got his panties all in a wad. His feelings got hurt."

"Fuck you, Trevor."

Trevor smirks. "So easily riled up, asshole."

"In other words," I say, "he was devoted to Carrie."

"Very," Nick replies. "He loved her. I just . . . I really can't see her killing him. She was too timid and sweet. And damn it, I can't believe he's dead." His voice cracks. "I need to go to my room. What else do you need from me, Agent?"

"Anyone here have a different opinion about Carrie?"

"She was quiet and timid," Cade says, "but sometimes those are the ones to worry about."

"Ignore him," Trevor orders. "He hates everyone."

"You said she killed him, too," I point out.

"Because she did it," Cade asserts. "He's just feeling guilty for stabbing her in the back. I don't. She stabbed Oliver all over his fucking body. Don't expect me to defend her."

"We don't know what happened yet," I state, eyeing the group. "Was Oliver in any kind of trouble?"

The general, quick consensus is no. No one knew of Oliver being in trouble. I move on. "When was the last time any and all of you saw Oliver?"

"I saw nothing but the blonde with big boobs once she got here," Cade says, flippant considering why I'm here, but I find people, men especially, often hide their feelings.

"He was with me," Nick says. "He wasn't into the women. We both felt like our women were going to be pissed. We ended up in a corner drinking expensive whisky. As to when he left, I took a call from Sharon and when I got back, he was gone."

"What was his mood?"

"He had some work project bothering him," he says. "But he was happy as hell about the wedding."

"Was there anyone that might want to hurt Oliver? Anyone he had a dispute with?"

The entire table bristles to such an extreme you'd think I'd just told them to bend over and cough. "Who?" I press.

"No one," Nick bites out.

"Oh, come on, Nick," Cade chides. "Why are you protecting him?"

"She needs to know," Trevor agrees, his attention on me now. "Brody and Oliver had a falling-out. None of us knew what it was about, but they didn't speak for months."

"And yet he was here?" I query.

"Josh invited him," Cade offers. "And Carrie was not happy."

"Why not?" I ask.

There's a lot of shrugging that follows. No one has an answer for me.

"How did the surprise invitation work out?" I ask.

"Oliver and Brody were hanging out together," Trevor says. "At the early part of the party. They made peace."

"Brody isn't here with you now," I observe. "Why?"

"Once he and Oliver had that falling-out, he disappeared," Cade states. "He cut us all out. We hadn't seen him in months."

And yet Josh, the best man, invited him. He had to have known Oliver wanted to mend that broken fence of friendship. I eye Josh over at the bar now. "How's he holding up?"

"Like shit," Trevor says. "He was off with the Lana chick and didn't see Oliver much last night. He's feeling pretty guilty."

Guilt.

*It can kill,* I think.

Nothing about this group interests me right now. Josh is another story.

"Expect to talk to me again back in Denver. And if any of you have anything I need to know, call or text me." I set a stack of cards on the table and move toward Josh.

# Chapter Thirty-Eight

As I near Josh, his energy says that he knows I'm approaching him, but he doesn't turn to greet me. Instead, I claim the seat next to him and we both just sit there staring across the bar. His eyes meet mine in the bar mirror and he turns to look at me. "Agent Castle. Do you know how I know you're Agent Castle?"

"I'm fairly certain at this point the entire hotel knows who I am," I reply.

"Oliver told me. He told me before I ever came in contact with you. He was freaked out about you being here. As his friend and attorney, he wanted me to make sure there wasn't a problem. I told him he was paranoid. Obviously, he wasn't."

"I didn't attend this event for professional reasons," I assure him.

"And yet, he thought you did," he retorts. "Why?" There's anger bubbling beneath his surface.

His anger doesn't unsettle me. Death breeds guilt and guilt breeds anger, especially in those close to the person, and usually in those with regrets. I want to know what the source is for Josh, but I'll go slow and let him lead me there.

"My badge tends to make people nervous," I state. "It could have been nothing more than that."

"Or it *was* more and I was too busy chasing a skirt to find out for him. And now he's dead. Now it's obvious to me something was going on. What did I miss? Why did you being here freak him out? And don't repeat that badge makes people nervous bullshit."

"You tell me. You were his attorney and best man, which I assume translated to the best friend."

"Like a brother," he says, downing his whisky. "He was like a brother."

"And Brody? Was he like a brother?"

"Yeah," he confirms. "We were all close. Real close, but they'd had a falling-out."

"And you tried to bring them back together?"

"I did. And it worked. They made peace. I guess I can have some peace myself that I made that happen."

"What exactly was the falling-out about?"

"Brody pulled him into a wild-card investment with a hedge fund, and Oliver lost a shit ton of money. In the end, that was Oliver's decision to participate, which I know he was mature enough to know, but they had words. I wasn't there, but it was bad."

"Do you know what the context was?"

"Aside from Oliver saying he was done with him, no."

"But they were close?"

"Yeah. The three of us were inseparable."

"Did you remain friends with Brody?" I ask.

"I did, and before you ask—all Brody said was that Oliver was being unreasonable and had his panties in a wad. I went from meeting them both for lunch or cigars to meeting them separately. It took months, but I could see them both wearing down, wanting to make amends."

"So you invited Brody here," I assume.

"I did," he says. "And I don't regret that. They got past that shit, whatever it was."

"Did you make the same mistake?" I ask. "Did you invest?"

"Hell no. I told Oliver not to invest. The hedge fund involved made me nervous."

I hand him my card. "Can you email me the hedge fund info and manager?"

"Uh, yeah, but what does that have to do with Carrie stabbing Oliver to death?"

"Is that what you think happened?"

"Lana told me she was covered in blood in the attic," he says. "Of course she did it."

"You're not going to tell me how much she loved him and how sweet she is?"

"Did she appear sweet? Yes. Did she make him happy? Yes. Did she love him? I don't know her heart, but I believe she did, and most importantly, he did. And that's the bitch of this. I've seen a lot of things. People are not always what they seem."

Truth, I think. "Anyone else you think might have wanted to hurt Oliver?"

"I know you have to do a complete investigation, but let's just be clear. No one else hurt Oliver. She killed him."

# Chapter Thirty-Nine

I don't have to track down Brody.

I exit the bar and he's about to enter. "If it's not the boss bitch herself," he says. "Agent Castle. I had no idea I was talking to an FBI agent last night. Or maybe I did. I was drunk. But whatever the case, I fucked up. A pretty badass move, and I definitely didn't even make the moves on you."

He looks like shit, and I mean truly like death warmed over. He's in sweats, a thick stubble hugging his jaw, his eyes bloodshot. And while his words are in jest, his tone is rough and raw, and it's pretty obvious that he's sheltering in place, hiding beneath his flippant attitude.

"Good thing I can see through you," I say, "or I might think hitting on me makes you coldhearted, even callous enough to kill."

His expression tightens but he doesn't blanch. He's not fazed by a potential accusation one little bit, but he's trouble in another way. He motions to the bar. "I don't suppose you could go get me a drink so I don't have to see those assholes just to get drunk?"

"Why are they assholes?" I ask, seizing on this little tidbit.

"Ask after I get that drink."

"Maybe you should get drunk after we talk," I suggest.

"I'm a multitasker. You get me a good bottle, and I can down half of it by the time we're done talking. And I'll even share if you want."

A waiter walks by and Brody waves a hundred-dollar bill at him, and when the man halts in front of him, he palms him the cash. "That's for you. Can you grab me a Macallan 25, three fingers, and charge it to room 318, brother?"

The waiter's pleasure with his tip perks him up with a happy vibe, and he quickly agrees, but Brody holds up a staying hand and eyes me. "I showed restraint, Agent. A glass, not a bottle. And I did it all for *you*."

"Am I supposed to be impressed?"

"Try it. You will be, if not in me, in my choice of whisky. Twenty-five is the sweet spot. It's on me."

"I'll pass," I say, but I eye the waiter and lift a finger toward the main hotel. "We'll be at the couches in the lobby."

The waiter nods his understanding, and I motion Brody in the intended direction. Once we're settled on a brown leather couch, a good space between us, he lifts his chin toward the main stairwell directly in front of us. "It's supposed to be haunted. I hope like fuck Oliver won't be stuck in this shithole for eternity."

"You were close," I say.

His eyes meet mine. "Like brothers from the day we met at a charity walk, twelve years ago."

"And yet you hadn't spoken in months until this weekend," I comment. "Why?"

"I slept with Carrie," he blurts out with no hesitation.

# Chapter Forty

Brody slept with Carrie.

I blanch with this unexpected discovery, and he adds, "It's not as bad as it sounds. They were on a break, and I didn't know who the hell she was."

"How did you *not* know who she was?" I ask. "I thought you were like brothers?"

"I went to Germany for three months for some medical training I combined with some rest and relaxation named Sheila. When I got back, I went to an all-night coffee shop and bar, got down and dirty in the bathroom with some chick, and that was that."

"It was Carrie," I assume.

"Yeah, but I wouldn't know that until weeks later. Oliver and I go to drinks to catch up, and I find out he and some chick named Carrie had gotten hot and heavy and then broke up, but he was pretty messed up over it. It was the first time I'd ever seen him let a woman get under his skin."

"Why'd they break up?"

"From what he said, she felt intimidated by his family. Natalie, his sister, is a bitch, and while his parents are great people, they're intimidating as fuck. You'll find out soon enough."

I almost laugh. The Phoenixes have nothing on my father.

The waiter arrives with his whisky, and Brody, for all his bravado, is gracious with the man. Once we're alone, I press for more. "What happened next?"

"A month after I'm back from my trip, Oliver invites me to dinner. Imagine my surprise when Carrie is not only there, but she has a ring on her finger."

"That was fast," I comment.

He snorts. "She knows how to get to the point, as proven in the coffee shop bathroom."

An accurate statement, I think. "What did you do?"

"Played it cool that night. Told her she was a bitch when I had the chance. And then I kept my mouth shut. And thus, the birth of my hostility for Carrie."

"Were they actually broken up at the time she slept with you?"

"I couldn't ask him that question and not be found out, but from what I pieced together, it's a maybe yes and maybe no. But either way, he was crying over her, she was fucking me. I get the vibe from her. She'd do it again, me and someone else. She's a bitch."

"How'd she react to seeing you again?"

"Pretended it didn't happen while holding on as tight as she could to Oliver. I wanted to tell him so many times, but I knew we wouldn't come back from that. Either way I went was wrong. I seethed, and he felt it. The secret hurt our friendship. And when we had a blowup about a financial deal, at its core, it was about Carrie. I was out of his life, and believe you me, she was happy about it. Ask me how I know?"

"How do you know?"

"I ran into her at that same coffee shop." His gaze is back on the stairwell, lingering before he looks at me. "She told me I lured him into that financial deal because I couldn't lure him to another woman." He laughs bitterly. "I should have done just that. Lured him to another woman."

He's right. He should have. "Why did you come to the party?"

"Josh is close to us both." His jaw clenches. "*Was* close to us both." He slugs back a long swallow of his drink before he adds, "He told me Oliver wanted me at the party but knew Carrie would freak out. I said fuck that bitch, and here I am."

"When was the last time you saw him?"

"He left about two, said Carrie would expect him."

"And when did you leave?"

"Later, and not alone. I was with one of the dancers. Sherry the cherry. And she was. We went to her room, and I didn't leave until dawn. We made a video. It's time stamped. You can see it if you want."

"Out of fear I'll have to bleach my eyes afterward," I say, "keep it. If I can't confirm your alibi outside your Pornhub tryout, I'll get back to you."

"At least look at the time stamp."

"Fine. Show it to me."

He pulls up his phone and hands it to me. I watch about ten seconds in which the female is already undressing and check the time stamp. I hand him the phone back.

He smirks. "Was that enough?"

"That was more than enough."

The corners of his mouth lift slightly. "Just let me know if you need more. I promise to come through."

I ignore his tasteless remarks. "Why are you on bad terms with the rest of the men in the wedding party?"

"I got drunk one night after the fight with Oliver and critiqued each of them," he says. "Cade, the arrogant prick who can't find a good investment any more than he can find his own dick. Trevor, who tries too hard. And Nick, who can't commit to anything but his wallet, proven by the fact that he's proposed to three different women but always gets cold feet."

"That wasn't very friendly of you," I observe.

"Apparently, they agreed. They didn't like my assessment."

"What do they say about you?"

"That I'm an asshole, which is fine. I'm all about keeping it real."

"Then keep it real with me right now. Do you think Carrie killed Oliver?"

"I have an ER background, so do I think being covered in blood makes her guilty? No. Do I think she's capable of killing? I don't know. I spent a lot of time hating her, but my time away from Oliver gave me perspective on a lot of things, namely her. She didn't know who I was when we met, either. I do believe that. Hating her was hurting us all. She loved him. I believe that, but isn't it usually the ones we love who hurt us?"

"Sounds like you speak from experience?"

"Observation," he amends. "My father's a politician and an expert at what I call BDSM mind fucks. Ask my mother, the nurse."

A nurse.

Like Carrie.

As for what BDSM mind fucks are—I can imagine, and that description explains so much about Brody. My question is what exactly it says about his "brother" Oliver and Oliver's fiancée, Carrie.

"I'll be in touch," I say, standing up and walking around the coffee table, only to turn back to face him. "I might never have known about Carrie. Why'd you tell me?"

I expect him to say he was beating Carrie to the punch, but instead, he says, "Because I didn't tell him."

# Chapter Forty-One

## CARRIE

One. Two. Three. Four. Five. Six.

I count to try to calm my mind. It's something my counselor, Mr. Jordan, taught me right after my brother died. While I'm counting, the things that scare me can't find their way into my head. I control them. They don't control me. Once I have control, I can decide how and when I allow myself to see beyond the numbers.

But it's not working.

I sit up, eyeing the TV playing a remodeling show about a forever home, the happy premise of family and home almost too much to endure. I will never have the perfect life I once dreamed of—no, I was living the perfect life. It's been stripped away from me. Oliver is dead. I reach for the remote and cry out with the pain in my stomach. It rips through me, and with it, any control I'm harnessing fades. I'm back in the attic, covered in blood with Andi leaning over me. No, Agent Castle. She's not my friend.

"How did you end up naked and in the attic, Carrie?" she demanded.

Why was I in that attic? And naked?! I wouldn't ever, and I mean *ever*, walk around naked. *I was scared.* I remember being scared. I repeat those words over and over in my head, and they are meaningful, even if I can't understand the root of their creation. I was scared. So very scared.

My mind flashes with images of me and Oliver in the hotel room. I was still in my party dress—a red, sparkly dress he'd loved—and he'd removed his suit jacket and tie. We were fighting, screaming at each other. The room starts to spin and spin. I squeeze my eyes shut, willing away the idea of that fight, and yet, I can see myself shove his unmoving chest. I can see him grab my wrists and pull me to him as he says, *"Calm down, Carrie. You know I love you."*

And then I'm just blank. I don't know what happened after that.

I had on my clothes. He had on his clothes.

Make-up sex, I think. We always had make-up sex.

But that would mean I was with him when he died. That would mean I killed him, and I didn't kill Oliver. God no. I love him. I want him back.

Dampness clings to my cheeks, tears pouring in sheets now. I didn't kill him. No. No. *No.* I know I didn't kill him. That is not who I am. But I can't tell Agent Castle we had a fight. I can't tell anyone. I'm alone. I'm so damn alone. My body quakes with tears bursting from my eyes. The room goes dark, and then I'm transported back to the moment I ran into the hotel room and found Oliver dead and covered in blood. Monitors start going off and suddenly a nurse is beside me.

She sputters out, "Oh . . . God," and then calls out, "Help," and then louder, "I need help!"

It's then that I realize I'm on the floor and don't know how I got there. There is a sharp pinch in my arm, and I look down to find my IV has ripped from the vein, blood spurting everywhere. I try to grab it and stop the bleeding, but my hand catches. My gaze jerks with my arm, and I find the silver cuff. Oh God, I'm cuffed, a prisoner in my own hospital bed. They think I killed Oliver. I look down again to find blood seeping through my gown over my belly. There is just so much blood. I'm drowning in blood, mine and Oliver's.

# Chapter Forty-Two

*I'm sitting at our kitchen island staring at a box with a red ribbon. I don't know who the box is from. I don't know why I am just staring at it and not opening it. Surely it's from Oliver. He's always surprising me with little gifts.*

"How's the soup?"

I jolt from the haze of a memory. Or—no. That wasn't a memory. A dream? I don't know. The drugs are working a number on me. No more drugs. I'm going to tell the doctor no more drugs. I can't even figure out what is real and what is not right now. For a moment, I almost ask if Oliver is really dead. Some part of me hopes I'm just so drugged I'm having nightmares. But then the ache in my belly, the very real ache, assures me that no, this is not a nightmare. Someone stabbed my fiancé to death, and apparently they came at me as well.

"Do you want me to get you something else?" the nurse asks, snapping me out of my reverie and back to her. "We have a few choices," she adds. "I can show you the menu."

The last hour comes back to me. The doctor came to see me, standing at the railing of my bed. "Tell me what drugs you take."

I'm still far from clearheaded, but I am also a nurse. I understand that he needs to know my medications. "I treat migraines and a bad back with beta-blockers, a muscle relaxer, and a cocktail of supplements for inflammation and general wellness. As an ER nurse, I'm exposed to quite the bucket of germs."

"How often do you get migraines?"

"Since I started on the beta-blockers last year, about once a month. Prior to that, they were once a week. Stress brings on the migraines and, again, the ER. It gets to me at times. I assume I'm presently too medicated to deal with that problem." What I don't tell him is that I often use beta-blockers for panic attacks. That's not his business or anyone else's. No one knows. No one will ever know.

I'm hazy on the rest of our conversation, but I do remember him arguing with the police officer outside my door about my cuffed arm. Now I have some long plastic thing around my wrist that connects to my IV stand. It's more comfortable and probably not very secure, but it's not like I plan to run. Plus, it seems I have a full-time nurse guarding me, at least at the moment, which can't be a good use of resources.

"The grilled chicken is quite tasty," the nurse adds. Katy, I believe she told me to call her.

"No," I say, feeling as if I was more clear minded with the doctor than I am now. They must have drugged me again. "No, thanks," I add again, my voice a bit stronger. "The soup is fine." I reach for the bread on the plate, hoping it might soak up some of the drugs in my system, too drugged to know if that is really a thing. I'm a nurse, yes, but I'm a loopy nurse.

The TV is back on the home channel, and the very idea of all it represents punches me in the gut. I motion to the screen. "Can you please turn that to something like cooking?"

"Of course," the nurse replies, graciously doing as I ask. She's young, maybe twenty-five, new to her life and career, probably full of all the dreams I've now lost. Because Oliver is dead. I have to repeat this in my mind, *Oliver is dead*, just to actually grasp the content of the words and as a way to force myself to adjust to this reality. I have to believe it is real to accept it and fight through it. I know this. I've been through grief counseling.

I dip the bread into the soup and start eating, little moments of the past flickering in my mind, far back in my past. I start reliving that day me and my brother, Eric, rode our bikes to Dairy Queen in the scorching heat. Our reward had been the delicious chocolate-covered cones we'd ordered, the ice cream beneath the rich chocolate cooling us off. The laughter in between each lick, nothing but pure joy. My parents wanted two kids but were only able to have one: Eric. I was adopted at only two years old. At that point, we'd been together ten years. We were family, brother and sister. Nothing could touch us. And we were young and had not a care in the world. We could never have known how it would all end. How *soon* it would end.

That memory shifts to the joy I felt with Oliver last night at the party. We'd shared a shot of whisky and toasted to our party, our friends, our future. He'd been so handsome in his suit, and I'd felt prettier than I'd ever felt in my red gown. Red. I'd chosen red. Almost as if I'd been foreshadowing the blood that would follow.

"You ate every bite."

With those words, my gaze jerks to the nurse. I glance at my bowl and realize she's right, but I barely remember eating. I do, however, feel better, the haze lifting at least a hair. "I think I should go to the bathroom. Am I allowed to walk myself?"

"Of course," she says. "Let me help you just to make sure you're steady. You do have a concussion and plenty of drugs in your system."

"No more drugs," I say. "I can't stand how I feel right now."

"I'll talk to the doctor," she promises, lowering the railing next to me and helping me rid myself of the heavy blankets. Rotating and setting my feet on the ground brings a head rush, but I fight through it. I need control. I need to stand.

It's a bit of a battle, but a few minutes later I'm in the bathroom, though of course, she makes me leave the door cracked. I don't know if she thinks I'm going to fall or kill myself. There's a part of me that craves that relief, to just end the pain of living life without Oliver. I don't know how I will ever bury him.

This idea stabs at me, and I barely manage to go through the motions and finish why I came in here in the first place. I've just washed my hands when I hear voices outside in the room, muffled as if the nurse is speaking to someone in the hallway. I shove open the door and enter the room. She shuts the main door and turns to face me.

"Your parents are here," she says. "Are you up to visiting?"

I now remember her and the doctor asking me if I wanted them to call anyone. No had been my answer. Why in the world would I want to put my parents through this hell? They lost a son. I don't want them to feel they've lost me. I wanted to somehow make everything okay before I talked to them. But the truth is, now, as my mind clears, I know nothing will ever be okay again.

"Yes," I say. "Please send them in."

"Do you want me to help you get back in bed first?"

"No, thank you. I'll sit in the chair." I motion to the light-blue leather seat in the corner.

She nods and hovers to ensure I'm safely seated before she hurries to the door. I steel myself for my parents to enter, for the rush of emotions. Yes, I'm adopted, but I have never in my life felt I didn't belong, like they weren't my real parents. I'm loved almost too much. My mother especially worries to the extreme. It's hard to live under that much scrutiny. It's hard to ever live up to the expectations of that kind of attention. They didn't want me to leave Texas. They didn't understand why I couldn't stay. They don't know everything there is to know about why I left, and they never will.

The door opens and my fingers dig into the arms of the chair, and when my visitors appear, my lips part in shock. Adrenaline and emotions, even fear, surge. The two people standing in my room are not my parents.

They're Oliver's.

# Chapter Forty-Three

## ANDI

Both sets of parents—Oliver's and Carrie's—will arrive later this evening. To protect them from the press, York and I will be meeting them in their hotel rooms, or in the Phoenixes' case, the private house they arranged.

With this knowledge in mind, and the need to just feel fresher and sharper, I take a quick shower and change clothes. With not a lot of options in my bag, I manage a professional-enough look in black slacks and a button-down white shirt. Yes, the FBI agent in me sneaked in some basics last minute that I swore I wouldn't bring for a weekend of fun. Almost as if I had a premonition. Talking to the parents of both Carrie and Oliver will be explosive and emotional. They need to feel confident in more than my badge. They need to feel confident in me as an agent.

Since they aren't expected until this evening, my goal is to be armed with knowledge for those encounters.

On that note, York and I spend quite some time chatting with forensics, with not much new discovered. The ME pretty much summed up what there was to be discovered, at least before the evidence hits the lab for processing. The cause of death will be obvious. Oliver was stabbed to death. The security checks contain no grand revelations beyond Trevor's DUI back in college. There are a few other hits related to hotel guests, but no one with any real connection to the case, at least on the surface. Per the investigator covering Natalie, her being a bitch is apparently legendary, but so far there are no red flags.

With all of this in mind, the key question for me is whose DNA is in that room, or on Oliver's person, that might not belong to Carrie. Investigation is, at its core, a process of elimination.

I'm sitting at a table in a small conference room where I've been doing one-on-one interviews on my own, reviewing my notes, when York enters and sets a cup of coffee in front of me. "Don't you just hate the process of building a case when it's obvious who did it?"

"Is it?" I ask, lifting the cup and adding, "Thank you. I need this."

"What does that mean?" he asks, sitting across from me. "Isn't it?"

"Is it obvious who killed Oliver Phoenix?"

He groans. "Of course it is. Carrie Reynolds killed him."

"You have your opinion, and that's all it is until we have facts. I'll reserve mine until those facts arrive."

"You can't be serious."

"My father said the same to me when I was fifteen," I tell him. "We were sitting at the kitchen table, eating pizza, going through one of his case files for a double homicide when I—"

"Holy mother of God. Your father let you look at a double homicide file?"

"I had a regular Beaver Cleaver kind of family life, but aside from that, *my point.* I'd just told him he was screwing up his facts."

"I hear he doesn't like to be told he's a screwup. Did he beat your ass?"

"He only beats asses of criminals, and assholes," I assure him and quickly add, "Not that I'm defending him. I'm not."

"Good thing," he says. "From what I hear, he's a real bull in a china shop, and everything gets broken."

Protectiveness bristles. That's the thing about me and my father. I have a lot of feelings where he's concerned, too many feelings. Sometimes I want to punch him, but I don't because I'm not him. But damn it, he's my dad. No one else can punch him, either, literally or figuratively.

I bite back an improper response and say, "Right. Well, the story has a point. He'd assumed the teenage son innocent of the crime of killing his parents, but as I told him, he was assuming kids think like adults, and they do not. Which of course, I knew, because I wasn't an adult. And I'd been right. The teenage son had been the killer."

York smirks and sips his coffee. "And he told everyone he solved the case, I bet."

"He solved the case. I just gave him an idea. But no, he didn't take credit for it. He, in fact, told everybody I'd solved the case and bought me a Beretta I couldn't even hold in my hand to celebrate, but again, we're off track. Finally, to my point, everything isn't always as it seems. I know you know this, but your eagerness to solve the case is getting in your way." *Otherwise known as retirement fog,* I think, before I add, "We can't be sure Carrie Reynolds did this. Not yet."

"You've got to be kidding me," he mutters.

*Again with this,* I think and say, "'You can't be serious' means the same as 'you've got to be kidding me.' You know that, right? And the answer is yes, I'm serious, and no, I'm not kidding."

"She was covered in his blood."

"Her stomach was sliced and she was hiding, afraid for her life."

"Is that what you really believe?" he challenges.

"Is that the only way you can counter what I just said? Because that's what her attorney is going to tell the DA and a jury if it gets that far."

York grimaces. "Point made. There are no shortcuts."

Right, I think. Point made. And don't be throwing punches at Eddie Castle.

*My dad.*

# Chapter Forty-Four

York's phone buzzes with a text, and he glances at the message and sighs. "Someone needs me. The story of my life. I cannot wait for sandy beaches and no one but my wife making demands. And she will make demands, but soon my hearing will go. I'm sure of it."

I manage a laugh because, you know, I don't hold a grudge, though Eddie Castle would. But I'm also not sorry when York pushes to his feet and heads to the door. He exits the room and I've already moved on. I'm about to begin my next interview when my cellphone rings. I glance at the caller ID to find my tech lead, Hazel—otherwise known as "the supreme master of the internet"—calling. Hazel is petite, with a giant attitude, an Asian mom, and a Russian father. It's a combination that delivers a whole lot of attitude and sass in three languages.

For now, she smacks gum in my ear and greets me with, "Hello, Agent Castle. Beat any asses today?"

Of course, she knows I hate the reference to my father, which is why I say, "No, but if you were here, that might change."

She snorts. "Whatever. You ain't your father. He's more, shall we say, *colorful* than you are. He reminds me of a guy I dated. He was such a rebel he wouldn't even put the toilet paper on the holder. I bet your daddy shreds it before he uses it."

"Actually, he doesn't shred it or put it on the holder at all. I grew up with him, remember? And it has to be the softest kind they make because his ass is delicate." With that, I move on. "Outside of discussing my father's toilet paper habits, what else have you got for me?"

She laughs. "God, I love your attitude about your father, but I actually called with that info you wanted." She gets right to the point. "Carrie was adopted when she was two."

"No one claimed her as an infant?" I query. "That is odd."

"She wasn't handed over until she was eighteen months old, and as for who the mother or father is, that information is sealed. However, her parents, Sue and Joe Reynolds, seem to be lovely people. Interesting thing. They had a son. He and Carrie were riding bikes and he was hit by a car. Carrie was twelve and he was fourteen."

"I heard about that," I say. "What about his parents? I don't know enough about them."

"Oliver's father is a rich white boy. His mother is a rich white girl. And those aren't my words. I'm reading from a forum on rich people I dug up."

"A forum," I repeat, grabbing the box sitting beside me and snatching a doughnut from inside, which I stuff into my mouth—yes, it's cliché, but it's also really good, and chocolate. "Which forum?"

"Reddit."

"The Phoenix family is on Reddit?"

"People talk about them on Reddit, yep," she says, smacking her gum a little harder. "Rich—"

"White boys," I supply. "Got it."

"Right. This forum considers the Phoenix father, and therefore his family, as gossip worthy as Michael Dell, Donald Trump, Bill Clinton, Steve Jobs, and so on, and so on, and so on. There are stories about all of them there. And the general consensus is that Natalie is a bitch. A lady who works at Saks said she offered to help Natalie pick a dress, and Natalie looked her up and down and then asked her if she could get someone who had better fashion sense."

"I can see that side of her, but it doesn't make her a killer. What else do they say about the parents?"

"Robin and Mike Phoenix are private, but people of high standards," she says. "Very few people get inside their inner circle. Chatter says they don't tolerate scandal."

"And now," I say, "they not only lost their child, they're about to be on every news station and probably true crime media outlet in existence."

"Exactly," she says. "They're going to come at you hard. Be ready."

There's a knock on the door, and York pokes his head into the room. "We have a problem." He steps inside the conference room and shuts the door. "Oliver's parents have arrived."

"Good luck," Hazel says. "I'll keep working." She disconnects and I stand up.

"I thought we were meeting them at their rental house?" I ask, already anticipating the press nightmare we're living in.

"They aren't here," he says. "They went to the hospital. A nurse I know over there was reading up on the families right after they arrived when she realized what had happened. She saw Oliver's parents walk in. She heard them tell another nurse they were Carrie's family. The nurse let them into Carrie's room. Agent, they're in her room now."

I'm already around the desk, motioning for him to open the door. "Let's go," I say. "And let's pray we don't have another homicide on our hands."

# Chapter Forty-Five

York and I arrive at the hospital and Carrie's floor just as a man and woman step out of her room. The woman is petite, with shoulder-length brown hair and delicate features, and her pantsuit is black. The man is tall, rather thin, with thick silver hair, his pants black and his shirt a crisp white. The two of them have a regal air about them, dripping of money in that unidentifiable way that is just understood in some people's presence.

"Check on Carrie," I instruct York before I step directly in the Phoenixes' path. "Mr. and Mrs. Phoenix," I greet them, taking my assumption to the bank. "I'm FBI Special Agent Andrea Castle, with a specialty in criminal profiling. I was actually in attendance at the party. I'm greatly sorry for your loss but thankful that I'm here and able to expedite the investigation in a proactive fashion."

"How is it that my son knew an FBI agent and we didn't know?" Mr. Phoenix asks, and while his eyes are bloodshot, his tone is accusatory in a way that has me curious. It reminds me of my chat with Josh and his indication that my presence had been unsettling to Oliver. It's also the same question Natalie pressed when we met.

So once again, I say, "I recently solved a high-profile series of homicides, and the press has been stalking me. The escape felt necessary."

Mr. Phoenix's expression pulls so tight I think he might suffocate in his own skin. "Your escape from the press failed. The bastards are all over this town, vultures ready to sink their teeth into the story of my son's murder."

I don't point out the fact that the press loves them more than they do me. They have a Reddit board. But he's still got a point. The press and vultures are synonymous. "We'll do our best to control them," I assure them both. "And obviously I'm sympathetic and aware of the problem."

"We have a lot of questions," Mr. Phoenix informs me, his voice hard now.

"Of course you do," I say. "I thought we were meeting at your rental?"

"We're just trying to make it through this day, Agent Castle," Mrs. Phoenix replies, avoiding a direct commitment.

York reappears by my side and gives me a nod to tell me Carrie is safe, before introducing himself to the Phoenixes. "Detective York," he announces. "I'm a local. We were fortunate that one of Carrie's friends invited Agent Castle to the weekend events. She's bringing the big guns in to this investigation."

Avoiding the bad subject of me being at the party he's just introduced once again, I move on. "Can I ask why you were in Carrie's room?"

"I needed to hear what she has to say," Mrs. Phoenix explains, folding her arms in front of her chest, a protective stance. "I needed to know if I believed she did this."

"Do you?" I query.

"Do *you*?" she counters. "Is it Carrie? I mean, who runs naked through a hotel, covered in blood, and wounded? It's illogical. Is she crazy, or is our son's killer still on the loose? Do you even know?"

Her voice has lifted, her hands cutting through the air.

I don't find her anger and frustration inducing the same in me. I was young when my mother died, but I remember the pain. Sometimes I remember it more than I do her, which is never a happy realization.

This is exactly why my response is calm and honest. "Our job is to not only get you an arrest but to get you a conviction. I need you to remember that. An arrest, especially a premature arrest, does not equal a conviction. I don't promise to be fast, but I promise to get the job done right."

"In other words, you don't know who killed our son," Mrs. Phoenix ascertains.

"What is obvious is not always the answer," York states, playing on our earlier conversation. "If it was, our jobs wouldn't exist."

"You can't hold her long without an arrest," Mr. Phoenix states. "What is it? Seventy-two hours? You have to have a plan. What is it?"

He's correct, of course. I'll be pressured to arrest her before we've collected proper evidence. That turns out badly more often than the general public recognizes, but right now, I turn the tables on the Phoenixes, and do so looking for additional motives for their visit with Carrie. "Have you talked to Natalie?"

"We have," Mrs. Phoenix replies. "And I'm aware of her inappropriate behavior. Carrie has vowed not to press charges."

And there it is. The reason they cornered Carrie in her room. They want to protect Natalie, which I understand. They've now lost a son. They want to shelter their last living child. And yet, the meeting with Carrie still sits oddly in my gut.

"What did Carrie tell you happened?" I ask.

"I'm Carrie Reynolds's attorney," a female voice indicates. "I need to speak to her immediately."

I can almost hear the door slam in my face.

Talking to Carrie, at least without extreme supervision, is over.

# Chapter Forty-Six

I turn to find a petite, pretty blonde in a smart black dress and heels, talking to the woman I know to be head nurse on this floor.

What comes next is not what I expect.

Mr. Phoenix steps around me and heads straight for the woman who's just announced herself as Carrie's attorney. The nurse is dismissed, and Mr. Phoenix and the attorney speak to each other in low, hushed voices. This conversation lasts about sixty seconds, before Mr. Phoenix waves at his wife, and she hurries to his side. She speaks to Carrie's attorney, says something short and fast, and then Mr. and Mrs. Phoenix walk away.

"All right, then," York queries. "What just happened?"

"What indeed," I concur. "Catch the Phoenixes and confirm our meeting. See what else you can get from them. I'll handle the newcomer on the scene."

"Yeah, well, I get the feeling that one is trouble," he comments. "Don't get your throat torn out."

"I'm a Castle," I comment. "Much like my father, I'm not easily cut." It's a reminder to him that I might not be my father, but I am still his daughter.

He smirks. "You gonna beat her with a bat like your papa would?"

"My father doesn't beat people with bats," I say and then add for effect, "*usually*. There was that one time, but that story has been blown out of proportion because my father wanted it to be blown out of proportion. You underappreciate the simplicity of his motivations." I don't give York time to accuse me of being one big contradiction about my father. He wouldn't be wrong, but then, as Eddie Castle's only child, that's my God-given right. I step around York.

I focus solely on Carrie's attorney, who's oozing enough Eddie Castle–style attitude to be my long-lost sister. I stop in front of her, and she reaches for control by saying, "You must be Agent Castle."

"And you'd assume that why?" I ask.

"You look like your father."

"You know my father?" I counter.

"Eddie and I have done a little business," she informs me, offering me her hand. "Danielle Littleton."

Since my father hates attorneys but loves blondes, I don't doubt she's telling the truth. If he was forced to work with an attorney, he'd choose her. I don't take her hand. "Small world," I say. *Or not.* "How exactly did you end up as Carrie Reynolds's attorney?"

Her hand falls away and she says, "Full disclosure. I heard about the case—scandal travels fast, especially when the FBI agent that broke the Spider Man case is on the scene—and I called Carrie's parents. I asked to represent their daughter."

*Of course you did,* I think. High-profile cases mean money, attention, and book deals. Lord knows I've had offers. "And you used your connection to my father to assure them you could handle me," I assume. My lips quirk as I add, "The one problem you have is that I'm not going to try and get you in bed like my father would."

She bristles. "That's between me and your father."

"That's a yes," I say, "and far from a first. But for the record, I didn't ask. I don't care who you slept with, Ms. Littleton. I care how you handle this case."

"Danielle," she corrects.

I don't extend the same courtesy. We are *not* friends. "Let's talk about Carrie, *Danielle.*"

Her spine stiffens. "Yes, let's talk about Carrie. Is she under arrest?"

"I'll let you know when I can actually question her."

"When the doctor allows it, I'll allow it. For now, I'm going to speak to my client."

"I'll wait," I say. "I'll grab some delicious coffee from the machine and be right here."

She turns to leave. I'm not ready to let that happen. "Why would the Phoenix family talk to the attorney of the woman who may have killed their son?"

Danielle pauses and turns to look at me. "We'll talk." She closes the space between her and Carrie's room, speaks to the police officer guarding Carrie, and then enters the room, shutting the door behind her.

I head into the waiting room and do exactly what we both expect me to do. I call my father.

# Chapter Forty-Seven

My father knows his faults and he taught me to know my own as well, which is a complicated topic I'll avoid for now. Among *his* declared faults, his words, not mine—he's loud and prideful. I don't mind the loudness at all. I guess I'm just used to it. The pridefulness does get him in trouble and rubbed off on me a bit too much.

Really the only flaws I'd assign him are, despite his good intentions, his vigilante attitude and willingness to beat people up. He'd argue those things are necessary for the greater good. Whatever the case, for all his real or perceived faults, communication is not one of them.

After my mother was killed, I had a regular nanny, but despite her presence, he swore that if I called, he'd answer. And he did. When I was twelve, he picked up the phone in the middle of a shoot-out. He'd taken a bullet in the shoulder while telling me that yes, he'd take me to the movies Saturday night. I'm fairly certain he killed someone while talking to me. But he'd promised to answer.

So as expected, he answers my call on the first ring now. "Sugar Bear," he greets, and there's loud breathing and panting in the background. He's having sex or fighting. Or arm wrestling. He does love his arm wrestling. It's his way of showing he's a superior alpha no matter his age, which is a young fifty.

"Dad," I say tightly, ignoring the endearment for more important things. "What are you doing?"

"I'm giving Frank, a local bookie, a chance to remember where my client's missing brother might be." There's more grunting, and knowing my father, I'm fairly certain Frank's face is planted on the floor.

"Is your boot presently on his back?"

"Exactly, daughter. You learn so well. I've always been proud of that. It's the perfect way to take a breath before the conversation continues, don't you think?" He doesn't give me time to answer. "I hear murder followed you all the way to Estes Park. I hate those press-grabber cases, but if you need backup, I'll pack a duffel and be there in two hours."

"The last thing I need is you giving the press something else to talk about."

"No?" he challenges. "Seems like that might be just what you need."

He makes a good point. If I were planning to stay in this tiny town, a distraction might be just what the doctor ordered, but I'm not. I'm getting us the heck out of here. "Danielle Littleton," I say. "Three words. Go." The three-word thing comes from my childhood, a game we used to play.

"Beautiful. Scrumptious. Devious." He goes further and adds more than I need to know. "All things that make for a good bedmate, but a bad friend or adversary. Why?"

"She used you and your connection to me to convince my top suspect's family to hire her as a defense."

"Told you. Devious. Or smart, however, you want to look at it."

There's more grunting and a low grumble of, "Castle, damn it."

"One minute, Frank," he says. "It's my daughter. You know how I feel about my daughter." He returns to me. "Okay, Sugar Bear. Back to Danielle. You might have to go kung fu on the likes of her before this is over. Like you did that Nelson dude at Quantico."

I frown because yes, Nelson got handsy with me. And yes, I put my knee in his groin and drove it to his throat, but I didn't tell my father. "How do you know about that?"

"Friends in high places, daughter of mine. Too bad I heard it from them, not you, but I get it. You didn't want me to beat the ass you already beat. Well, not the ass. I think you chose well. A man's personal baggage is very, well, personal to him. In Danielle's case, I'd punch her in the boob—just my opinion, but I do know a little about pain management."

"Good Lord, Dad," I groan, glancing out the window at the parking lot, where Mr. and Mrs. Phoenix are presently standing next to a car in an animated argument.

"Handle her, baby," my father urges. "I know you can. Unless you want me to show up. I can handle her."

I ignore that ridiculous offer, focused on the moment Mrs. Phoenix loses her regal carriage and shoves the hell out of her husband. "I need to go," I say, hanging up, on alert in case I need to get involved with the Phoenixes' dispute.

Mrs. Phoenix continues her assault on her husband, slapping him in the face, but he doesn't react violently. He does grab her, but all he does is pull her into an embrace, hugging her as she sobs. My chest tightens, a flash of myself punching at my father after he told me my mother was dead. I blamed him for no good reason. Just in that moment, I needed to blame someone. And he did just what Mr. Phoenix is doing to his wife. My father held me and told me he loved me. He told me we'd get through the pain, but neither of us ever did. We're both screwed up. He's never remarried. I've never even considered getting that close to anyone.

But focused again on the here and now, I decide that Danielle isn't my problem. The Phoenixes are. As they should be. The problem is that when powerful people need and want resolution, they tend to push in all the wrong ways. They tricked the staff into believing they were Carrie's parents in order to see her.

I want to know what happened in that room between them and Carrie.

# Chapter Forty-Eight

Danielle isn't quick with Carrie.

After forty-five minutes of waiting, I send York back to the hotel to manage the interviews. I pass much of my wait at the nurses' station, munching on way too many Reese's Peanut Butter Cups for my own good, but they are my favorite and I'm hungry. At some point, the doctor dodges me and heads into Carrie's room, and he's not quick, either. Obviously, Danielle has a plan, and it won't be one that pleases me, but I'll handle it and her.

At present, Carol, the head nurse, whose pink hair is twined neatly at her nape, is chatting with me about how shocked she was to find out that the Phoenixes were not the Reynolds family. "When I found out," she explains, "I was terrified they'd hurt her." She finishes that statement by hugging herself. "I've never seen anything like this." Because despite being in her midthirties, a decade into her career, she's well seasoned by small-town standards.

Whatever happened in that room was not the expected, and my urgency to find out is rapidly growing. My answer might be coming soon, as Dr. Mendez exits the room, his gaze finding mine.

I push off the counter I'm leaning on and he's in front of me quickly. "Agent Castle," he greets me.

"Doctor," I reply.

"Whatever happened to her was traumatic. I've spoken to Carrie's parents, who are on their way, and I'm recommending a psychologist evaluate her before you talk to her."

"At the parents' request?"

"Mutual agreement," he replies, avoiding a real answer. In other words, the evaluation is at Carrie's attorney's recommendation, but for good measure, it seems, he adds, "I believe this is in the best interest of her health."

*And Danielle's best bet of setting up an insanity plea,* I think. "When?" I ask.

"Soon. I called in a woman whose opinion I value. She's driving in from Denver."

"I'm going to need to review her credentials."

He bristles. "She's highly qualified."

"I'm sure she is, but I have enough to charge Carrie. I'm about two seconds from doing so. If I'm holding back, I need to show those who will be pressuring me to take that action why I'm holding back." I hand him my card. "Please email me her credentials. When will she arrive?"

"Not until about eight p.m., which I understand is the timeline for Carrie's parents to arrive as well."

I glance at my watch. "It's five now. When the counselor is done, it will be closer to ten."

"I would agree with that timeline. It's inconvenient but necessary."

*Is it necessary?* I think. Maybe. Maybe not.

But there is no denying the fact that it squeezes my window to question Carrie, as well as her parents, before choosing to charge or not to charge.

Before I can ask a few more questions, Danielle exits the room.

The good doctor—or not so good; I'm undecided—is quick to get lost, while Danielle joins me. "I assume Dr. Mendez explained the situation," she says.

I don't confirm or deny anything. "You explain it."

"All right," she replies. "Carrie's suffering post-traumatic distress, as would be expected. From what she's said to me, I believe she was attacked and ran for her life. We believe the right doctor, one who specializes in such things, can help get to the core of that trauma. Perhaps that doctor can even help her remember what happened last night. Of course, that's what we all want."

"Is it?" I ask.

"The unknown is no better for me than it is for you," she argues. "Knowledge solves this case, the knowledge locked in Carrie's mind. This is a win-win for both of us, and we both know you don't want to charge an innocent woman."

"What I want," I say, "is to charge and convict the person who brutally stabbed Oliver Phoenix over and over and over again in a fit of passion. And mark my word, *I will.*"

"It's not her."

"We'll see," I say.

"Charge her and destroy her life, and we'll sue you personally."

"You're forgetting that I'm a Castle. I don't intimidate easily. And as a plus, I'm not my father. No one has seduced me into anything."

Her cheeks heat. "I didn't seduce him. Quite the opposite."

"I'm not sure that's a good thing, either. I'll be here at eight." I turn and head for the exit.

I've just entered the lobby when I notice a middle-aged couple fretfully talking to the nurse. "We need to see our daughter. Immediately," the woman demands.

It's rather obvious these two people are Carrie's parents, and Danielle's claim that they will arrive later tonight was a bunch of baloney.

I approach them and say, "Mr. and Mrs. Reynolds?"

They turn toward me, both of them in casual wear, jeans, and T-shirts, both of them a bit disheveled. The petite woman's round face angles toward me, piercing blue eyes meeting mine. "And you are?"

The man, who towers over her, his eyes deeply lined, settles a hand on her shoulder. "Yes. And you are?"

I reach into my bag and offer them both cards. "Special Agent Castle. I'm investigating the murder of Oliver Phoenix."

"What about the attack on our daughter?" Mrs. Reynolds demands. "What about that?"

"I'm investigating the case in its entirety," I reply.

"We're not talking to you without our attorney present," Mr. Reynolds declares.

"All right," I say easily, quite used to these kinds of roadblocks. "But please know that I have to decide whether to charge Carrie within the next forty-eight hours. I'll be pressured to charge. Everything you can do to help me, and give me a reason not to do so, is in Carrie's best interest."

"She didn't do this," Mrs. Reynolds maintains, her voice cracking in the aftermath of her sharp tone. "And she was cut. She was hiding. Carrie was naked and hiding."

"I'm the one who found her," I explain. "I'll be happy to explain the details if we can just sit down and talk. I'm not her enemy right now."

"Right now," Mr. Reynolds states. "But you might become her enemy."

"It doesn't have to be that way," I respond. "Even if she did this, there could be more to the story than I can see now."

"She's not insane," Mrs. Reynolds interjects. "She's not insane, and I hope like hell no one is saying that to her."

It's an interesting thing to hope for. "Why?" I ask. "Would that suggestion upset her?"

"We're done here," Mr. Reynolds announces. "Let's go, Sue." He physically moves her and sets her in motion.

They leave without a formal conversation, and yet they've told me so much.

There's something in Carrie's background. Something that makes them fear the stigma connected to a plea of insanity. That doesn't work in Danielle's favor if that's her defense for Carrie killing Oliver. Of course, it won't matter if Carrie's innocent.

All I can say to that is, we'll see. We will definitely see.

I'm headed out to my car when my cellphone rings with a call from Lana. Aware she's freaking out, and with good reason, I pause long enough to take her call. "How are you doing?" I answer.

"I can't stop seeing him on that bed. And her all covered in blood. Did she do it? She did it, right? How can this be happening?"

Earlier, she insisted that Carrie didn't do it. I have no idea why her flip-flop bothers me, but it does. I wonder if all of Carrie's friends will start doubting her now. "I thought you were sure she didn't do it?"

"Are you?" she asks.

"I don't know her. You do."

"I know, but I just kept thinking about her covered in blood. It's hard to get past that part of all of this."

*Because we shouldn't try to get past it,* I think. It's a clue. It's telling us something. It's telling me something. I'm just not sure it's telling me anything obvious.

# Chapter Forty-Nine

## CARRIE

Still cuffed to my IV pole, I sit in the hospital chair by the window, trying to get a grip on exactly what is happening to me. I've lost the man I love and it's destroying me, but I can't just grieve. No. No. I need an attorney. I need to protect myself.

My mind replays the meeting with Danielle Littleton.

I'd just started escaping the haze of the drugs, not as much as I'd have liked, but I was improving, when she entered my room and announced her name and declared herself my attorney. I said, "Who hired you? I don't . . . I didn't—"

"You did. Your parents and I talked on your behalf. As soon as your parents arrive with your checkbook in hand—"

"They don't have my checkbook."

"They're going to your house, and as I was saying, when they arrive, you're going to write me a check that I'm going to cash before the Phoenix family freezes your bank account and accuses you of murder."

"They're not going to do that," I argued. "They were just here. They told me—"

"It doesn't matter what they told you," she snapped. "They're manipulating you. You killed their son."

"I did not kill Oliver!" I shouted at her.

She grabbed the railing at the end of my bed and said, "They need to charge someone. Help me make sure it's not you."

That's when I sobered in all kinds of ways and reality set in. No matter how many times I say I didn't kill Oliver, no matter how unfathomable such a thing is to me, it's not unfathomable to anyone else. Everyone else, probably even my own parents, think I killed Oliver.

I have to assume Danielle does, too. Maybe even the Phoenixes.

"Oliver's parents want—"

"A lot of things," she said. "We'll see how that aligns with your best interests and go from there."

Returning to the present, I have to thank Danielle for reminding me why I must retrieve my memories. Those memories could hold the truth to what happened to Oliver. They could very well allow us to catch Oliver's killer.

This as my focus is all I have now, but it's a mighty and necessary goal. That means no more drugs. That means finding that calm, cool self I find in the ER who defies the hell around me. I can do this. I have to do this. For Oliver. Everything is for Oliver.

With that goal in mind, I'm frustrated as Ava, my fiftysomething nurse, kneels beside me to check my vitals. I'm frustrated with the throb in my head that tells me I'm far from recovered.

I rub the back of my neck. "I'm ready to have my head stop hurting anytime now."

"Of course you are," she says. "You took quite a knock on the head. You know from your own experiences caring for patients, I'm sure, that time is your best friend. Each day it will get better."

I like Ava. There's a worldliness that comes with her gray hair and the deep lines fanning her green eyes. Green eyes that tell a story, too. She understands pain, and it shows in that indescribable way that only a good nurse offers in support. I've always tried to be one of those nurses.

"I know the answer," I preface my next question as she wraps a blood pressure cuff around my arm, "but just because I need to hear your answer, Could the concussion be causing my memory loss?"

"It's a good question to ask the doctor."

The answer is frustratingly evasive, but understandable. She's not a doctor, and I'm tied to my damn IV pole like a criminal. I'm not exactly the person you want to get involved with right now. Therefore, I don't pressure her. I simply ask, "When can I do that? When will the doctor be around again?"

"In about an hour," she answers, reading my vitals and removing the cuff from my arm. My blood pressure is 120 over 70. Perfect. Nothing will ever be perfect, or otherwise, for Oliver. My chest squeezes with emotion, and when Ava goes to move away, I catch her hand. "I didn't do it. I didn't do this."

She settles back into her kneel beside me. "I'm not assuming you did anything. I see how much you loved him."

"But?"

"There are no buts," she says. "At least not from my perspective. My job is not to judge. You know that. You're a nurse as well."

"Funny how I can remember everything I learned in nursing school, but not the events of last night."

"You'll remember. Have faith." She fans herself. "They have the heat up so high. Are you hot?"

"Very."

"I'll get you a little fan, too, and crack the door just to get some air in here."

"Will they let you?"

She nods. "Of course. I'm in charge of my patients' comfort."

Someone knocks on the door and Ava pops to her feet. "That's probably the dessert I ordered for you. That broth you had earlier and a little bread wasn't much. I'm hoping to entice you to eat a bit more with chocolate cake. Believe it or not, it's really quite good. I'll be right back."

She rushes away, exiting the room and leaving the door ajar.

And for just a fleeting moment, I think about running.

# Chapter Fifty

I actually stand up as if I might really make a run for it, but pain erupts, like thunder in my head, and sits my butt right back down. Not that I want to run, but as my fingers grip the armrests, I amend that thought. Well, maybe I do. I want to run away from my new reality. The one without the man I love. And I do love him. Forever. I will always love him. *Always.*

Willing tears and the thunder in my head away, I lay my head back and shut my eyes, counting again. One. Two. Three. Four. I get to ten when I hear, "Chocolate cake has arrived."

I lift my head to blink Ava into view. "I'm still trying to find a fan," she adds. "Apparently, we all agree—the heater is on overdrive today. Everyone wants a fan." She pulls the tray up in front of me and sets the cake down. "But everyone doesn't get cake. I had your piece set aside special. Try that. If that doesn't make you feel better, we need more testing."

"I'd laugh," I say, "but it would hurt. Imagine me laughing. And thank you, Ava."

"No thanks needed, honey. Eat. You need to eat."

*I need Oliver,* I think, but in silent submission, I pick up the fork.

Ava watches me closely, and satisfied that I've complied, she announces, "I need to get vitals on another patient, but I'll be back to check on you in a few." She fans herself. "And hopefully with a fan." She hurries out of the room and leaves the door open a bit wider than last time.

I don't consider running this time. Where would I go? I'm in hell, and I've always felt that no matter how many I help, I doubt I'll ever make it into heaven. And yet, I try to change that feeling. I do try.

For no reason but to please Ava, I jab my fork into the cake and slide a bite into my mouth. It's a thick, rich chocolate, with a bittersweet icing. I don't want to like it. How dare I like anything right now. But I do. I like it, and for that reason and that reason alone, I set my fork down and slide the tray away.

Squeezing my eyes shut, I reach for my memory of last night, desperately trying to remember something, *anything*. And a few little details splatter across my mind, a bit like spilled sour milk, hard to digest. I'm back at the party and I'm laughing with the girls, feeling a bit light-headed from the champagne, when normally I handle my champagne quite well. Next thing I know, the girls are dragging me to the stage in front of the male dancers. My eyes pop open, and despite the ache of my stitched belly, I sit up straighter. *Oh God.* I was sticking money in one of the dancers' G-strings. Why would I do that? That's not like me at all. The dancer, a bald, muscular man, had even grinned at my fingers at his hip and blown me a kiss.

Muffled voices lift outside the door, drawing me out of the convoluted memory that I'm not sure is even accurate. The voices grow closer and despite the soft tones, I make out my parents' distinct tones in the mix. My gut clenches. Oh God. This is the moment I've dreaded, and that dread has me flashing back to a similar moment.

*I'm standing with two police officers in the parking lot of the Dairy Queen where my brother and I just ate a few minutes ago, the one by our house, shaking, hugging myself, trying to form words to explain to them what happened to my brother. I can't look to my left, where he's in the street, his broken body sprawled out on the pavement.*

*I don't want to tell them what happened. I don't want to tell them, but they push me for more. "We need to know what happened."*

*"It was so fast," I whisper. "We were roughhousing and he'd taken off across the road, trying to beat me across the intersection." My lips curl around my teeth. "Suddenly the car was just there, and . . . and . . ." My gaze lifts and my words fall away as my eyes lock on the navy-blue Chevy that pulls into the parking lot, my parents' car. I sob at the sight of it and sob some more. Eric was their son. I'm just . . . I'm the outsider. They're going to blame me. They're going to hate me.*

*I suck in a breath as my mother exits the passenger side of the car and manages two steps before I watch in horror as she collapses. My father rushes to her side, and I sob harder now, sinking to my knees on the hot Texas pavement.*

I blink back to the present, but I'm still thinking about that day.

I never finished telling my side of the story, not then, not to the police or my parents. Not everything. I couldn't talk about it, and my mother couldn't bear to hear about it, either. So I just didn't explain what happened to anyone. Not even to Mr. Jordan, the counselor I saw soon after and for years to follow. I never could talk about it, not if I was going to survive it.

I never even really knew if I remembered anything right or wrong.

# Chapter Fifty-One

Another set of voices lift from outside the door, and I land solidly in the present, leaving the past and the day my brother died with it. I can now identify Dr. Mendez and Danielle as part of the conversation. I can't really hear what they are saying, but of course, it's about me. My mother's voice comes next, and all I can make out is her frustration.

I shove aside the tray and stand up. This time the thunder in my head doesn't win. Dragging my IV pole with me, I walk toward the door and lean on the wall by the door as my mother says, "She didn't do this. My daughter did not kill anyone."

She's always been the one who defended me. Always. It hurts my heart to even think about disappointing her. "What about the cut on her belly?" she demands. "She has to be terrified right now."

"On that note," Dr. Mendez says, "I'm concerned for your daughter's mental well-being."

"My daughter is not insane." My mother cackles. "Do not even think of going there. She didn't do this."

"Honey," my father coos. "Honey, he's just looking out for Carrie."

I can almost see his calming hand on her back and feel her deep breath that follows. "Go on, Doctor," he urges, which tells me he's succeeded in bringing down her stress.

I breathe out as well now. She's calm. I'm calm, too. For now, at least.

"For my part," he continues, "medically, she has a head injury that can affect her memory, as can a psychedelic reaction to certain drugs, which she certainly was symptomatic of when she arrived."

"Wouldn't that show on a drug test?" my father asks.

"Not if it's a synthetic drug." He moves on. "Additionally, we have to consider that mental trauma can cause memory loss. In my book, if she's innocent, her best defense is her memory. Furthermore, I'm not a psychologist, who might be better equipped to help her retrieve those memories. That's why we have Carrie lined up to speak with a qualified psychologist. I'll compare notes with that person, and I believe we'll agree to have her further evaluated upon her return to Denver."

"All of this is good," Danielle chimes in. "We're building Carrie's defense. We're protecting her."

"Defense?" My mother's voice cracks. "You think she killed him?"

I wait for the answer, and Danielle doesn't make me wait. "We don't know what happened," she explains. "But her best defense is one that prepares for an insanity plea, if it becomes necessary, even one that is drug-induced, and not at her own hand."

"She didn't kill him," my mother says. "This is ridiculous. She's a nurse. She cares for people. She loves Oliver. She didn't do it."

"We have to consider all options," my father says, as if he's considered the possibility I killed Oliver.

And he's what gets to me. He sets me off.

There is a pulse in my jaw that vibrates through my entire body. He is always the one who turns on me. He never really saw me as his daughter. He blamed me for the accident. I tell myself to let it go, but before I can stop myself, I'm dragging my IV pole and shoving open the door, intending to do nothing but quietly defend myself.

To start, that's what I do. I step into view. "I didn't do this," I say, finding my father just a foot away. "I didn't kill Oliver." His eyes meet mine, and the doubt I find in his stare cuts me. "I didn't kill him!" I shout. "Do you understand me?! I didn't kill him!"

All eyes are on me far and wide, and of course, now I look like a crazy person, just like they claim I am.

I step toward my father to plead for his support, the way I'm always pleading for his love, but the police officer grabs me, holds me. My gaze collides with Danielle's, and I swear there's a glint of satisfaction in her stare. This is what she wanted. She's painting the narrative of me being crazy. Insane. Guilty by insanity.

I want to grab her and shake her.

I want to scream.

I want Oliver to be alive.

I draw a breath and will myself to calm, only to have my mother throw her arms around me and hug me. Now she's helping Danielle with her narrative, because having my mother hold me right now is really going to make me crazy.

# Chapter Fifty-Two

My mother begins to sob and does so to such an extreme there is a kind of howling sound coming from my shoulder where her face is buried.

Her meltdown makes mine look tame at best and my father steps behind her, hugging her and murmuring in her ear. My new attorney I didn't even hire responds a bit more fiercely. "In the room," she demands, pointing. "And hands off, Officer."

The officer looks toward Agent Castle, who I'm just realizing is by our sides at this point and here for the show.

Castle motions to the officer. "Let her go. She's not going to run away in a hospital gown with an IV pole attached to her arm."

She's right. I'd remove the IV, cut the line, and change clothes if I were going to run, but of course, we've established that I'm not going to do that.

Nurse Ava appears by my side. "You know it's not safe to walk around yet," she says. And as if I didn't just scream in the middle of the hallway, she ushers me inside and orders me into my chair. Her gaze goes to my cake. "You should have eaten the cake. It would have kept you out of trouble."

Now she's scolding me like a child, but it's a deserved scolding. She's right. I should have eaten the cake and stayed in my chair.

There's a bit of chaos that follows, and a shifting of bodies, before finally my parents, Danielle, and the doctor are in the room as well. Danielle shuts the door on law enforcement and watchful eyes.

The doctor motions for Ava to leave. She nods and turns her attention to me. "I'll be back to check on you," she vows, and even before she departs, my mother is on one knee by my side.

"How are you?" she asks, her cheeks streaked with mascara, her eyes bloodshot and weary.

"I'm just trying to survive, Mom," I whisper.

"I can get you another dose of Valium," the doctor offers. "It's certainly reasonable under the circumstances."

I shake my head. "No more drugs that numb and cloud my mind. I don't want to feel what I feel right now, but I need my memory to return, and drugs are not going to help."

"Agreed," Danielle interjects. "No more drugs. And we need a few minutes, Doctor."

He ignores her and remains focused on me. "How is your head feeling?"

"Throbbing," I say. "But I'd rather feel that than other things right now."

"You're clearly improving," he observes, vague on his definition of *improving*. "And while that's good," he continues, "it's okay to need some relief."

"I'm an ER nurse," I say. "I know how to check my emotions. I need to be clearheaded to do that."

He studies me a moment, and I wonder if he's judging me for my cocktail of drugs, but nothing I take causes mental impairment. If he is, thankfully he lets it go. "Understood, but I'll approve meds if you need them." He nods at me, before he heads toward the door and exits.

Now it's just me, my new attorney, and my parents in the room. I wish I could say this is when I can finally breathe again.

It's not. I can't catch my breath.

# Chapter Fifty-Three

I find myself doing what I often do with my parents. I withdraw, arms folded in front of my chest, a shiver overtaking me, followed by another, and yet another. "You're cold," my mother assumes, quickly grabbing a blanket from the bed and wrapping it around me.

There was a time when I wanted her to take care of me, especially after Eric died. If she fussed over me, she didn't blame me—that had been my logic. But somewhere along the way, that shifted, changed. I started to realize that her "fussing" wasn't about love but rather distrust—in my actions, my choices, my ability to take care of myself and others around me.

I'm self-analytical enough to know that's exactly why I became a nurse. Not to follow in her footsteps but to prove that not only can I take care of myself, I can take care of others, and I'm good at it. Really good at it.

I snuggle into the blanket and my mother asks, "Better?"

"Yes," I oblige. "Thanks, Mom."

She squeezes my arm. "You never have to thank me for taking care of you."

*Because it's not for me,* I think. It's for her.

My eyes meet my father's. He appears concerned, but I still see blame in the depths of his stare. It's always there. It will always be there.

They never got over me living and him dying.

The truth is, neither have I.

"We have a lot to talk about," Danielle states, breaking up any and all parent/child interaction being displayed by setting a contract and a pen on the table by my chair. "One hundred and fifty thousand dollars. That should ensure I'm paid in full if your accounts are frozen."

"That's so much money," my mother says, casting me a concerned look. "Honey, if you can't do this, we'll see if we can get a loan."

It's a lot of money, but Oliver and I have that and a whole lot more in our account. Still, as silly as it might seem in these circumstances, it feels excessive and somehow wrong to spend so much without his input.

"Joe," my mother urges, tugging my father's arm. "Tell her we'll take out a loan."

"It's okay, Mom," I say, allowing the blanket to fall from my shoulders, the chill gone as I force myself into that ER state of mind, where business comes before emotions. Or at least I give it a champ's effort, as my father often says. "I've got this," I promise her, my attention returning to Danielle. "It's a lot of money."

"Unless you're going to spring a memory and produce a killer that isn't you, it's not even close to how much your defense is going to cost, but it'll get you a long way. And Agent Castle as well as the Phoenixes need to know they can't cut you off and therefore cut off your defense. They need to know they can't pressure you to talk."

"They can pressure me all day," I say. "I can't remember what happened."

"You were covered in his blood, honey," she reminds me, as if I need to be reminded. "They can charge you right now, and if I don't work my magic, they will."

"And injured myself, and in hiding," I add. "I was hiding. I was scared. I just can't remember of who. But I will. I know *I will*."

"It better be before they come for you."

"The Phoenixes aren't going to come after our bank accounts," I insist. "They told me they believe me. They know I wouldn't hurt Oliver."

"Sign the contract and write the check," she urges. "Then we'll talk about what's really going on with the Phoenixes."

"I know nothing about you," I argue.

"We reviewed her references," my father interjects. "She's handled, and won, a great many high-profile cases."

Danielle quickly adds, "The Phoenixes want a conviction. They'll be going to pressure law enforcement to charge someone. That someone will be you."

I want to object. I outright want to reject the idea, but she's right, of course. They're going to charge me. They're going to say that I killed Oliver, despite the cut on my stomach, despite my love for him.

With a resistant hand, I write a check and hand it to her.

Satisfaction glows in her eyes, and she places the check in her purse. "Now. Let's talk about the Phoenixes."

"They suggested I get out of town and away from the press while the police find out who really did this," I say. "They said they'd pay for some private resort to keep me safe. They insisted that protecting me is protecting the family and Oliver's legacy."

"Resort." She smirks. "Some might call it that. What they offered to pay for is a high-end rehab facility. And transportation to get you there. I said yes."

"Rehab?" I demand, at the same time as my mother. I wave that off. "I'm not going to rehab. I have no addiction to treat. It'll make me look guilty. No."

Danielle sits down in the chair next to mine. "Hollywood does this all the time. You're rehabbing your trauma. You're working with a professional to retrieve your memory, and this looks good to the courts. Agent Castle will never slap you in handcuffs when you're showing a willingness to aid in her investigation."

"It's *a hospital.*"

"Rosewood is a resort-style rehabilitation facility. Heck, I went to one of those places after my ex-husband started seeing his secretary. I needed the emotional support. It's not about drugs. And as the Phoenixes pointed out, this keeps you away from the press. As a bonus, it keeps you away from law enforcement. You'll have a solid week of solitude while I work my magic on the outside."

I'm about to ask why the Phoenixes would protect me if they want me arrested, but a cold sensation fills me with realization. "The will states that if I'm declared insane, or incapable of caring for myself, Oliver's family will manage my money." I shove a hand at her, pushing away the very idea. "I don't want the money. They do. Just give them the money."

"Don't be ridiculous," Danielle chides. "You're not giving them the money. You need to pay for your defense."

"How much money are we talking about?" my father asks.

"It's a lot of money, Dad," I say, and leave it at that, focused on Danielle. "The money makes me look guilty. I wanted him, not his money. I didn't do this. Give them the money."

Her refusal is instant. "No. And yes, before you even say it, I'm sure the Phoenixes plan to have someone in the facility rule you incompetent. But I have a plan to protect you. The most important thing right now is for you to meet with the psychologist Dr. Mendez has lined up. I'll handle the rest. Agreed?"

"Do I really have a choice?" I ask.

"You always have a choice, honey," Danielle says. "But this is what is best for you." She eyes my parents. "Carrie and I need to talk one-on-one."

"Can we have a moment with her, please?" my father asks.

"I'm fine, Dad," I quickly say. "Let me do what I have to and then we can talk."

He gives a stiff nod. My mother hugs me, scoffing at the cuff that restrains my movement before turning and presenting a plea to Danielle. "Can you do something about this?"

"Let's not press Agent Castle until I have all the legwork in place," Danielle replies. "Then we'll get the cuff off."

My mother's expression twists in disapproval, but she nods her acceptance. She kisses me and then joins my father where he stands. He holds his ground, with no attempt to kiss me. I don't want him to kiss me anyway, but I hate the jolt of emotions inside me that defies this truth.

"We'll be close," he says simply, before guiding my mother toward the exit.

Once the door opens and shuts and I'm alone with Danielle, she pins me in a stare. "You now have attorney/client privilege. Tell me what I'm dealing with. Did you kill Oliver?"

I go cold inside again, bitterly cold, so this time I'm withdrawn, a bit like I am forced to be in the ER at times. "I did *not* kill Oliver." I enunciate the words precisely.

"Then tell me," she says. "Who did?"

# Chapter Fifty-Four

## ANDI

I hang out in the waiting room of the hospital, where I've apparently taken up residence, while Carrie is evaluated, cramming down food one of the nurses brought me. I'm proving myself to be my father's daughter by going all in, elbows deep in an egg salad sandwich, when Dr. Penny Norton, the psychologist doing the evaluation, appears in the doorway.

Wonderful. I look like a heathen, not that I really care. Impressing someone with my eating habits is not why I'm here. Catching killers is my game, and I play it well. I toss the last of the sandwich in the trash, clean up, and meet Dr. Norton in the middle of the room. She's forty-something, brunette, with soft features and a hard attitude.

"She's traumatized," she states, her voice stern. "Whatever happened in that room that forced her to hide in that attic has a strong hold on her."

"'Forced' is a strong word," I observe, sipping my Mr. Pibb all the way to the slurp-worthy bottom and with a purpose, as my father's words play in my head: *"If someone has a stick in their ass, stick it further on up there. It'll get them to talk. Or not, and that tells you something about 'em, too."* My father can be crass, but if you look beneath the roughness, there's a lot of working strategy to be had.

And as expected, Dr. Norton bristles. "Please," she says. "Do you have to do that?"

I act completely baffled by her request. "Do what?"

"Slurp your drink."

"I'm a real big advocate of no waste," I say. "And time lost is waste. I feel like that's where we're going."

She ignores that comment and circles back to the prior topic. "I chose a strong word, Agent Castle, as is appropriate. Carrie's suppressing the events of last night to protect herself from the extreme duress, which is not uncommon. The mind is a miraculous thing."

"So her mind is coddling her," I follow along, adding my own observation. "I thought that was her mother?"

She charges onward to defend her position. "I could list study after study that supports Carrie's mental impairment."

"Now it's an impairment?" I challenge.

"It absolutely is," she declares.

I give her credit. She's not flustered, not by my slurping, pushing, or prodding. That tells me she's done this before. I'd be interested to find out just how many cases she's testified on.

"And how long will this impairment continue?" I ask.

"She needs help recovering from the trauma to latch on to her suppressed memories."

"And what exactly do you recommend?" I ask, but I already know the answer. I bet myself a chocolate cake the answer is a treatment facility.

"A treatment facility," Dr. Norton states.

And there it is, folks. The winner and my chocolate cake. If only it were as filled with calorie-free bites as she is with bullshit. "How long?" I ask.

"At least thirty days, with a staff that has experience in this area. I've discussed this option with Carrie's attorney, and she's lined up an appropriate facility."

"Do you have any connection to this facility you recommend?" I ask.

"I do not," she replies primly.

"Does anyone you know have a connection to the facility?"

"They do not. I'm not trying to play a game here, Agent Castle. I have the patient's best interest in mind."

"And what about the victim's?"

"Carrie getting her memory back is in the victim's best interest. I'll let Ms. Littleton handle giving you a copy of my written report." With that, she turns and walks out of the waiting room.

I'd assume Oliver's family would object to this and demand an arrest, but as Danielle, Ms. Littleton herself, appears in the doorway, a gleam of satisfaction in her eyes, I know that's not how this is going to play out.

# Chapter Fifty-Five

I stand my ground and force Ms. Littleton to come to me.

"You talked to Dr. Norton, I assume?" she asks, stepping toe to toe with me, her way of telling me my badge doesn't intimidate her.

"Do you know what they say about attorneys who are overly confident?"

"I'm not overly confident, Agent Castle."

"That's what every overly confident attorney says until they find out that, guess what? They were overly confident. You know my problem with an overly confident attorney?"

"*What*, Agent Castle?"

"Nothing. Did the Phoenixes agree to this treatment facility?"

"They're showing support for the woman their son loved. They've offered to pay for the outrageously expensive facility and provide transportation to get her there."

"I'll agree with the terms. I'll ride with her, with her in my custody, held for questioning, until she's checked into the facility. She doesn't leave the facility without me being able to fully complete that questioning."

"Which I'll be present for," she reminds me.

"And," I add, ignoring her, and holding up a finger as she opens her mouth to speak, "I want twenty-four hours' notice before her release, in which to decide if I want to arrest her. All of these things will be put in writing tonight."

"Agreed," she says, but her tone is pure sour grapes.

"How much money will Carrie inherit?"

"She's offered to give the money to the family."

"How much?" I press.

"It's excessive."

"That's not an answer." I let it go. I'll find out. I have a point, which I make. "The family isn't supporting Carrie," I say. "They're trying to control that money. You're trying to make that work for you, but you should know that I'm going to make it work for me as well."

"If you had enough to arrest her, you would."

"I have plenty to arrest her," I say, "but I'm not a rookie. I know when to make an arrest and how to make it stick. I'll be at the hotel when you have that paperwork." With that, I step around her and leave.

# Chapter Fifty-Six

By the time I return to the hotel, York and our team have been clearing guests to go home for hours. I check my email, which includes a note from the ME: I'll have a report to you by tomorrow night, but don't expect any surprises. Thus far, all of the studies and testing done by myself and the forensics team support my on-site findings.

In other words, he still believes a woman killed Oliver. It's hard not to be swayed by medical findings, but I still believe there's something going on here that defies what meets the eye. Therefore, I remind myself to keep an open mind.

I head to Lana's room with the news that I won't be traveling back to Denver with her. I suspect that's why she's called me twice in the past hour. I knock on her door to find her anxiously waiting for me.

"What's happening?" she asks, motioning me into the room.

I follow her inside, only to discover that we're not alone. Brody is with her. He gives me a grin from the end of the bed, where he's sitting. "Howdy there, Agent Castle," he greets.

"Brody," I say as Lana reclaims the conversation.

"They said we're free to leave," she informs me, folding her arms in front of her and watching for my reaction.

"That's correct," I reply. "That's why I'm here. I won't be traveling home with you."

She glances at Brody and lifts her chin toward the door.

He pushes to his feet. "Yeah, yeah, I'll get lost." He saunters forward but stops a reasonable distance away, still close enough for me to smell the booze on him. "Don't worry," he says as if he's read my thoughts. "I won't drink and drive, Agent Castle." It's a strange thing to stop and pointedly tell me, but with that, he heads for the door.

The minute it opens and shuts, Lana is in front of me. "What's happening? Everyone keeps calling me because they know we're friends. It's making me crazy."

"I'm not going to talk to you about the investigation, and you can tell them as much."

"Right," she says. "Right, I know. I know you can't." She presses her hands to her face. "I hate that this is happening. I liked her. We were friends."

She not only speaks as if Carrie is guilty, she speaks as if Carrie is the one who died. "She's far better off than Oliver," I point out.

"I don't know," she says. "Is she? If she's innocent, she's lost the man she loves, and the world believes she killed him. If she killed him, she'll rot in jail." She doesn't wait for an answer. "Did you find out about the box?"

"We're following up on that lead," I confirm. "Try and rest. Are you going to be okay to drive home alone?"

"I'll be fine. Don't worry about me. Or I can stay if you like and try to help. Carrie talks to me. Maybe she'll say something helpful to me? And there's another friend of hers back home that didn't attend the party. Erin Sterling. She's a nurse as well. She didn't like Oliver. She talks to Carrie quite a lot."

"Do you know why she didn't like Oliver?"

"Not really. Erin works in the cardiac unit. I never really got to know her. I just know what Carrie told me."

"Which is what?" I ask.

"That Erin thought he was arrogant and that's about it. I think her and Oliver had some sort of a clash at some point. I can get you her number."

"Text it to me," I say. "Right now, I just want to get everyone home safely—you too."

"Home does sound good," she replies. "I'm sure it would to you as well."

"The sooner I get back to work, the sooner that happens. I'll be in touch when I'm back." I turn for the door and she halts my progress.

"Andi?"

I rotate to face her. "Yes?"

"You won't tell Carrie I told you about the box, right? I don't want her to feel as if I stabbed her in the back. And if she's a killer and gets off, I also don't need another enemy. My ex is enough for me."

"For now, there's no issue with discretion, but we'll talk about what needs to happen and when once we're back in Denver."

"You can't tell her I told," she insists.

There's a panicked desperation to her words, and I certainly get it. She's in an awkward position, but my job isn't to ensure everyone's comfort. It's to deliver justice for all.

"We'll talk," I say, and this time when I turn, I leave.

I head back to the conference room where York is working with the team. "Interesting news," he announces as I claim the seat across from him. "The Phoenix family made arrangements to transport Oliver when his body is released and then jumped on a chopper and left without talking to us. You'd think they'd want to be here, pressuring us to make an arrest. Most parents want to control the investigation."

"They've now arranged to have Carrie exactly where they want her, in that treatment facility. They think they're in control."

"I'd still think they'd want to be right here, asking questions, driving answers," he argues.

He's right, of course, but I'm beginning to think the Phoenixes have something to hide, and that something may or may not have anything to do with their son's murder. It's time to start digging around in the Phoenixes' lives. And that's exactly what comes next. I make the calls and give the directions that will allow us to see behind the Phoenix family curtains.

# Chapter Fifty-Seven

Twenty-four hours later, it's headed toward midnight, and I'm in a hotel conference room, surrounded by detectives and with a bag of Funyuns in front of me, looking through the interviews. "Those things are disgusting," York says, eyeing the big onion curl I stuff in my mouth.

"Funyuns are not only good, they smell like onion, and then so do you, therefore everyone stays away." They won't keep my father away, I add silently, but of course, I'm speaking of normal humans.

"I bet it won't keep Ms. Littleton away. She's been here how many times?"

"Three," I say, sipping my Dr Pepper. We're out of Mr. Pibb, and no matter how many times York tells me it's the same thing, he's wrong. "We finally agreed on the paperwork for Carrie's treatment facility. I shot it over to my boss."

"She's inheriting millions," he says. "We know who did this. Do we even need to finish our data on anyone else?"

*That's like asking my father if he really needs the baseball bat,* I think. The answer is yes; we still need to see this through. Inheriting money goes to motive, not evidence. "The defense will try to redirect the attention of the jury to someone else. We have to be able to counter."

"Of course" is the answer I receive, and we all go back to work.

I talk to Erin, the nurse Lana said talked to Carrie often, and who she thought had a dispute with Oliver. Erin chats with Carrie at work but has never had a problem with Oliver. Of course, few people will admit to a conflict with a man who was murdered. I have the team look further into her with not much to find.

My attention turns to studying the car accident that killed Carrie's brother.

After which I manage to talk to the now retired detective in charge of that case.

"I'll never forget what the driver said," he tells me. *"I swear I thought that other kid pushed him."*

He seems to shiver with the words.

I do, too. The idea of a child dying—being here one day and gone tomorrow—is brutal, and that's at best.

"I see the driver got off?" I ask.

"It was a no-fault accident," he replies.

"Unless it wasn't," I surmise.

"Exactly," he says tightly. "The kid, the brother, he was a talented athlete even at a young age. He had a bright future."

He's just driving in the knife. I do not like this part of my job—the death, the pain. "I don't see anything about your suspicions in relation to Carrie in the files."

"Of course not. The family's wealthy. I had boatloads of pressure to leave it alone. You know going after a rich kid isn't a good way for a DA to get reelected."

We end the call, every word of the exchange sitting like rocks in my belly.

My mother was killed by a man who was late to work and ran a red light. Losing her still torments me, as it does my father. The driver went to jail for manslaughter but not for long enough. The driver who killed Carrie's brother did not, but he will never forget being behind the wheel of the vehicle that killed a little boy. I'm sure Carrie's parents have suffered plenty. But has Carrie?

I dial Carrie's parents' attorney and get sent to voicemail. I leave a message. "Let's talk about Carrie's brother," I say. "Call me back."

Obviously, he listens to the message but chooses to text his response: Don't go that low. And if you even bring this up to the parents and open that wound, they'll sue.

In other words, I'm getting nowhere with this lead, but it's ammunition the DA can use during the trial to stir the jury's emotions. Now I just have to ensure that trial happens.

My cellphone rings with Aiden's number. I stand up and, without excusing myself from the rest of my team, exit the room and enter the hallway.

"Hey," I greet him. "You read the agreement?" I shut the door behind me.

"I did," he confirms. "I think it's a win for us even if Carrie's team thinks it's a win for hers. We're building a case. On that note, I expect to have the warrants for Carrie and Oliver's home and offices. His office was tricky. The Phoenixes have a lot of power. Getting a judge that didn't fear them was no easy task."

"I'm gathering that," I say dryly.

"A good reason to just get the searches done quickly, but how do you feel about the timeline? Do you want us to roll with those or wait on you? When are you coming back?"

"If the doctor approves it," I say, "tomorrow afternoon, but as much as I want to be there, don't wait. I don't want to give Oliver's or Carrie's parents a chance to tamper with anything beforehand."

"We can lock down the locations if you really want to be here," he offers.

"No," I say, but having already discussed the case with Aiden in detail early this morning, I add, "I want evidence sooner than later, and I'm hoping like hell you find that box I told you about."

"That would be interesting," he says. "I'll take a look myself as well during the searches. And I've got a team here helping Hazel dig for dirt anywhere we can find it."

"Let me know before you do the searches," I say. "Since I'd like as much cooperation as possible, I'll give Carrie's attorney and Oliver's parents a short heads-up just before you do."

"That works," he agrees. "We can go into the Phoenixes' business discreetly, in plain clothes."

"Echoing your words," I reply, "that works. I'll let them know."

"How are you doing on getting an interview with Carrie?" he asks.

"Nowhere. I told you the doctor's protecting her."

"Sounds to me like someone is paying him off," he comments.

"Maybe," I say. "Or it could just be that the doctor relates to Carrie in ways that aren't exactly healthy. I know he's a former addict. He's defensive of her. She's personal to him. I don't think this is about money to him."

"Don't underestimate the power behind the Phoenixes' excess of money," he says. "They clearly don't trust us to conduct this investigation. And we can assume they not only want to break her for us, they believe they have someone in that treatment center that will make it happen. They needed Dr. Mendez to ensure she left Estes Park and landed there."

"Their desire to get her to that facility still feels off," I say, thinking out loud. "Unless . . ." My mind races with a new angle on their motives.

"Unless what?" he presses.

"Unless I'm more right than I know. They really do have something to hide, and they're afraid Oliver told her. Maybe they have no choice but to protect her."

"Or control her," he suggests. "I think you're onto something. Keep me posted. And when you get back, I'll come by and bring dinner, and we can look over the case."

"I'll call you," I promise and hang up, without committing to the dinner.

One day, maybe I'll be ready for more, but I swear the dead man stabbed over and over while celebrating his upcoming nuptials isn't exactly a selling point for an expanded relationship. Then again, I'm not sure what really happened to Oliver Phoenix. I don't think anything is as it seems.

# Chapter Fifty-Eight

It's just before eight the next morning when York and I load into the department-issued black sedan we'll be using to escort Carrie to the airport. His face is shadowed with gray stubble. My eyes are puffy, my hair clean but damp. I'm walking death and he dares to ask, "Any morning thoughts on the case?"

"Coffee." It's the logical answer with both of us running on no sleep. "Just need coffee. Then ask for thoughts."

"Right-o, Madam FBI Agent." He starts the engine and jokes, "You're cranky without your coffee. I bet your father beats you with a baseball bat if you talk to him before his coffee."

"Before his morning whisky," I reply, and irritated at his constant jabs, I add, "and if you keep going at my father like you are, I'll ensure he's brought on as a consultant on the case and have him start here with you. Then you can ask him about his morning habits all by your lonesome without me as a buffer." I glance over at him, and his eyes are wide.

"All right, then," he says. "No more talkie without the coffee."

"Thank you," I say. "And for the record, I'm not cranky. Not at all." I could tell him that my dad is a good man, and a single father who was always there for me, but why? I just want York to stop talking about the wrong things. Right now, his discomfort is almost as refreshing as my morning coffee will be.

Still, thankfully, York swings us by a local-brand coffee shop, which is about all there is up here. Shortly after, we're at the hospital, entering the parking lot through an area closed off to the press. The police presence is as solid as this little town allows. Once we're by the door where we'll exit the hospital with Carrie, York eagerly offers to stay behind and wait on the second car and detective that will be backup today. He's uncomfortable now, and I say that's what he gets for running his mouth about my father. I head inside, cup in hand, downing the remainder of my coconut mocha by the time I'm forced to deal with Ms. Littleton and her coconspirator, Dr. Mendez.

The three of us gather at the nurses' station for a cordial interaction. "Doctor," I greet him with a nod, before shifting my attention to add Carrie's attorney. "Ms. Littleton."

"Danielle," she reminds me.

I don't agree or disagree with the name.

This morning, using her first name just feels plain unnatural, too casual and quite fake friendly. If it feels weird on my tongue, and *Danielle* does, I'm not speaking it. I'm simply not keen on false narratives, and anything that involves her and me is a false narrative. It's bad enough we're twinsies today, both in black pants, boots, and silk blouses. One of those blouses is red, though, and it's not mine. I tend to stick to black when I'm wearing my badge. That way it's the star of the show, not me.

"She's approved for travel," Dr. Mendez states on Carrie's condition, "but she is not approved for questioning. Her mental state is delicate."

"Which is why I'll be by her side the entire trip," Ms. Littleton replies, in an obvious warning shot.

"Of course you will," I reply dryly, but my focus is on Dr. Mendez. "When will she be discharged?"

"She's dressing now and we're preparing her paperwork," the doctor replies. "I'd say give us twenty minutes." He shakes both of our hands and departs.

"Can we skip the cuffs?" Ms. Littleton asks. "She's not going to make a run for it."

"No," I say, and I don't explain myself. She is aware that there's a protocol to follow for the one and only prime suspect in a violent murder, who I've yet to even properly question. And furthermore, I'm not about to send either of them the wrong message. I don't know if Carrie is our killer, but there's more of a chance that she is than not, and my job is to give her reasons to cooperate.

"Once she's on the helicopter?" she presses.

"You already know my answer, but she'll be well protected on our exit from the hospital," I state. "I assume the chopper's ready?"

"The Phoenixes have confirmed it's on standby when we're ready."

"Then if you'll excuse me, I need to notify our team of transport." I step around her and speak to the officer at the door, eager to get things moving. If I get my way, I'll be talking to Carrie before this trip is over.

# Chapter Fifty-Nine

## CARRIE

I stand under the hot water of the hospital shower, free of my cuff long enough to clean up and dress. This after I was allowed my normal drug cocktail with my morning juice and coffee, but Dr. Mendez warns me that will likely change at the treatment facility.

I dislike the fact that he's been added to the short list of people who know my dirty little secret. The truth is that I've been having panic attacks for most of my life. My parents think they started over Eric's death and ended a year later. Oliver knew they never ended, as does my doctor back home.

But no one knows, and no one will ever know, that they started before Eric was ever hit by that car.

Ever. It's one of my flaws. It's part of what makes me, me, and I don't even know where that originates. I'm not a Reynolds by birth. I don't even know my real last name. I just know that being a Phoenix, connected to Oliver, felt almost necessary—it felt like survival. I have a flickering memory of Oliver and that box, and I'm instantly stabbed with the sense of betrayal I felt when his office door was locked. When he locked me out.

I try unsuccessfully to shove away that memory. I don't want to remember that night and how I felt, but I decide it's about a sense of being alone. Outside that door that night, that's what I felt. Alone. So very alone. And that is what I am now.

Alone.

By the time I've dried my hair and dressed in my own jeans and a teal blouse from my suitcase someone brought me, I'm ready to head to the treatment facility. I'm not going for Oliver's parents, who I believe have an agenda that is self-serving. They've never felt I was good enough for Oliver. He swore differently, but I saw it in their eyes past and present. I'm not even going to this facility for Oliver's legacy, because that's a bunch of bull. None of this is about his legacy. It's about the family reputation. And their reputation doesn't matter to me.

How Oliver died is what matters.

Who killed him is what matters.

Remembering is what matters.

And while I'm in that facility, I'll talk to counselors and doctors, not family and the press. The time will give me a chance to do just that: remember, and do so without other people confusing me with their agendas and memories. It will give me time to figure how I move forward. How I do what is right. And God, I hate that I have to think about this when my mind should be solely on Oliver, I really do, but I need to figure out how to protect myself.

There's a knock on the door and my nurse calls out, "They're ready for you."

I draw in a breath. Everyone is ready for me. I'm just not sure I'm ready for them. As an adopted child, there is a tendency to feel flawed, as if I am being judged as not good enough.

I don't need a counselor to tell me this. I've lived with that sense of existence every day of my life. I'm certainly being judged right now and coming up exactly as I always fear: flawed. What they don't understand is that I was never flawed in Oliver's eyes. He was my rock, my soulmate, truly my better half. Ironically, considering the circumstances, this would all be so much more tolerable if he were by my side.

But facing this alone is my only option. I open the door and find Nurse Ava standing in front of me. She gives me a quick inspection as the door closes behind her. "You okay, honey?" she asks.

My eyes burn, but somehow, I contain the tears. "I don't think I'll ever be okay again," I whisper, but I offer her my wrist. "Go ahead and cuff me. The sooner I finish the walk of shame the better."

"The cuff is silly," she says. "I'll let the fools forcing this on you cuff you. I won't do it."

This is the first time she's shared an opinion on anything to do with me, and it gives me hope that she, and others, won't believe I'm a horrible person capable of bad things. There's a knock on the door, and Ava squeezes my arm before heading in that direction. About thirty seconds later, my attorney, Ms. Littleton, or Danielle, as she prefers I call her, steps into the room.

Ms. Littleton, as I will continue to call her—we are not pals or friends—is wearing black pants, which are neutral enough, but her blouse is a bright red silk, which is not what someone who is trying to be discreet wears. That's the problem with the Phoenix family that even the Phoenix family calls a problem. Someone is always using them for money and/or fame. I don't know what I think about my new attorney's skills just yet, but her motives are clear.

I represent money and fame.

The only good thing about that is that she gets more of both if she handles my situation with positivity attached.

"Ready?" she asks.

"For this to be over," I say. "Now what?"

"We get the heck out of town," she says, "and we do so quietly. Agent Castle will be escorting us. That doesn't mean an interview. No talking to her. None. You understand?"

"Why can't I get it over with?"

"Because you need time to heal, and we need time to prepare."

There's another knock on the door and Ms. Littleton opens it. She then backs up to allow an officer to enter. He steps to me and says, "Wrists."

I inhale and present my hands. He uses a black zip tie of some sort and shackles both of my wrists this time. At least before, one was free. I'm even more ready now to be done with this.

At that moment, Agent Castle walks into the room. "We're ready to move," she states, her eyes meeting mine, and I know she's trying to read me. I'm trying to read her.

But I can't.

I wonder if she can read me.

And if she can, does she see a woman who loved her fiancé, or a woman who killed him?

# Chapter Sixty

## ANDI

Per York, the chopper is confirmed and the airport security arrangements are coordinated. Additionally, the hallways are cleared for the walk to the car.

When Carrie steps out of the room, she's framed by Ms. Littleton and me. Two officers walk before us and two behind. Once we're at the exit, we're halted while one officer clears our path. She gives the go-ahead, and the door is opened. I motion for Ms. Littleton to go ahead of Carrie.

"I need her in my sight," she states.

"I'm not attempting to talk to your client," I reply dryly. "I'm ensuring that if anyone starts shooting at her, I have a visual to shoot back."

She pales. "You think someone is going to start shooting?"

"You want the fame," I say, eyeing her red blouse and matching lipstick. "It comes with risks. Let's move."

"I'm not going to be the target," she argues.

"You're not willing to protect your client?" I challenge.

"Isn't that your job?" she counters.

"Exactly. That's why you're going first." She opens her mouth to object and I hold up a staying hand. "There are police ahead of you, and Carrie will be directly behind you."

"I'll go first," Carrie offers. "If she's afraid—"

"I'm not afraid," Ms. Littleton replies. "I'll go first." She stiffens her spine, sinks into the expensive winter coat that's covering her expensive pantsuit, and marches onward, her high heels clicking on the tile.

I motion Carrie forward and she draws a deep breath, distress in her eyes, but she doesn't complain. Like a good little soldier, she charges onward. York motions them to the rear of the sedan. Ms. Littleton wastes no time climbing inside, under cover, but when Carrie would follow, she pauses and turns to face me. "Are you going to charge me?"

"Are you going to talk to me?"

"I want to. They won't let me."

"Unless you plan to be ruled incompetent, you make your own decisions."

"I'm not incompetent and I'm not a killer. I'll tell you whatever I can remember. I want to help. I want to catch the killer."

"I'll believe that when you actually start talking."

Ms. Littleton climbs out of the vehicle and steps in front of Carrie, facing me. "I said no conversation." She rotates and all but shoves Carrie into the car.

Carrie is a hard nut to crack, and not because of her silence.

Because she appears sincere, gentle, and even kind.

But sometimes, looks can be deceiving, which in my book can work for or against her.

I'm still undecided.

# Chapter Sixty-One

Everything goes as planned, until it doesn't.

The ride to the airstrip is short, with me in the front passenger seat of the vehicle and York in the driver's seat. In light of the small, private airstrip hosting this trip, we haven't asked for the airport to be closed but for visitors to be limited to those traveling. Once York parks us near the door of the main building, we all exit the vehicle, and he lingers, offering us an escort inside.

I don't attempt to grab or hold Carrie, and when York makes a move to do so, I wave him off. She's cuffed. It's enough. Carrie's eyes meet mine, appreciation in her stare, an innocent quality to them. I've met people like her. People who come off like lambs but are really tigers, bears, or alligators, depending on their flavor of killing.

I motion everyone inside and we find the lobby to be all but empty, which serves us well. We're met by a staff member, who directs us to a small break room and waiting area, out of the view of the main lobby, and we are quick to make that our destination. With three small tables framed by snack machines, Ms. Littleton and Carrie have a seat. "I'll go arrange boarding." This from York, who heads toward the counter.

My phone buzzes with a text, and I snake it from my pocket to find a message from Whit: SOS. You aren't going to believe this case I'm working on. Come by your pop's place tonight. You need to hear this.

He's not luring me into the trap of actually responding. He's of course trying to do my father's work and get me over for a visit. It's only been two weeks. You'd think I'd been avoiding him for months. And the truth is, I'm still pissed at Whit for acting like a dimwit and almost getting us both fired. My father is not the influence he needs right now, and he knows it.

"Problem," York says, rejoining us. "The pilot's currently throwing up. They're having to call in a replacement."

"Of course they are," I say, but I'm not all that disappointed. More time means more opportunity to assess Carrie, and once we're on the chopper, chitchat won't be possible. "How long are we looking at?"

"An hour at most," he replies. "I'll hang out with you until you leave." He claims the seat across from Carrie. "I hear you're going to Rosewood, that place where the rich and famous rehab. There's a rumor a certain actress I like will be there with you. Think you can get me an autograph?"

He's trying to get her to admit she's been in rehab before, or to just talk and give us something. It's pretty smart. I let him do his thing and walk to the snack machine and plug in my card and choose a Snickers bar for breakfast. It's not the best of choices, but I'm starving, and if I have to hunt down someone, shoot someone, or battle the press, chocolate is my kind of zippy energy.

Behind me, Carrie replies with, "I don't know how it works in there. I've never been to rehab, but I'm sure autographs won't be allowed."

I rotate to face them, opening my Snickers but focusing on Carrie. "One day costs more than my mortgage. Or so Google told me."

"I had no idea," she replies. "But I'm not surprised. The Phoenixes set this up."

"Was Oliver as extravagant as his parents?" I ask.

"Enough, you two," Ms. Littleton warns. "She's not answering any questions."

"He treated me like a princess," Carrie says. "Always good to me in every possible way."

"At least you have the money to keep living the same lifestyle," York adds.

"I don't care about the money," Carrie states.

Ms. Littleton stands up. "I'm going to have to ask you both to step out of the room."

"But I just got here."

At the sound of a familiar male voice, all the attention goes to the doorway, where Brody—dressed in jeans and a T-shirt that reads I'm Your Huckleberry—is now standing.

# Chapter Sixty-Two

"What are you doing here, Brody?"

I ask the question at the same moment that Carrie does.

"I come bringing peace, love, and happiness," he says, "and thanks to the Phoenixes, I'm keeping my promise to you, Agent Castle. I'm not drinking and driving. I turned in my rental, and I'm hitching a ride with you guys."

"He can't be here," Carrie says, her voice lifting, her gaze going to her attorney. "Can he be here?"

All eyes go to me. I motion for Brody to follow me, tossing my Snickers bar in the garbage and then stepping out into the waiting room, in a corner area by the window. "What the hell is this, Brody?"

"I'm just hitching a fast ride home."

"And you thought riding with us was a good idea?" I demand. "How did you even know when to be here?"

"I called to check on the Phoenixes, and they spared me booking my own bird. They offered me a lift."

"Are you spying for them?" I challenge.

"I'm not, but I wouldn't be surprised if Carrie's attorney is on their payroll."

"She'd lose her license."

"And get rich doing it," he counters.

"Is that your game?"

"I'm already rich, Agent Castle. I'll show you my bank account if you'll have coffee with me back in Denver."

"This is not a negotiation, and unless you're involved with Oliver's murder, I do not care about your bank account."

"I'm not even going to get defensive. I have no reason to be. We both know the night he was killed I was miles deep in—"

"Stop. If you have some vigilante idea about getting back at Carrie—"

"I'm not Eddie Castle," he comments, and when my jaw clenches, he says, "I can google. I know who you are. Do I want to make her uncomfortable? Sure. I'll enjoy that. She cheated on him and killed him."

"We don't know that."

"I do," he says. "And she's in cuffs. Obviously, you know something or you wouldn't be arresting her."

"We're escorting her to the hospital, not arresting her," I counter. "Once we've formally questioned her and examined the evidence, we'll make that decision."

"I get it now. That bitch of an attorney of hers isn't letting you question her and now they're stashing her away in a hospital. Fuck." He scrubs his jaw. "Am I allowed to ride with you?"

I should say no, but I'm interested in how Carrie reacts to stress. "If you behave."

He grins. "Behave is almost my middle name. Sometimes. Almost never, but today it's my almost middle name. As a bonus, I'll be useful. You want to talk to her. Don't you worry, I'll make it happen. I'm your Huckleberry."

He starts to turn and I say, "Stop."

He doesn't listen. He walks back to the break room.

I sigh and follow him, ready to go kick him to the curb. I find him at the coffeepot, pouring himself a cup. York arches a brow, and Carrie's attention is on me. "He's staying?" she demands.

"Once we're in the air, he won't be able to run his big mouth," I say.

"My mouth is far more popular than any of you give credit," Brody chimes in.

Ms. Littleton stands up. "Can we talk, Agent Castle?"

York, proving he's smarter than the average bear, stands up. "I'm the local lead. You can talk to me." He motions to the door.

Brody sits down at Carrie and Ms. Littleton's table. "If you want to leave her with me and Agent Castle, that is."

"This is harassment," Ms. Littleton complains.

Brody pats the table. "I promise to be gentle. Sit." He eyes Carrie and adds, "Tell her I'm gentle."

I expect Carrie to react with a push of some sort, but she doesn't. She just looks at him, her expression unreadable. I walk to the machine again and grab another Snickers, irritated at myself for wasting the last one. By the time I'm sitting, so is Ms. Littleton, and I have just enough time to take a bite before Brody has spilled his coffee in her lap.

She jumps to her feet, yelping, and snaps at Brody. "You fool!"

"Holy balls," Brody exclaims, standing as well. "Let me get you some paper towels."

"I have to go to the bathroom," she says, eyeing Carrie. "Don't speak to anyone," she orders, before pointing at me. "She has a right to counsel." With that, she walks around the table toward the door.

"I'll help," Brody offers, and he's gone, on her heels, but not before tossing me a quick wink and motioning to the front of his I'm your Huckleberry shirt.

York follows in their wake, giving me and Carrie one-on-one time.

I don't get up. I don't move to her table. I just sit there and take another bite of my Snickers. Carrie said she wants to talk. Let's see if she does. And true to her word, she doesn't make me work for what comes next.

"Yes, I slept with Brody," she says, "but I had no idea who he was at the time. And Oliver and I were new and on a break. It was just before we got really serious. I was shocked to discover he was a friend of Oliver's."

The story matches what Brody told me, and I don't have time to press for many more details. I home in on what might be important. "Did Oliver ever find out?"

"No," she says tightly. "*God, no.* It would have devastated him."

"Could Brody have told him?" I ask.

"I'd have known," she insists. "Oliver would never have been able to hide that kind of hurt from me."

"So you weren't fighting over Brody?"

"No. Absolutely not."

"Were you fighting at all?"

"I don't have any idea what we would fight about," she states, an evasive answer I don't miss, but I can't risk pushing the point and her clamming up on me. Not now, not this talk.

"Did you kill Oliver?" I ask, looking for a reaction.

"No. God, no," she says again. "I loved him. I loved him so very much." Her voice hitches. "I will do anything to help you catch the real killer. *Anything.*"

"Tell me about the box he received."

Surprise flickers in her eyes and then interest. She leans forward. "Who told you about it?"

"Tell me about the box," I counter.

"Do you know who sent it?" she pressed.

"Do *you?*"

"No," she says easily. "Oliver said a groomsman sent it and that it was a crass gift that would make me hate that person. He didn't want me to see it or know who sent it. I pushed. He was weird about it."

"Weird how?" I ask.

"Secretive. He even went into his home office and locked the door. That was not normal at all."

"Who did you *think* sent it?"

"Honestly, I got insecure. I thought he was cheating, but I went to his office when he was working late and surprised him with dinner. He was so happy to see me, and I just decided I was being that old insecure me."

"Why are you insecure?"

"The curse of being an adopted child," she says. "There's always a little part of me that doesn't belong. Oliver knew that. He really knew how to make me feel like I was where I belonged. And that was with him."

Ms. Littleton appears in the doorway with a huge wet spot on her pants. "Tell me you aren't talking."

I take a bite of my Snickers.

Brody appears in the entryway, a smirk of satisfaction on his face. I don't know what to make of him, but he and Carrie have a past. And he just keeps showing up in all the right places at the wrong time. Including the party, it seems.

# Chapter Sixty-Three

My version of a chat is not the same as Eddie Castle's, but it's certainly more than ruminating about the weather. Despite lifting off a full two hours later than expected, there is never another opportunity to "chat" with Carrie. I do use my time wisely by allowing York to babysit Carrie and Ms. Littleton while I step into the outer waiting area and instruct my team to do some extra digging on Mr. "I'm your Huckleberry" Brody.

Once we're finally cleared to take off, York is more than eager to wish me a farewell. He's off and then we're off. It's a fast thirty-five-minute trip home, and we land at a small airstrip in Denver, where, thanks to my prior planning with Aiden, one of our field office agents, Marcus Lowry, is waiting on us. Marcus is a big, bald Black man who's mastered a stone face that reads more like an assassin than an FBI agent. In true form, he offers that expression up today and intimidates Ms. Littleton into silence. I gotta love Lowry. I really, really do. Unfortunately, Brody isn't quite as taken aback by Marcus, greeting him with, "Beast Master. You're a weapon of mass destruction."

He's not wrong. Marcus really *is* a beast, and big isn't just big; it's really big. As in he likes the gym more than pizza. He's a little crazy like that. He also ignores Brody, eyes me, and then motions the group of us—me, Carrie, and Ms. Littleton—toward a black SUV. We leave Brody in front of our arrival terminal.

But I'll be seeing him again soon. I have questions for him.

Once Carrie and Ms. Littleton are loaded inside the car but we aren't, Lowry makes his critical observation. "You're really bad at taking time off. No wonder you have a shit love life," he says as he throws all the bags in the trunk.

My love life, or lack thereof, gets far more attention than it should.

"Everyone isn't as lucky as you, Lowry," I say, referencing his wife and two adorable kids. He loves his family. He'd kill for his family. I'm not jealous. I know what it's like to lose someone you love, and so does my father.

The ride to the treatment facility is short, and the silence is broken by Ms. Littleton chattering on the phone about some other case. I get the feeling she's discouraging our conversations, which is fine by me. Carrie and I will talk again, and the next time will be on my terms. In the meantime, Whit keeps texting me and I keep ignoring him.

I'm still ignoring him when Marcus pulls us into the parking lot of what reads more like a luxury resort than a treatment center. Oliver's family is paying big money to put their son's potential killer in this place, and I can't get over the fact that they're avoiding me while helping her get a lesser sentence. Something doesn't sit right.

We all exit into what has turned into a brutally cold afternoon with the wind wicked and punching at us. Marcus heads to the trunk to retrieve Carrie's luggage, and I indicate the building. "We'll walk you inside."

Ms. Littleton bristles but says, "All right, then." She urges Carrie forward. "Let's get out of this wind."

Finally, something Ms. Littleton and I can agree on.

The lot of us make a run for the door, and once we're in the lobby, all of us shivering from the cold, Ms. Littleton motions Carrie toward the front desk, and the pair walks in that direction. I join them and flash my badge. I follow that by making our agreement clear, and even presenting a signed copy. "I'm to be given twenty-four-hour notice of Carrie's departure and allowed to question her before she leaves."

The receptionist is now the one bristling. "I'll have to talk to the medical director."

"I signed the agreement," Carrie states. "I'm fine with the arrangement." Her eyes meet mine. "You know I want to talk to you."

I don't reply. I simply eye the woman behind the counter. "I'll still need to have the medical director involved," she says, and stands. "Ms. Reynolds, I'll take you back now."

Ms. Littleton steps in between me and Carrie and hurries her away. It sure seems as if she's afraid of Carrie speaking to me, more afraid than Carrie is, which is interesting. Whatever the case for Carrie and me, our time is coming. Sooner than later.

# Chapter Sixty-Four

Moments before I walk into a meeting with Ms. Littleton and the medical director, I get a call from Aiden. The search warrants are a go, but I've decided against any early warning. "There are too many players running the game board in the wrong directions," I tell him, standing outside the building and freezing my ass off for a little privacy. "But let's move in this evening, after work hours, to allow the Phoenixes some privacy. I want to take lead."

"This is your baby," he says. "I'll meet you at the Phoenix offices. I'll have Marcus run the team going into Oliver and Carrie's place. Unless you want me to call in Whit."

"No," I say tightly. "I don't want you to call in Whit."

"You're going to have to forgive him."

*The man beat a witness,* I think. His reasons don't matter. It was wrong. But what I say is, "Yeah, well, I have things to say to Whit right about now, but that's for another time."

I've barely walked back into the lobby when the medical director enters and waves me and Ms. Littleton to the back offices. At least this goes well, and an understanding is achieved about how and when Carrie will be discharged. Actually, a little too easily. It's clear Ms. Littleton is eager to keep me on board with this plan.

After the meeting, Ms. Littleton arranges her own ride home, and in the process, I learn that she choppered into Estes Park. Brody's suggestion that the Phoenixes might be funding her actions in some way is starting to check out. Considering their bizarre behavior in general where Carrie is concerned, it's not hard to believe and certainly worthy of further exploration.

I leave Ms. Littleton in the lobby of the treatment center waiting on her car. Marcus and I settle into his car, and he groans. "Lord help the man who marries Ms. Littleton. She's as ripe as a fresh crime scene with a dead body."

He's not wrong.

Not at all.

There are a lot of things not right about Ms. Littleton.

# Chapter Sixty-Five

I've learned naps are all about the survival of the fittest.

Marcus drops me at my door, and the minute I'm inside, I head to the bedroom, declining a call from Whit, and collapse on my mattress. It's new, a gift from my father after I told him I wasn't sleeping well during the prime of my search for the Spider Man. He'd surprised me and had it delivered, ironically, with a big red birthday bow on it with a note that read: *This one sleeps so well, even the boogeyman won't keep you awake at night.* The boogeyman was the worst of my fears as a child. Oh, how I wish that were true now. We never talked about the note, or my nightmares, but that first night on that bed, I slept like the boogeyman slayer or a baby, however you want to look at it.

Puffing up my pillow, I sink into it and then shoot off a text to Hazel and ask her to find out if the Phoenixes paid for Ms. Littleton's travel to Estes Park before I set my alarm for forty-five minutes later. By the time I'm up, I have a message from Hazel telling me that no, Ms. Littleton's transportation was not paid for by the Phoenixes, at least not on the books.

I still think they paid for it.

My next move is to unpack and shove down a microwave dinner, some sort of pasta with chicken. If that stuff they call chicken is really chicken. I wonder sometimes. Whatever the case, I'm no worse for the wear by the time I arrive at the Phoenixes' building twenty-five minutes ahead of time. I'm unsurprised to find Aiden leaning on the hood of his black BMW, waiting for me.

Aiden is tall, with dark hair and a good build, his face chiseled and handsome. He's also a good listener, a great negotiator, and a problem solver. On top of all that, he's a good friend. Most would say I'm crazy for keeping him at a distance. Maybe I am, but he's also my boss.

That's usually my reason for keeping him at a distance.

It's more about monsters, most of them my own personal variety.

I pull into a parking spot and kill the engine. Since my house was my splurge and is now a hefty monthly expense, my economic little Jeep is rather simplistic compared to his fancy car. I exit the vehicle and meet him at the hood. "How's it going?" he asks.

"It's always better when I'm working, which is exactly why you shouldn't have placed me on leave."

"You're very confrontational, considering I'm your boss," he teases.

"You should have considered the risk of such empowerment when you got me naked."

"Hmm," he says. "Point made." He glances at his watch. "The team's twenty minutes out. I assume you want to go in first and talk to the Phoenixes before we swarm the building." It's not a question. He knows how I operate, because it's generally how he operates.

As for the swarm, he's not exaggerating. The FBI tends to handle warrants in an excessive way. It's just how they operate, and to some extent, we're all just part of a machine working at high levels of expertise. "That's the plan."

"You want a sidekick?"

"I think a one-on-one chat right now works best. Anything you've dug up on them that I need to know?"

"Hazel went back a good twenty years and discovered Mike Phoenix was accused of stealing his technology from a friend in college. Said friend raised a stink that lasted about twenty minutes before he got paid off, and the scandal was basically wiped off the internet. If Carrie knows, that could be a reason they want to silence her."

"Maybe," I say. "That somehow feels too obvious. I think there's more to whatever is going on with her and the Phoenixes."

"Hazel's still working her magic. More soon."

"And Brody? Anything new on him?"

"So far, everything he's said seems to check out. His father really is a politician and is still married to his mother. As for Brody himself, he's a big high roller in Vegas, likes the stock market and his investments, but there's nothing that looks shady."

I take that in but can't quite accept it as enough. The bottom line is that the idea of Brody being involved in Oliver's death really snagged me on the ride home, and I can't seem to let it go. Maybe the one-night fling with Carrie was more than one night. "I need to know if Brody and Carrie were having an active affair," I say. "The knife wounds on Oliver were made by a woman, but that doesn't mean he didn't help Carrie kill Oliver. And there is a cut on Carrie's belly that seems to support the idea that someone else might have been in the room."

"I can't get you Brody's phone records, but we should have Carrie's and Oliver's hit my desk tomorrow morning."

"The sooner the better," I say, motioning toward the door. "I'm going in."

He hands me the warrant. "Don't go Eddie Castle on them and beat anyone with a baseball bat."

I scowl at the bad joke. Aiden and my father are a whole other thing I try not to deal with. Eddie Castle and Aiden King in the same room is an explosion of bad Castle and King jokes mixed with too much testosterone. And that gets ridiculous.

For now, I suspect it's the Phoenixes who are about to explode. On me. And if Natalie, their dear daughter, is here, here's to hoping she doesn't try to beat my head on the ground. Or better yet, here's to hoping she doesn't have a baseball bat. Because no, I'm not my father, but I don't fight like a girl, either. He made sure of it.

As if I'm writing my own story, I reach the main door, open it, and enter, and before I ever make it to the security desk, Natalie Phoenix is standing in front of me, confrontation in her eyes.

# Chapter Sixty-Six

"What are you doing here, Agent Castle, at our offices?" Natalie demands as a bulky dark-haired security guard steps to her side.

She's in red today. A red dress. Red lipstick. Red eyes. The color of her outfit isn't to celebrate life but disguise misery. Pain radiates from her, sincere pain, but guilt can also equal pain. She will gain money and power with Oliver gone. Forensics says the killer was a woman. I can't rule her out, not yet. I hand her the warrant. "Look at that and then let's go somewhere private and chat," I suggest.

"It's a warrant, right?" she asks without looking at the document in her hand. "Why are you searching our offices instead of her house?"

I'm not a coy person. I know she means Carrie, and I don't ask her to explain. "We're doing that now, but motive matters for a conviction. I need to find out what was going on with your brother that got him killed."

"You didn't need a warrant. We would have helped." She eyes the security guard. "Jack, can you keep the staff out and allow the police in?"

"Of course, Ms. Phoenix," he replies, stepping around me.

Once he's gone, she says, "My parents are actually here right now. We were talking through my new role and just . . . you know, the funeral. There are a few things I convinced them just to tell you."

My interest is officially piqued.

She turns and starts walking. I follow her to the elevator we use to travel to the twenty-fifth floor. On the ride up, she glances over at me and seems to want to say something but presses her lips together. This is a different side of Natalie, a tamer version, and I'm curious about the source.

I text Aiden a hold until contact message to ensure our entry into the building does nothing to stop the flow of information I'm hoping to achieve in this meeting.

Natalie leads me to a conference room. "I need to talk to my parents for a few minutes. They've agreed to share this information, but they didn't know it would be now. I need to give them a moment to digest it all."

I nod and remove my coat, hanging it on the back of one of about a dozen chairs lining the long mahogany table. Tugging my phone from my pants pocket, I'm punching in Aiden's number even as I walk to the window. The horizon is a floating line of peaks and valleys of the Rocky Mountains. Much like the peaks and valleys of grief and recovery.

Aiden answers and I explain my hold request. "Interesting," he states. "Yes. Get in and get what you want, then we'll follow and do the same. On another note, Carrie's parents are at her house. They're cooperative, but they've called in Ms. Littleton."

"Of course they have." The door behind me opens. "Gotta run," I say, hanging up and sliding my phone into my pocket.

When I turn around, I find Natalie standing at the end of the table, framed by Mr. and Mrs. Phoenix. Both Mr. and Mrs. are dressed casually, him in tan slacks and a button-down, her in a floral dress and flats, as if they joined Natalie at the office after hours to avoid the staff. I'm also struck by how much Natalie looks like her mother—petite with the same green eyes and brown hair, and yet somehow Mrs. Phoenix is softer, gentler in her presence.

A man in a suit enters the room and joins the Phoenix family. He's perhaps forty, with brown hair and glasses. "I'm Larry Ward, Agent

Castle. I'm the family's legal counsel. They asked me to sit in, but I don't intend to interfere. I don't believe they have anything to hide, and I'm here for support and guidance should it be needed."

"Fair enough," I state. "Nice to meet you, Mr. Ward."

Natalie motions to the table. "Let's all sit."

There is a general consensus of this being a good idea as everyone moves to claim a seat. Mr. Phoenix is at the head of the table with his wife and daughter on his left and right. I sit down mid-table on Mrs. Phoenix's side, eager to allow myself enough space to study all facial expressions.

"I'll just say it," Natalie offers, "and get it out there. I know you have to think the way my parents have helped Carrie get into a rehab facility is illogical."

"I do," I agree. "A stronger conviction comes not from insanity but a straight-up conviction."

"As I've told them," Natalie assures me. "But they did it to protect me."

# Chapter Sixty-Seven

"What does that mean?" I ask, on alert now, my eyes keenly focused on Natalie. "They did it to protect you?"

"It means that Oliver was adopted," she informs me. "Which they feared would make me look guilty. You know, the jealous sister who wanted to be CEO, all the money, and attention, and so on."

Now the family's actions make sense. And it's certainly an interesting twist that does, in fact, turn attention, at least momentarily, on Natalie. "Were you?" I ask. "Jealous?"

"God, no. Oliver was good at his job. He was patient. People piss me off. He was a buffer. I'm going to miss that—*him*. So much."

"So much that you tried to kill Carrie," I point out.

Mr. Ward clears his throat. "That was an emotionally driven outburst. She was in shock, but she's aware of her poor choice to do such a thing."

"Not the smartest move," Natalie concedes. "But I'm pretty sure your father would approve. Don't you agree, Agent Castle?"

"Don't push Agent Castle," her father chides. "The adoption wasn't something we made public. We didn't even tell the kids about it until they were teens."

Mrs. Phoenix chimes in. "We didn't want Oliver to feel like he was the lesser child. We only did then because I read a book that hit an emotional nerve. I felt we were being dishonest with the kids. We wanted them to know. The rest of the world didn't need to know, but Oliver told Carrie."

"I loved Oliver," Natalie expresses eagerly. "I don't care what the world says about me."

"Our stockholders care," her father reminds her.

"I know you know how shitty that sounds, Dad." Natalie lambastes him, looking at me again. "He was my brother. I don't care what the word 'adoption' means. He was *my brother*. I was never in his room the night he died. I'll hand over my DNA, any data you want from me, and take a lie detector test."

I'm not going to decline anything I've been offered, but I'm inclined to believe Natalie is telling the truth. I glance at her parents. "You offered to help Carrie in exchange for her silence," I assume.

Mr. Phoenix bristles. "We didn't offer to help her lie. We offered to help her get proper medical care. We just reminded her of Oliver's legacy as a Phoenix."

"In other words, for her protecting Natalie's reputation," I say, and I don't give them time to reply. The motivation is clear. They can't afford to have the world believe Natalie killed her brother and is now running the company. "Did you offer to help pay for Ms. Littleton?" I ask.

"You obviously can't keep Carrie from slandering our daughter," Mrs. Phoenix states. "Unless you tell me that's a new FBI superpower, which I doubt. So no, we're not paying for Ms. Littleton's services, but we did offer her a bonus to protect our interests in the press."

I lower my chin and offer a keen eye. "That's unethical. At least on Ms. Littleton's behalf."

"We told Carrie," Mrs. Phoenix counters. "Therefore Ms. Littleton is protected."

Mr. Ward interjects. "I've told them that could end badly."

"Good advice," I reply. "And let me just reiterate what your daughter already did. When you help Carrie achieve an insanity plea, with fancy, financially motivated doctors, you ensure a lesser sentence. Don't you want her prosecuted?"

"As we told our daughter," Mr. Phoenix states, "we're not uneducated on such matters. We stay in tune with the world we live in. Too often, law enforcement either overcharges or rushes to charge, and this results in bad people going free. We bought you time to build your case and charge her properly."

"We don't want her to go free," Mrs. Phoenix declares. "We want her to rot in jail for the rest of her life."

And yet, they're worried about their stockholders.

I don't like the Phoenix family. But I believe them.

# Chapter Sixty-Eight

I collect the DNA sample from Natalie and arrange her lie detector test before I do my own little sweep of Oliver's office. Only one thing stands out to me: a picture of Oliver, Josh, and Brody on his credenza. I invite Natalie into the room. "When was this taken?"

"Oh gosh," she says. "Years ago. Why?"

"Were you aware that Brody and Oliver had a falling-out?"

"Oliver talked to me about it. He lost a shit ton of money over some stupid investment Brody dragged him into. I told him to stop investing with friends. Just be friends. Why?"

"Just trying to understand the dynamics of the relationships. What's the status of that big company deal Oliver was working on before he died?"

"Since it wasn't yet inked," she says, "who knows. I'm hopeful it stands, but Oliver was just so damn good with people. Losing him will be painful."

"Is there anyone who wouldn't have wanted that deal to close?"

"Maybe a competitor, but that's really unlikely."

I set the photo down. "Was that photo before or after Carrie?"

"Most definitely before. You ask the strangest questions, Agent Castle."

*She just doesn't understand the questions,* I think, but I ask, "You say you never met Carrie until she'd dated Oliver for a year?"

"I'm not sure of the exact timing, but it was close to that."

"Okay. Then I'm done for now" is all I say, but I'm bothered by the photo. Logically, Carrie saw it, and yet she claims she didn't know who Brody was when she slept with him. What if she did?

I leave the building and debrief with Aiden.

Once I'm in my car, I've yet to start my engine when my cellphone rings with my father's number. He always answers and so I answer. "Dad."

"Daughter! I hear you're back and serving search warrants."

"Which you shouldn't know about."

"Friends—"

"In high places," I supply. "Whit doesn't count," I add since Whit is still part of our team and most assuredly his source. "I know he's calling me for you, trying to get me to the house."

"Great idea. Come by the house, Sugar Bear. I can tell you all the dirty, *dirty* secrets of Danielle Littleton. And you know you want to know."

"No, Dad," I say. "No, I really don't want to know." There's an image in my head of the two of them I wish I could wash away. Lord help me, make it go away.

"Okay, honey. I'll order the pizza in, say, half an hour?"

I sigh in resignation. "Yes, Dad. Order in thirty."

"Got it. Extra cheese, lots of feta, and pineapple, which is disgusting, but whatever you like, honey. See you soon." He disconnects.

# Chapter Sixty-Nine

## CARRIE

Upon my admission into the clinic, I have a blood draw and CT scan, and I'm handed a sample cup. I don't need to pee, but I force the issue and soon I'm in a medical office reviewing my tests with my new doctor, Dr. Rogers. He makes me think of Mr. Rogers, from kids' TV, but with a bowl cut and dark-rimmed glasses. Apparently, my concussion is improved and nothing else significant shows up. Dr. Rogers feels I'm medically equipped to begin my therapy.

Whatever that means.

He hands me off to Nurse Naomi, who is youngish, friendly, and quite plump and sweet. *Plump* sounds insulting, but it's not. Unlike me, Naomi is comfortable in her own pale skin, so much so that she is radiant, glowing from the inside out. "This," she says, pausing at a fancy, glossed-over glass door, "is your private suite."

The next thing I know, I'm standing in what amounts to a luxury hotel room, complete with silk sheets, a fireplace, and a mountain view. "Your bags are in the closet, which is a full walk-in," she informs me. "Your therapy won't start until tomorrow, so just enjoy looking around and resting for the rest of the day. We encourage you to view the pool, the sauna, the gym, and tennis court, but not indulge until after your next CT scan." She motions me back to the door. "Let's go look around."

I'm given the grand tour, meeting numerous "guests" along the way.

The facilities are high-quality luxury, and there are even shops and a café, where the nurse leaves me to enjoy a decaf coffee, as no stimulants are allowed, and a delicious variety of macarons. I order to go and return to my room. Sitting down next to the gas fireplace, which is now casting flames of warmth on the room and me, I sip my coffee and decide I don't belong here.

I don't deserve this place.

# Chapter Seventy

## ANDI

I check in with Marcus on the search of Carrie and Oliver's home on my way to my father's Cherry Creek home, and there's not much to report, aside from Ms. Littleton giving him a hard time. At least, not at first glance. We'll see when all the evidence is collected. As for Carrie's parents, I'd like to talk to them, but I'll wait until Ms. Littleton isn't around. About the time I pull up to my father's house, Aiden calls. "No red ribbon in Carrie's work locker."

"Damn," I murmur. "Lana saw it there. Carrie must have moved it before the trip."

"Where are you at? You want me to pick up a pizza and we can talk about the case?"

"I'm pulling up to my father's place now. Come over."

"Your father hates me."

"He doesn't. Come over."

There are voices in the background and he says, "I have something for you. I'll be there."

He hangs up.

I park in my father's driveway, grab my bag that holds my MacBook and field notes, and head for the door. The moment I ring the bell, my father—in his standard jeans and a snug T-shirt with exposed tattooed arms—is flinging open the door. He really doesn't look his age, which I think has to do with his perfect, thick brown hair, which he colors. I haven't actually asked if he does, but of course he colors it. He's too old not to have some gray.

"Daughter!" he exclaims. "Come in out of the cold. We both know you hate the cold."

Yeah, well, there is truth in his words, but mostly because he always kept the house so damn brisk. I hurry inside and he holds out his arms. "Give the pops a hug."

I oblige. I mean, I love my dad. I just don't always love his ways. But he's also a towering force that is both big and strong, and he bear-hugs me. And I mean really bear-hugs me, to the point of me being about two seconds from needing resuscitation before he lets me go. "Get rid of the coat. It makes me feel like you aren't staying."

Obligingly, I slide out of my coat, hanging it on the coatrack by the door that is steel with a cool design if not for a huge Texas Star on top. I know. It's weird. And he doesn't even like Texas. He says it's too hot, but he won it at some arm-wrestling competition, and he's big on showing off his prizes.

He gives me a once-over. "You put on weight."

"Are you serious right now?" I demand. "You do know you aren't supposed to say that to a woman, right? And especially not before pizza."

"It looks good on you, Sugar Bear. Eat the pizza."

"It's like me saying your muscles look soft."

"My muscles are never soft. I know that. And you should know when you look good."

I'm officially lectured about self-confidence. Thank you, Dad. That's one thing people don't get about Eddie Castle. He really could slam his fist into a man while helping me with an algebra problem on the phone. That happened. More than once. I learned to tune out the background noise. He's actually very good at algebra.

He motions me toward a hall and starts walking down the corridor before me.

My father's massive home is far more than a man cave. It's a fancy seven-thousand-square-foot house with a media room and full gym. Vigilante work—I mean, PI work—serves him well.

He cuts left, as do I, into his fancy chef's kitchen with a giant island. My father doesn't cook. He barbecues, but somehow his fridge is always filled with homemade food. People bring him gifts. It's a crazy thing that is hard to explain. They either want to please him, bribe him, or thank him, and everyone knows Eddie Castle likes to eat.

Like father like daughter, thus the weight gain, I guess. I didn't actually think I'd put on weight, but I suppose I now have to step on a scale.

I claim the seat at the end of the island while my father calls out, "Whit!" at the top of his lungs, before grabbing a beer from the fridge, popping the top off, and setting it in front of me. "He's working out. I really love that you have all of us calling him Whit, like dimwit." He waggles a finger at me. "You're a chip off the ole block."

"Considering you like Danielle Littleton, I object to that comparison."

"Enjoying her is not the same as liking her," he corrects.

"Oh God." I hold up a hand. "No more talk like that." I chug back my beer.

Whit walks into the room. "There she is. Agent Castle, who can't stay away from work any more than I can but claims I'm wrong for working." He settles on the stool to my right.

"I didn't look for this," I say. "A man was stabbed fifty times at the party."

"I didn't look for my case, either. Get this." He pauses as my father hands him a beer, and he tips it back for a long swallow before he says, "My suicide cases tie back to the Spider Man."

I frown. "How?"

"They both have family with prior victims."

"Really?" I ask. "Okay, that's weird."

The doorbell rings and my father eyes his porch camera on his phone. "It's Jesús," he says, hitting the speaker. "It's unlocked, but don't come in unless you have my enchiladas."

Jesús is a detective at the Denver PD. I don't even ask what this is all about. I focus on Whit. "What are you thinking?"

"I'm thinking that Jesse Waller, who we thought might be a Spider Man protégé, really was just that. I'm watching him."

"Just don't go turning him into a punching bag."

He smirks. "I'll try."

A fit, dark-haired man enters the kitchen. "What's up, Jesús," Whit greets.

Jesús grimaces. "Just paying my debt." He nods at me. "Hi there, Andi."

"Please tell me you didn't arm-wrestle him." Jesús is a great detective in excellent physical condition, and a good ten years younger than my father, but my dad is six three and 225. Jesús is more like five ten and 170.

He scoffs, and follows it up with pure bravado. "I wasn't that stupid."

"You bet with him, didn't you."

"Fuck yeah." He rests the pan in his hands on the opposite side of the island. "On *Dancing with the Stars* of all things. My wife watches it. She was sure she knew who would win this season. I didn't think he really did, so she made his damn enchiladas, but did she make me any? No. No enchiladas for me."

"You can have some now." The doorbell rings. "That will be the pizza. Pizza and enchiladas. I love it."

A few minutes later, my father is sitting to my left, and we're all stuffing our faces with pizza and enchiladas, talking about my case. "Of course this Carrie chick did it," Jesús says.

I keep talking, sharing details of my investigation, and a few minutes later Jesús amends his thoughts to say, "It was Natalie."

Whit waves his slice around and argues, "It was Brody."

"Forensics says a female stabbed him," I remind him. I glance at my father. "Maybe it was *Danielle*," I say dryly, because Lord only knows the woman kills me every time I'm with her.

"I damn sure didn't shut my eyes with her."

I cringe. "Oh God, Dad," I snap. "Stop. I do not need the image in my head you just gave me. I am your daughter."

"Okay," Whit says, ignoring our chitchat about Ms. Littleton and getting back to business. "Brody's sleeping with Natalie and she did it," he suggests. "He just helped her clean it up."

"Carrie was covered in blood and in the attic," I argue.

"They were having sex when Natalie showed up," my father interjects.

I snort. "And Carrie answered the door naked?"

Whit runs with my father's theory. "Eddie's onto something. She hid in the bathroom while he tried to get rid of his sister," he says. "She was cut, right?"

"Yes."

"She runs out of the bathroom to save her man and gets attacked. She runs for her life and goes into shock, thus losing her memory."

I consider that a moment. "That's actually believable."

"See," he says. "You need me. Stop being pissed."

"Stop beating people up."

"She tells me that all the time," my dad says. "Don't listen."

Jesús stands up. "I don't need to hear this. I'm leaving." He turns and heads in the other direction.

The doorbell rings again. "Who the hell is that?" my dad grumbles. "Can I not just have dinner with my daughter?"

"That will be Aiden." I call out, "Jesús, let Aiden in!"

My father scowls. "Really, daughter?"

"Yes, really, Father. He's my boss."

"Your boss with the wrong intentions."

"Don't be such a father."

"I'm your fucking father. That's who I am."

"I can handle myself."

"And I can and *will* help," he counters.

Aiden walks into the room, and my father eyes him. "Aiden King, you're in my castle." He points at me. "And she's my castle. Remember that."

Aiden just shakes his head and slides into the seat beside me, holding up a small key in a baggie. "What is this?" I ask.

"Marcus found it taped to the bottom of the desk drawer in Oliver's home office."

My father motions to him. "That's a locker key," he says. "I know all the secret locker locations. Let me see that."

Aiden's jaw clenches, but he hands it to him. My father eyes it and then me. "I'll do some digging."

"No," Aiden and I say at the same time.

My father smiles. "I'll get right on it."

# Chapter Seventy-One

## CARRIE

My morning starts with fresh orange juice, a buttery croissant, and my parents.

We're in my room, around my fireplace, all in cozy chairs. I'm actually in my favorite black velvet sweat suit. I'm told "they" want me to feel at home here. "This place is lovely," my mother says, "and I have to say these are the best croissants I've ever had in my life."

"We understand you're starting therapy soon," my father interjects.

I blanch. "Are they supposed to disclose that to you?"

"It was part of the basic paperwork they hand out," he replies. "When *do* you start therapy?"

My eyes narrow on him, suspicion burning in my belly, but then, my father and I have a history. With him, there was no ability for me to grieve for Eric. It was always about me defending my actions that day, as if I wasn't just being a kid, roughhousing with my big brother.

"Did you talk to my doctor?" I ask.

"We did not," my mother quickly inserts. "We completely respect your privacy. Your dad's just interested in this process and your healing. Thankful they allowed us to see you before you begin your treatments. They tell us you won't be allowed visitors for a full week."

The very idea that I'm allowed to see them now sits uncomfortably with me, and I can't help but wonder if there are cameras in the room, eyes watching and judging my interactions with my mother. Because here's the thing. Darkness can hide behind pretty things. In fact, I think most dark things hide behind pretty things, and you never see their teeth until you're bitten.

"Have you remembered anything else?" my father asks. "About that night?"

"Nothing," I say, and it's the truth. Even the fight I remembered having with Oliver is now in question. So much so that I think it's actually a memory from the night we went to a black-tie charity event months back. I remember fighting over some woman flirting with him. And I most certainly remember the make-up sex afterward.

"Perhaps the counselor can help you retrieve your memories," my father says. "Therapy helped you remember what happened with Eric that dreaded day."

He's wrong. I don't remember. I never remembered. My therapist just re-created the memories for me, and I took them on as my own. "When are you going back to Houston?"

"We'll stay until you get out of here, honey," my mother promises.

"No," I say. "Don't do that. They could keep me here a week or a month. We don't know."

"Surely it won't be a month," my mother exclaims.

"Unless they do," my father says and he leans forward. "Will they?"

He's asking if I killed Oliver.

I stand up. "I think you should go back to Houston."

My mother grabs my hand. "I don't want to leave you."

My eyes are locked with my father's, and his tell a different story. He can't wait to leave.

There's a knock on the door, and Nurse Naomi opens it and steps inside. "Sorry to rush you, but Carrie's program is set to officially start in five minutes."

"What about the funeral?" my mother asks. "We need to be here for the funeral."

Every muscle in my body clenches. "I can't think about that right now. I *can't* think about burying him. Why do you have to even bring that up? *Why?* I can't even believe he's . . . he's gone."

I'm trembling, and the nurse rushes forward. "I think we need to give Carrie some time to finish her breakfast before her treatment." She steps in front of me. "You okay, dear?"

I fold my arms in front of me and say what I've said at least three times to her and others. "I'll never be okay again."

"We'll go," my mother says. "We love you, honey."

The nurse backs away and allows my mother to hug me. I hug her back. I do love my mother. I actually kind of cling to her. "You'll be okay," she promises. "We'll get through this."

"Thanks, Mom," I whisper, and when she pulls away, I see my father has already left the room.

My mother hesitates, but she backs away and exits the room.

Nurse Naomi kneels in front of me. "What can I do?"

"Turn back time," I whisper. "Give me a chance to save him."

"How about we help you remember who did this? Then you can at least feel a sense of justice."

*Justice.*

It's a word that settles with solidified comfort in my belly.

# Chapter Seventy-Two

## ANDI

Aiden stayed the night, but it's not what anyone would think.

My odd sense of a romantic, sexy evening is one of the many reasons I'm not good at relationships. I mean, I guess we do sleep together. Sort of.

I wake on the floor of my living room with my MacBook beside me, groaning with a crick in my neck. Aiden is sleeping on the floor by the couch, half sitting, half lying. This after an all-nighter reviewing the photos taken at the searches, as well as reviewing data on Brody, Josh, Natalie, and of course, Carrie.

Aiden must sense my alertness, groaning and straightening, cursing with the crunch of his body. I'm already thinking about all the data we've observed in the past hours.

"I keep going back to the death of her brother, Eric," I say, and thanks to Hazel, I have the police reports. "A few witnesses did say it looked as if she pushed him."

"And others said they were roughhousing and it was clearly kids being kids." He gets to his feet. "I'm going to make coffee."

An hour later, I've been caffeinated, eaten an omelet compliments of Chef Aiden, and I'm already at Carrie's treatment center with that key in hand. My father has one of his men carrying a copy of it, trying to find the locker it belongs to, but that's a long shot. My gut says this is important. I need to know what this key opens.

With early-season snow flurries in the air, I eagerly seek shelter inside the lobby of the treatment facility, making my way to the front desk. I flash my badge. "Agent Castle," I announce. "I need to speak to Carrie Reynolds."

"I'm sorry, Ms. Reynolds has started her treatment plan. She won't be available to visitors for seven full days."

"This is a law enforcement matter."

"I understand, but I have notes here that you agreed to respect her program. You'll need a court order to see her sooner than medically allowed."

I'd argue, but she's right. I also expected this, but I had to try. I turn away from the counter and dial Josh. He answers on the first ring. "Agent Castle," he greets me.

"How did you know it was me?"

"I put your number in my phone. You're now on caller ID."

"Something you need to tell me?"

"I wish there was something I could tell you that I haven't."

"Maybe there is. Oliver hid a key under his desk drawer. It looks like some sort of lockbox or locker key. Any idea where that might be?"

"He banked at North Central. Other than that, I haven't a clue. And I can't imagine he'd keep anything anywhere but the bank."

"Are the lockboxes at the bank key operated? Or do they use a combination?"

"I think most safe-deposit boxes are double keyed for safety, but I can't be sure. I keep my valuables in a safe."

"All right. Thanks. Oh, just one more thing. How was Oliver that night? What was his mood?"

"A little off because of the Brody thing, but after they talked, he was great."

"And he and Carrie?"

"Normal."

"Okay, then, I'll be in touch if I need anything."

We disconnect and I dial Brody. He doesn't answer. I'm about to leave when Mr. and Mrs. Reynolds exit the back offices, bristling with the sight of me.

"Good morning," I greet them. "This is well timed. I was hoping to chat with you about Carrie and Oliver."

"We've been instructed by our attorney not to talk to you," Mr. Reynolds states.

"It's just a few casual questions. If it helps, I'm not fully convinced Carrie is our killer. Your help will allow me to redirect my focus."

Mrs. Reynolds looks up at her husband, a silent question in her eyes. "No," he says to her and then meets my stare and repeats the word. "No."

"Then can we set up an appointment with Ms. Littleton present?" I ask.

"She said you'd ask that," he replies. "The answer is still no." He maneuvers himself and his wife around me and they exit the building.

I turn and watch the door shut behind them and in my face.

There's something they don't want me to know.

They've certainly driven home the point that what appears as obvious sometimes really is obvious. Carrie might just be our killer.

# Chapter Seventy-Three

## CARRIE

I'm in my sitting room on one of the most comfortable couches I've ever sat on, waiting for my new therapist—or technically, I believe, psychiatrist—to join me. I imagine Dr. Thompson will be an older man, with a depth of experience, and kind but judgmental eyes. I imagine he'll start where they all start and ask about my childhood. They all want to talk about my childhood. About me being adopted. And if they've spoken with my parents, they'll most certainly ask me about Eric.

Time ticks on, and I'm once again wondering if there are cameras in the room. Maybe the cameras are why Oliver's parents sent me here. They want to catch me saying something that might be used against me. Of course, my privacy and doctor-patient privilege are in play, but there are ways around that, sneaky, dark ways around just about everything.

Suddenly parched, I stand and walk to the water dispenser in the corner, filling a glass and drinking. I reach for my phone, but they've taken it. Their desire for me to feel at home obviously has limits. I walk back to the couch and sit down. There's a book on the coffee table called *Own Your Stress*. I own my stress. That's why I'm such a good ER nurse. The minute I find the page on yoga, I put the book down. Like yoga is going to help me cope with a double amputee in the ER.

The door opens and a stunning Black woman with perfect skin and a perfect body enters. She's in a cream-colored dress that only makes her perfect body all the more perfect. She's maybe thirty-five. No. Thirty-six. I'm very good at guessing ages.

"Hi, Carrie," she says. "I'm Dr. Thompson." My heart sinks. *She's* my doctor? This woman represents every insecurity I've ever owned in my life. It's as if Oliver's parents knew this and rather than sending me here to protect me, they've sent me here to torture me. But they can't know my insecurities. Only Oliver knew those innermost, personal thoughts of mine. Unless he told his parents? Surely not. Or—did he?

Dr. Thompson sits down in the chair across from me and slides a pair of delicate glasses onto her delicate face with her perfectly sculpted jaw. "Where do you want to start?" she asks. "I'd like to let you choose."

She's too perfect.

I now know that Oliver betrayed me. He told my secrets.

And that changes everything.

# Chapter Seventy-Four

## ANDI

Brody has no idea what the key is, either. Nobody does. I spend a week hunting for the secret locker. So does my father. Interviews get us nowhere. We still can't find the weapon used to kill Oliver. DNA will take months to come back, and no one can be completely sure whether Carrie's stomach wound was or was not self-inflicted. That could spell trouble with a jury. Bottom line, Carrie comes off as a sweet, heartbroken fiancée. A woman who lost the man she loved. A woman traumatized. A meeting with the DA's office has them on the fence right along with me. We agree we need to take our time and charge appropriately and be well armed with evidence.

When Lana checks in, an idea flares. I decide to get creative. I don't text back. I show up at the hospital and surprise her at work.

"What the heck are you doing here?" Lana asks, smiling when she sees me, only to frown. "Is this about Oliver?"

It's not an unusual response. This is Carrie's workplace and my first time on-site, but I wave that off.

"I'm feeling guilty about deserting you in Estes Park. I thought I'd just check in."

"We both know that's not why you're here, but hey, if you want to eat crappy cafeteria food, let's go."

I end up at a table with a group of nurses, and once they find out who I am, they don't clam up. Everyone tells me how wonderful Carrie is, how devastated she must be. Two nurses wonder if it was a patient who'd become obsessed with her, the first time I've heard of this.

Once Lana and I are alone at the table, I ask about this man. "He wasn't obsessed. That's silly, but I can get you his details and text them. I'm not supposed to, but I will."

A few minutes later, she sneaks me the info and says, "Did you find the box? I can't help it. I'm dying to know what was inside."

"Of course, you know I can't tell you most things. But no, we haven't found it. Any idea where it might be?"

At that moment, a doctor approaches. Lana is on instant alert. "Something I can help with, Dr. Cryder?"

"Lana, Mrs. Knight will not take her meds from anyone but you. And she needs to get them down her."

She sighs. "All right, then. I'm off to help Mrs. Knight. Sorry, Andi. Call me if I can help with anything else."

"I guess ER nurses are nurturing creatures," I comment. "Unlike the likes of us FBI agents."

"I don't know about that," the doctor says, unfazed by me being an FBI agent. "Lana isn't an ER nurse by trade. She's a pediatric nurse forced to work ER while waiting for a transfer. You almost have to find a cold place inside to survive the horrors of this place. I know I'm a coldhearted bastard. Or so all the women in my life tell me."

"Do you know Carrie Reynolds?"

"She's good at her job. That's all I have to say."

Someone calls his name, and he doesn't bother saying another word. He just turns and leaves.

How very cold of him.

# Chapter Seventy-Five

## CARRIE

I sit in my room, staring out at the mountains, drinking coffee. Real coffee now, with caffeine. The hospital wants to see if stimulation changes me or impacts how I react to grief. That also means over the next week I'll be allowed visitors. Even Agent Castle, who I've never really believed to be my friend. My attorney agrees. That must make it true.

As for Dr. Thompson's decision to allow Agent Castle any access to me at all, it's an example of her dictation over my well-being.

Dr. Thompson and I have never connected.

Only one of us knows that fact.

It's not that I don't want to remember what happened to Oliver, which she has told me is her primary goal—to help me do what I've told her I want to do: remember. And of course, I do, so very much, but I can't shake this feeling that anything I say will be held against me, no matter how much Dr. Thompson claims patient confidentiality.

With that feeling driving me, over the course of the next seven days, I eat my fluffy croissants, run on the treadmill, and meet with Dr. Thompson daily, sometimes twice a day. I don't socialize. I trust no one enough to chat beyond the weather. I also keep a journal at Dr. Thompson's prescription. I'm allowed to write anything I want to write about on an assigned subject. The first assignment is my brother. An easy assignment, considering I've been down this path. I know what she wants to hear.

> The day Eric died was the worst day of my life, until another worst day of my life stripped away the man I love. Eric was the best big brother I could ever want. He was funny, and sweet, and even when we fought, there was this bond between us. I knew that he could pick on me, but no one else could. He'd protect me.

I leave out the part where he teased me about being adopted and told me Mom and Dad loved him more. Oh, and the fat jokes. I didn't like the fat jokes.

The next assignment is about my parents. Another familiar assignment. My entry includes the following:

> My parents have always been my rocks. They adopted me at such a young age that they could have lied and hid the adoption from me but they didn't. They told me they wanted me to know everything between us was honest. They wanted me to know that they chose me.

The next assignment was about life with Oliver, to which I wrote:

> Heaven. Happiness. Friendship. There is nothing like having a partner you share everything with, good and bad. One of my favorite things was our Sunday cooking days. We are—were—both horrible cooks. But we had fun trying to make a meal

together. And we shared a love for wine. Trying
them. Drinking them. Collecting them.

I don't have to leave anything out about Oliver. I loved him. We
were perfect together.

The assignments have gotten harder, though. Suddenly Dr.
Thompson shifted her tone, telling me to write about how my parents
treated me after Eric died. I didn't fall for her tricks. I simply wrote
only a few lines: They were sad. We were sad together. We were all
we had left.

My final assignment is to write about everything and anything I
can remember from the weekend Oliver died. "Even what people were
wearing," she instructs. "Little details lead to big details."

I don't write about dresses and people. Only one person matters,
and that is Oliver.

What I write is exactly what I remember:

Oliver is dead.

He was covered in blood. I was covered in blood. I
ran. I hid. I was afraid for my life.

Later that day, I meet with Dr. Thompson, who is looking as pretty
and perfect as ever as she reads what I've written. She glances up at me,
shuts my journal, and just studies me. "This isn't enough."

"How can you tell me what is or is not *enough*?"

"You're not trying to remember," she accuses.

"I am."

"What are you hiding from? What were you hiding from that night
in the attic?"

"I don't know."

"Think," she commands.

"I have," I snap. "I *am*."

"What were you hiding from then and now?" she challenges yet again.

Tension builds inside me, and I tell myself to control it and myself, to contain the anger she's stirring inside me, but I can't seem to do it. Suddenly, I'm standing, shouting at her. "I don't know!"

The outburst is regrettable, an action she'll use against me to call me unpredictable, volatile even. "I'm sorry," I offer quickly. "I'm just frustrated that I can't remember. It's taking a toll."

She slowly pushes to her feet and says, "That's enough for now. We'll meet again this evening."

# Chapter Seventy-Six

## ANDI

I wake at 6:00 a.m., after sleeping two hours, to a call from Natalie. "We're putting off the funeral because we don't want that killer bitch present, but we can't disinvite her, either. In other words, we need you to hurry up and do your job and make an arrest."

"Good morning to you, too," I say.

"I'm serious. Another week has passed with inaction. Arrest that bitch."

By the time we hang up, I'm fairly certain the only reason Carrie's alive is because Natalie can't get to her. Maybe that should make me look at Natalie like a killer with a motive. I don't. And we've managed to find a few witnesses who placed her in the gym at the times she said she was as well.

Our stalker was ruled a nonthreat by Marcus, but we continue to follow up on leads, conducting new interviews and looking for the weapon. At this point, Carrie will be cleared for conversations in the next twenty-four hours, and once I've had the caffeine to stomach her, I call Ms. Littleton to set up my interview.

"Not yet," she pushes back.

"Now," I say. "Or I swear I'll just arrest her. This is not a court-ordered hospital stay. Now, if you want to have her committed—"

"Fine. I'll work it out with the medical staff at Rosewood."

After that call, I'm eager to prepare for the meeting. I head to the office, and after spending a few hours with Hazel, who's a five-foot, one-hundred-pound firecracker with a giant mouth, I'm swearing in Russian and Chinese. I practice, intending to test them out on my father. Of course, with my luck, he'll have a lady friend who speaks at least one of the two languages and he'll know what I'm saying.

Unfortunately, even with Aiden and Marcus helping, what the research comes down to is we're in limbo, waiting on forensic evidence. It's late, and I pick at a slice of our delivery pizza that just arrived.

"We don't even have the murder weapon," I say, snatching a piece of pineapple and popping it in my mouth.

"That's what I don't get," Marcus interjects. "Where is it? If Carrie killed him, she had to put it somewhere, and she was naked. It's not like she ran outside, hid it, and then ripped her clothes off, cut herself with the knife she already hid, and went to the attic."

And that's exactly what I assume Ms. Littleton will say to the jury.

We spend the next half hour eating and talking about the nonexistent knife. Aiden even checks in with the Estes Park team since York himself is checked out and unhelpful. Out of sight, out of mind. He's just riding the wave to retirement.

"I'm back to interviews," I say, when every angle seems exhausted. "And more interviews. I've done them."

"Do them again," Aiden says. "I got the forensics report on the weapon. It's a hunting knife. Find out who the hunter is in the group. Or who knows someone who's a hunter. Who has access to that type of weapon? Or go at it another way. Just go back at it. You know how this works. Keep working."

He's right. I know he's right. I just have to keep looking for new angles. "I'm not getting anything out of Carrie's posse," I say. "Believe me, I've tried. They all think she's the best thing since chocolate. I need to hit the men again."

"I can go talk to the cigar club they hang out at," Marcus offers. "I love me a good cigar."

"I'm in," Aiden offers. "I love me a good whisky and cigar."

The last thing I need is them drinking and smoking when they should be listening. "I've got it," I say, standing up and grabbing my bag. "Text me the address, Hazel."

She gives me a two-finger salute, her dark curls bouncing around her head as she dismisses me and reaches for yet more pizza. She's on slice four. If I had to describe her to a stranger, I'd call her a pretty, itty-bitty garbage disposal, with brains and a dirty mouth. I like that I always know what I'm going to get with her. She is who she seems to be: genuine.

Someone close to Oliver Phoenix is not who they seem to be.

Maybe Carrie did this. Maybe she didn't. But I'm no longer sure Carrie and Oliver were the only people in that room that night.

# Chapter Seventy-Seven

Surprise is my friend and eight o'clock is the magic hour, the hour when, per Trevor and Josh, Oliver's posse favors the cigar club. I arrive at eight thirty, giving the group time to relax and settle in before I slide into the picture.

I enter the members-only club to find a cozy little place filled with leather chairs, high-end carpeting, and expensive chandeliers, then flash my badge at the front. The woodsy scent of tobacco permeates the room.

I expect trouble I don't find. Turns out my badge works for a membership card. Every establishment is not so kind. This one happily allows my entry and even takes my coat. I find Josh, Trevor, and Brody sitting in leather chairs by the fireplace, sipping whisky and puffing on big chunks of tobacco.

I sit down in the one empty chair directly across from Brody, who lifts his glass in my direction, motioning up and down my body. "Black pants must be the agent uniform. Must get boring. Not that you're boring."

"Of course not," I say. "I know you'd never tell me I'm boring. You're too much of a gentleman."

"Exactly. Now we're getting to know each other. You've called me more than twice."

"Whisky, Agent Castle?" Trevor offers.

"I'm not good at drinking and catching killers," I say. "I'm sure you can all understand that."

"Any good news?" he asks hopefully.

I sidestep a real answer with "We're just piecing it all together."

Josh casts me a glare. "Why haven't you arrested her? She was covered in his blood."

His words are angry and heavily slurred, which tells me he's drinking his pain away. That's never a good answer, but sometimes it's a necessary interlude. "Investigative work sometimes takes more time than we'd like, but it's better than a not-guilty plea."

"She's fucking guilty." He stands up and walks away.

Trevor sets his glass down. "I'll go reel him in and get him back."

Brody leans forward. "What did you expect? He was our friend."

"Help," I say. "Did he own a knife?"

"You asked me that about two phone calls ago. No. He doesn't hunt."

I have called Brody a number of times while digging through the case, but I'm not sure why that's problematic to him. "Who does?" I ask.

"You asked me that, too. That's not our thing. Not this group. I hope like hell you've got more than 'who likes to hunt?'"

"Tell me something I don't know, Brody."

"She's a bitch. Wait. You know that."

"You're very angry with her."

"She killed my best friend. Do you expect me to be her cheerleading team?"

"How many times did you sleep with her?"

"Three times in one night. Yes. I can do that. And no, never again. I know you've checked my phone records. I wasn't having an affair with her."

"I can't access your phone records."

"Now you can." He grabs his phone, keys in something, and my phone beeps. "That's my log-in to my cellphone account. Have at it. I have nothing to hide."

I reach in my bag and pull out the key. "Do you recognize this?"

He sets down his glass. "That's for a locker here."

"Here?"

"Yeah. We have lockers here. Some of the married men dabble in different flavors, and I don't mean whisky or cigars, and shower up before going home. Others just like to keep a few things here now and then."

"Why didn't you say that when I asked before?"

"I didn't put two and two together."

"Show me Oliver's locker," I say, because obviously from this conversation he has one.

"Yeah, sure." He stands up and motions for me to follow.

Our path is down a set of stairs that leads me to the men's locker room. Just outside it are a couple of rows of lockers. The key reads 221, and I find that locker. I glance at Brody. "I need to do this alone."

"That's screwed up. I showed you the locker."

"Brody," I snap.

"Yeah, yeah. I'm going."

Impatiently, I wait for him to leave. Once he's out of sight, with my heart racing, I fit the key into the lock and it turns. Excitement fills me and I open the door. Inside are a folded-up box, a red ribbon, and a folder. I grab the folder and open it, and begin to scan the documents inside.

I'm halfway down the page when I literally gasp. I'm not a gasp kind of girl. I'm looking at Carrie's adoption papers, and they are one big shock attack. Her biological father is Norman Morrow, whose name anyone who's studied true crime knows all too well.

Norman Morrow is a serial killer.

He killed ten people, at least that we know about.

Another interesting tidbit about Norman: he stabbed his victims to death quite brutally.

Logically, you'd think this means Carrie is the killer, but it's not that simple. She didn't send this documentation to Oliver. Someone else did. And that someone could have been in the hotel room the night Oliver died with every intention of us finding out about Carrie's father.

# Chapter Seventy-Eight

## CARRIE

Journal entry number twenty:

I remember—so little. Too little. But what I do remember is how much I loved Oliver. I remember making love to him on the very bed where he died before we ever went to the party. I remember the tenderness in his eyes when he told me I'm beautiful. When anyone else tells me I'm beautiful, I don't believe them. But it's there, in Oliver's eyes. He thinks I'm beautiful. Or he did. I'll never see that look in his eyes again. We will never wake up and declare the morning "pancake morning" again, create yummy treats and top them with whipped cream. We'll never sit by a fire while we each enjoy a book together again. We will never be us again. I'm not sure I'll ever know who I am without him.

I'm not sure I'll ever know my purpose in this life.

I mean, I'm an ER nurse, and my job is to save lives, but I couldn't even save my fiancé. I keep thinking that. That I had a chance to save him and didn't. I'm not sure what that means, but just as I believe in my heart I ran to that attic, fearful for my life, I believe I could have saved him. I don't know how. I don't know how. But I know that just that feeling alone makes me hate myself. If they convict me for a crime I didn't commit, I'll still deserve the punishment. Because I could have saved him but I didn't.

# Chapter Seventy-Nine

My morning session with Dr. Thompson is my final one before I'll be allowed visitors.

She sits across from me after reading my latest journal entry, a solemn expression on her face. She finishes it, her gaze lifting to study me, several seconds passing before she sets the journal on the table.

"Guilt is a normal emotion. Blame is easy to put on ourselves. We've talked about this."

"That doesn't change how I feel," I tell her.

I've found myself surprised at how I've opened up to Dr. Thompson. She doesn't cast blame, and she doesn't ask the same stupid questions I've been asked in the past. She lets the journal guide me. She lets me guide the conversations.

"That is true, and I'm glad to hear you say that," she says. "No one gets to tell you what you feel is wrong. Not even me. In fact, I'd say that what you feel is normal."

*Normal.*

How many times in my life have I ever felt normal?

Never.

But I almost do with her.

"However," she says, "I'd like very much to guide you to a healthier place emotionally. And I hope that you'll agree to stay with us for the full month commitment. I believe we're making progress. I want to keep on this path."

Considering what lies ahead for me out there—life without Oliver, Agent Castle, Oliver's parents, and the tug-of-war for money they'll surely present, if Agent Castle is right about them—I am all about this plan. "Me too," I say. "I'll stay."

"Good," she approves. "Now let's talk about your conversation with Agent Castle today. I'd like to sit in, if you're okay with that. I'll act as a moderator. I'll protect your interests, and I'll put a stop to it if you become overly distressed."

"I'd like that, but Dr. Thompson, I want to talk to her. I want to heal, but I need to help her find Oliver's killer. I have to help. Maybe she'll say something that will trigger me."

"That's the worry."

"I mean in a good way. Maybe she'll tell me something I need to know, something that will help me remember. I want to remember what happened that night."

"Very well. I'll keep that in mind. I won't hold you back."

But she will.

She and I both know she will.

# Chapter Eighty

## ANDI

My interview with Carrie will be held in what is far from a normal interview setting.

The receptionist for the treatment facility, Jeananne, takes my coat and then leads me to a cozy room lined with book-filled shelves, with a crackling fire in a fireplace. Four chairs circle a coffee table, with a plate of cookies on top. I sit facing the door, setting my bag on the floor at my feet.

"Would you like a latte, Agent Castle?" Jeananne offers. "We have a full coffee bar."

"Oh. Well, sure. Can you make a white mocha?"

She offers me a small smile. "We can make you a delicious white mocha."

And she's right. A few minutes later, I'm left alone in the room to enjoy one of the best white mochas I've ever had. Carrie is living the life of luxury, if you can call being captive in a treatment facility while recovering from the murder of your fiancé living a life of luxury.

The door opens and a tall, attractive Black woman enters, followed by Carrie and Ms. Littleton. Ms. Littleton is in a hot-pink blouse and skirt, always doing her best at an attention grab. Carrie is in black like myself, but while I'm in a pantsuit, she's in a simple, loose-fitting dress. I stand and the tall Black woman offers me her hand. "I'm Dr. Thompson," she greets me. "I'm Carrie's doctor, and for her safety, I'd like to sit in today."

"Of course," I say. "I'm more than fine with that."

"For her safety," Ms. Littleton says, "I'm also sitting in."

"Sorry, Agent Castle. They want to protect me, but I do want to talk to you. I just don't want to become the fall guy, either."

"Let's sit," Dr. Thompson suggests. "And I highly recommend the cookies. They're amazing."

The shift in topic is one I accept reluctantly but willingly. Patience is a virtue. We'll shift back to Carrie. I'll get to ask my questions. "If the coffee is any indication of how good the cookies are, I have no doubt," I say, making small talk, but I'm aware of the bombshell I have to lay on Carrie today. I can't warn the doctor or Ms. Littleton. I need to know if Carrie knows about her father. I need a genuine reaction.

"What have you remembered?" I ask.

Dr. Thompson reaches for a notebook on the shelf and then says, "When she hides, she has a reason to hide. I need you to understand that, Agent."

"All right," I say. "I'm clear on that point."

"Good," she says. "I'll assume you're sincere in that response." She offers me the notebook. "Carrie wants you to have her therapy journal."

*Interesting,* I think, accepting the journal. Surely someone on Carrie's team knows a written journal holds liability. Or maybe they don't. "You wrote this, Carrie?" I ask, needing her confirmation.

"I've been writing things down as I remember them," she confirms, and now, seeing her in a calmer state, I'm struck by her sincere and gentle nature. And I certainly see why so many people close to her stood by her. "There's not a lot there, but the one thing that really stands out," she continues, "is a sense of me needing to save Oliver and failing him. I just . . . I don't know what that means."

Dr. Thompson chimes in. "I've explained to Carrie that this feeling could be guilt oriented, which is normal in the aftermath of a tragedy. We blame ourselves."

"Do you remember anything else at all?"

"I have these weird flashes of memory, but none of them make sense," Carrie replies. "One of the memories I realize was actually from months back. I don't remember drinking a lot. And Dr. Thompson tells me there wasn't a high level of alcohol in my system."

"But there was a high level of trauma," Dr. Thompson states. "Carrie has agreed to stay with me for another three weeks. I believe we can make progress if we can keep working together."

"I'm sure you can see how this helps us all," Ms. Littleton adds quickly. "We all want and need Carrie to remember what happened the night—" She catches herself before she says something she obviously thinks will traumatize Carrie, and finishes with, "Well, that night."

I don't agree or disagree, and I won't until after I finish reading Carrie. "Do you know your biological parents, Carrie?"

"What does that have to do with this?" Ms. Littleton pipes up.

"I have to agree, Agent Castle," Dr. Thompson interjects.

"Of course not," Carrie states. "I'm adopted."

"You've never looked for your biological family?"

"Never even considered it," she says easily.

"Agent Castle," Ms. Littleton warns.

"We found the box," I say.

Carrie sits up on the edge of her chair, her energy eager, not fearful. "You found it?"

"We did," I confirm.

"It was a gift Oliver received before he died," Carrie explains. "I told Agent Castle about it. He was upset about the contents. He said it was a gag gift gone wrong. He wouldn't tell me who sent it. He was afraid I'd hold it against him."

"Him?" Dr. Thompson asks.

"One of his groomsmen," Carrie explains, and then her attention returns to me. "Where was it?" she asks, her voice lifting. "What was inside? I know it's silly, but it just feels relevant. It was something that upset him before . . . you know." She swallows hard and adds, "Before."

"It was in his locker at the cigar club," I reply, and give her a minute to let that sink in.

"Oh." Her expression transitions from momentary confusion to realization. "Well, I guess that does make sense. He said it was a gift from one of his groomsmen. He must have taken it back to him. As I said, he was pretty upset over whatever was in that box."

I reach into my bag and hold up a folder. "Your father's identity was inside that box, Carrie."

"What is this?" Ms. Littleton demands.

"I think this would be better handled a different way," Dr. Thompson interjects. "Can we talk outside, Agent Castle?"

"I don't understand why he would have that," Carrie says, her eyes on me. "How would he have that? Oh God. Did his parents have me investigated? Did they hate me that much?"

It's a question I'd asked them as soon as I left the club last night. The answer had been no, which doesn't mean they didn't, but I believe I would have heard from them about this information right away had they known. "Oliver's parents didn't investigate you. Someone else did."

"Oliver?" she asks.

"I don't know, Carrie." I hold out the folder containing the documents we believe were in that white box with the red ribbon sent to Oliver. "But you have a right to know what others now know."

"Let's wait on this," Dr. Thompson states, clearly seeing something in Carrie that worries her.

"What stunt are you pulling, Agent Castle?" Ms. Littleton demands.

Carrie snatches the folder from me and rounds the chair to stand by the door, opening the folder and reading. And then just staring down at the page. Seconds tick by, and she starts to tremble. "No. No." Her gaze rockets to mine, and her voice is low, taut. "This is a lie. This is a *lie*. Why are you doing this? Why? He is *not* my father." She throws the folder away, papers fluttering about. "This is not who I am," she declares. "This is *not* who I am!" If I expected an explosion—and I did—that's not what follows. She sinks to the ground and begins to sob.

# Chapter Eighty-One

I agree to keep Carrie's father's identity a secret, at least for now. I also agree to allow Carrie to stay at the facility for another three weeks. At the end of that three weeks, we'll see where we stand.

Once I leave the facility, I text Aiden an update, decline his offer to come over, and head home. I need some alone time to process what just happened and to decide where I stand on Carrie Reynolds. I'm leaning toward believing she's more victim than killer.

And then I head to the office with a theory in mind.

What if someone at that party is related to one of her father's victims?

————

A few hours later, I'm at my kitchen table, with my laptop open and a steaming cup of coffee next to me. There's also a doodle mess on my notepad, my unproductive method of expelling excess energy and frustration.

I toss down my pen and sigh. So far I've made no connections between the hotel guests or staff and Carrie's father, but it's a tedious research process. It takes time we don't have. While those who kill in the heat of the moment rarely kill again, at this stage of an investigation, nothing is certain, and the threat of another murder has to be considered. Since Carrie's father killed across three states—Colorado, New Mexico, and Texas—we've blasted a special alert and request for information to those states and beyond. We hit the NCIC, which will cover the entire US, with additional information, on top of our initial submission.

But I'm missing something that's staring me in the face. I feel it in my bones, and it's driving me crazy. My cellphone rings with a 615 number, and I'm hoping for a lead. I answer with, "Special Agent Castle."

"This is Detective Boone out of Franklin, Tennessee." His twang says "country boy" all the way.

"Tell me you have something good for me."

"I have *something* for you," he replies, "but I'm not sure if you'll think it's good."

I breathe out. "Hit me with it."

"Your crime with the box and red ribbon you posted on the NCIC system."

I sit up a little straighter. Having my team send out a national law enforcement request for information was longer than a long shot. "Yes. What about it?"

"One of my guys is obsessed with those damn alerts. He brought it to me, and it's a good thing. I had a box of my own, too. Red ribbon and all."

"Really? And?"

"The woman who received it is now dead. That seems to be the common denominator between the two cases, along with the box of course."

I'm standing now. "Tell me more," I say. "What was in the box, and how did she die?"

"The box included proof that she'd been stealing from her company. What was in your box?"

"Our key suspect in the murder we're investigating is adopted. The box held proof that her father's a serial killer."

"Okay, you one-upped me on that one," he drawls. "Who did she supposedly kill?"

"Her fiancé."

"Interesting," he says. "The crime scene was set up to look like a suicide on our end, but it was a shoddy cover-up, easy for a seasoned detective to spot. I'm one hundred percent certain this case was a one and done, which is why I didn't list it in the database."

"And yet we're talking?" I comment. "Who killed her?"

"Did I mention she was going through a nasty divorce?"

"The husband," I conclude.

"Bingo. We nailed him wicked fast. She had no idea he knew she'd stolen money from her employer. We found the bank account where she'd stashed it all."

"I assume he did, too?"

"Oh yeah. Ripe for his taking. She never touched it. Just took it. Can't figure that part out, but the ex is a dick. Must have been her escape plan to get away from him."

"And yet she filed for divorce?"

"He did. He had a side chick. They wanted the money."

"How are these two cases connected?" I say, thinking out loud and settling back down in my chair.

"I think you have yourself a copycat killer, which means there has to be a connection to my case, even in passing. I'm going to send you my case files without you asking. I'm not one of those guys who doesn't like to share. I'm the guy who wants to catch bad guys. If you want to connect me with your team, I'll get them whatever you need."

"Thank you, Detective Boone. This is helpful and a bit bizarre."

"That it is. If you head in our direction, I'll show you around, so give me a shout."

"Where exactly is Franklin?"

"We're roughly twenty miles from downtown Nashville and a whole lot less to the outskirts. Nashville has a boatload of small cities surrounding it, all close enough that people live in those cities and still work and play in Nashville. In other words, I'd be searching for a connection in Tennessee, not just Franklin."

I'm already processing theories. "The wife is a nurse. She could have a connection to the hospital. Can you email me the files, including that information?"

"You got it. You want me to send the files to anyone else?"

We connect our two investigative teams and then end the call. I dial my supreme master of the internet, Hazel. "If you called to ask me to work a miracle," she says, "I'm the closest thing to a miracle I got for you right now."

"Well, let me give you a chance to be the miracle maker. We've got another box in Tennessee, but it appears there's no real connection. It's a copycat. Which means someone at that hotel knew about the case and has a link to Tennessee. Carrie's a nurse. I'm guessing the connection is her. Find a link. Look at where she's been."

"You want me to hyperfocus on Carrie?"

"As much as I want to say yes, that's a bad investigative move. Tennessee is sending you the case files. Look at everyone who was in that hotel. And look for any and all connections to the place, people, crimes. But speed this up by looking at Carrie and the rest of the wedding party. Don't leave Oliver's family out of the mix."

"Still worried about Oliver's sister?"

"Not really, but she had a lot to gain by his death. We'd be fools not to look at her again."

When I've sent Hazel off to do her magic, I trade my coffee for wine. I'm way past coffee and sit down to read the data sent over by Boone, because the truth is, no matter how much I want what I want, this kind of search on this many people takes time.

An hour later, I haven't even touched the wine. I'm engrossed in the Tennessee case file, which to me reads like a well-wrapped book. Boone is good at his job. He covered every investigative base. But is this a copycat case? I won't know until we connect dots, and somewhere there *is* a dot that connects.

My cellphone rings on the table next to me. I grab it and find Hazel's number, trying not to get excited about the quick callback that could mean good news or no news at all. "What do you have for me?"

"I'm not sure I'd call this good news."

"Okay. Well, hit me with it."

"Carrie went to a medical conference in Nashville."

My spine goes ramrod stiff. "Why is this not good news?"

"The entire cigar club also went to Nashville two weeks before her conference, Oliver included."

I throw my pen in the air. "Oh my God. Could this get any more complicated?" I don't wait for an answer. "Any connections to the hospital where the Tennessee victim was taken?"

"The only one I see, and this is a quick glance, is Carrie. Elsa Ward was taken to a Nashville hospital, and a huge portion of the staff can be assumed to have been at that convention. I haven't had time to check except for one person. I checked the attending doctor for Ward."

"And? Was he there?"

"No. He was not."

# Chapter Eighty-Two

## CARRIE

*I must be a killer. My father's a killer.* I write that in my journal over and over. When my mother, my *adoptive* mother, calls, I decline to talk to her. I decline to talk to Dr. Thompson. She allows me a short break, an evening to myself.

Then she comes to my room.

I'm standing at the window when she enters. I can feel her energy. That's another reason I'm a good nurse. I can read people's energy. I know when they're going to freak out. I know when they're living in a tunnel of darkness. Maybe I know those things for all the wrong reasons. Maybe I even enjoy all the blood and pain the ER produces. Maybe I need it.

Of course, I've never thought any of these things in my life, but my God. My father is a *killer*.

"Carrie."

I turn at Dr. Thompson's voice and face her. She's in her white jacket, and she motions to the chairs. "Let's sit."

I nod and reluctantly sit. Sitting is just too calm right now. My thoughts go crazy.

"Listen to me and listen to me now. You are not him," she declares. "Stop doing this to yourself."

"Doing what?"

"Turning yourself into a killer. Clearly you were set up. Someone used your father against you. Don't demonize yourself. Fight back. Let's get busy remembering. Then you can give Oliver justice. You can tell the police who killed him and hurt you."

"What about genetics?" I ask. "I have his genes in my body."

"You have your mother's, too."

"There's nothing about her in the file Agent Castle gave me."

"Good news. That must mean there's nothing to tell. And whoever compiled the data on you and your father did so maliciously. Fight back. Remember what happened that night. *Remember, Carrie.*"

She's right. My God. She is right. I don't know who did this, but I have to pull myself together and help Agent Castle find them. "Yes. Help me. Help me remember. Now, please."

# Chapter Eighty-Three

## ANDI

The morning after the Tennessee revelation, Hazel has found at least thirty people in the hotel who have a Nashville connection, out of the three hundred who were present the night Oliver died. Over coffee, not wine, I spend hours going over the details with her. As for the search for a connection between Carrie's father and Oliver's murder, it's a complete bust.

I'm halfway through a pot of coffee when I start calling the cigar club, starting with Brody.

"Agent Castle. Good morning."

"You're way too cheery for a man who just lost a close friend."

"I handle things my way," he says, his voice noticeably tighter.

"Why were you in Nashville last year?"

"Holy hell, do you want to know my underwear color, too? I thought I was cleared?"

"I haven't cleared anyone. Why were you—"

"It was a guys' trip. We saw Jason Aldean perform, then went over to Kid Rock's place. Why?"

"Did you see Carrie there?"

"No. Hell no."

"Did anyone see her?"

"She was at home in Denver. Oliver was with us. It was a guys' trip."

"Did anyone act funny?"

"We were wasted. We all acted like idiots. That's the joy of walking around Broadway and not being worried about getting in a car and driving drunk."

"Did anyone disappear?"

"I mean, not really. Cade scored with some hot chick and went home with her."

*Cade the doctor,* I think. I type a message to Hazel: Look for connections to Cade.

She replies back: Done. There are none.

"Agent? You done with me?"

"Probably not. I'll be in touch."

I disconnect and curl my fingers in my palm. *What* am I missing?

———

By Friday, late afternoon, two days after my interview with Carrie, I've read her journal entries, and as I suspect she knew, nothing in them helps us. I'm also officially in need of rest. I have started to believe lack of sleep is affecting how I process information. By midmorning, I head home and sleep two full, wondrous hours. After which I slide into my favorite baggy jeans and a sweater and ignore my growling stomach. I'm eager to put my fresh, rested eyes on the file.

I'm only about an hour into my work when my cellphone rings and I glance down to find my father, who's been surprisingly quiet for a few days, calling. He doesn't even know about the new serial killer in the mix. "Hi, Dad," I answer. "What trouble are you in?"

"I'm here with your pal York."

I blink and sit up straighter. "What? In Estes Park?"

"That's right. Imagine me standing right here in Estes at a bar with my big, muscled arm around York's shoulders. He's loving having me here. Aren't you, York?"

"Help," York pleads. "Andi, help."

I swear I laugh. I can't help it. York deserves this.

"I'll be right back, Yorkie baby," my father declares, and I can hear shuffling about in the background before he returns and says, "All right. I let York breathe a little. He's got concrete retirement shoes on. You better be glad I was feeling guilty about not finding you that locker key and decided to try to find your weapon. York doesn't do heavy lifting."

Nail on head. And obviously, Whit has been talking to the team and my father, because I didn't tell him about the missing weapon. "And?" I urge, eager to know what he found, praying he found our knife.

"No luck on the knife," he says, "but I got something."

"Meaning what?"

"There was a ghost-hunting operation that sneaked cameras into the hotel. They had them all over the place. They didn't come forward because they were afraid of being connected to the murder."

"But they did now?"

"After I got one of them drunk and introduced him to Mandy, the waitress I got friendly with—I'll spare you the details—but bottom line. I have the tapes."

"Have you looked at them?"

"Nope. But I'm going to get out of here before Mandy leaves and he starts thinking about the videotapes in my hand again. I'm on my way to you. You at your place?"

"I am."

"Good. Order me that burger I like. I'll call you when I'm a half hour out."

I stand up and start to pace. This could be our big break.

I have a good feeling about this.

Maybe, just maybe, I'm about to figure out what I'm missing and solve this case.

# Chapter Eighty-Four

It's one o'clock when the burgers arrive—and just in time. My father explodes into my house with all the fierce energy that is Eddie Castle five minutes later.

Ten minutes after that, we're both on the floor in front of my coffee table stuffing our faces. These times alone with my father are the ones where he's gentler, quieter, more analytical. He doesn't perform for me. He's just with me.

"Holy mother of insanity," he says, of Carrie's father's identity. "Is she as crazy as him?"

"I'm on the fence," I say, stabbing my fry into the ketchup. "At the least someone wanted Oliver to believe she is. I mean, the info on her father was sent to Oliver."

"Assume that's true, because we're presuming everything—with what endgame?" he asks. "To have him leave her? Who wanted them broken up?"

"His family," I say. "The friend, Brody. Maybe others. Believe me, I've been considering the options. But wanting them split up and wanting Oliver dead are two different things."

"Well, if he decided to leave her, she could have lost her shit."

"Why tell her at a party to celebrate their wedding?"

"Maybe he just found out about the father," he offers.

I sip my soda. "He got the box weeks before."

"What if he figured out who sent the box while he was at the party? He confronted that person. That person came to the room, and it got bloody."

I think back to my meeting with Carrie two days ago. "Carrie did say she feels like she should have saved Oliver. She can't remember what happened, but that feeling won't let her go."

"Hell, I still feel that way about your mother." He gives me a sad smile. "Remember how she used to crinkle her nose? Cutest damn thing."

"I actually don't remember. I can't remember her face. I hate it."

"I know, Andi baby. And I feel guilty as shit for that."

"It's not your fault."

"That's my point," he counters. "Guilt—and that feeling of 'I should have done more'—is normal. Carrie feeling it is normal. But that feeling means nothing about what happened that night."

"Unless it does," I argue, clearing my food away and grabbing my computer. "Let's find out." I stick one of four data drives he's brought me into the side of my MacBook.

He stuffs what seems like half a burger in his mouth and grabs his own MacBook and we get to work.

Two hours later, I'm seeing double. We've both watched so much worthless video footage I want to scream. I get up, stretch, make a pot of coffee, and it's not long until we finish it off. I've now had to go pee three times. "No more coffee," I say, after I go to the bathroom time number four.

Three hours in, my dad hands me a bowl of dry Cap'n Crunch cereal. "The crunch keeps you alert." He winks. "And it's good. Try it. Dad knows best."

He's correct, at least about the cereal. The crunch does help. So much so that I eat way too much cereal. Finally, four hours into our little project, something on the film finally catches my eye. I frown and sit up straighter. I pause the film and rewind. I play it again. "I think . . . I think I have a situation," I say. "No. A problem. A very unexpected problem."

My dad moves to the couch cushion behind me. "What are we looking at?"

I play the video for him of the woman who crosses paths with Oliver in a hallway outside the main party room. They talk and then she snuggles up close to him. He sets her away from him, clearly declining her advances.

"You're looking for a woman," he comments. "And she looks like a woman who might be scorned. And you know what they say about a woman scorned. Who is she?"

"My friend who invited me to the party. *Lana*."

Instinct kicks in, and I grab my phone and dial Hazel. "What's up?"

"Did you check out my friend Lana? I don't remember seeing her in the notes, now that I think about it."

"I didn't," she admits. "I guess I should have, but she was with you and . . . *I'm sorry*. I was so hyperfocused on the wedding party. I'll do it now."

"Yes. Do it now and call me back."

I lower my phone and sit there thinking. I can't blame Hazel for not prioritizing Lana. I didn't, either. I should have ruled her out in the beginning.

"What's going on?"

I glance over at my father. "I think I might know why I've been feeling like I'm missing what was in front of me." I push to my feet and start pacing, waiting for Hazel's callback. "And right now, I need to think."

"Understood," he says. "I'm here if you need to talk it out, baby girl." He stands up and walks out of the room, and in this moment I respect his experience. Because that's why he respects my need to silently process.

My cellphone rings and my stomach twists in knots. Hazel wouldn't call this fast if she didn't have something for me. I answer the call. "She has a connection," I say.

"She worked at a Nashville children's hospital before she went to Boston. Her ex still does. He's in pediatrics."

Which fits perfectly considering Lana told me she prefers working in pediatrics. "The hospital where Elsa Ward was taken?"

"No."

"What else?"

"He was at the same conference as Carrie. Lana was not."

I digest that with a rush of adrenaline. "Get me everything you have on him plus his number and keep digging."

We disconnect and I start pacing. I'm so close to the right answers but not quite there. If the ex is in pediatrics at the wrong hospital, he can't be the one who told Carrie about the Elsa Ward murder. Unless he heard it from a friend. But how does Lana play into this? Did Lana find out her ex and Carrie met, and therefore plotted Oliver's murder? Or did she come here to protect him? Was that why she was trying to get close to him at the hotel in the video footage? And he didn't want to hear a warning from her? She did invite me to that weekend in Estes Park. Maybe she wanted me to help her protect him.

I text Hazel: Look for a connection between Lana's ex and Carrie.

Right about then, my phone pings with a phone number, a name, and a short bio. Lana's ex, Derrek Montgomery, has a scholarly and impressive medical background. He's smart enough, and educated enough, to pull off an unsolvable crime, but I won't let that happen. My finger hovers over his number to call him, but I decide better. If Lana is here to undermine a crime, I could put her at risk. If she is involved in that crime, working with Carrie and Derrek, or even just Carrie, Derrek might alert her I'm onto her.

My father returns and sits next to me, but he says nothing. He understands my process. He'll talk when I'm ready to talk, which is not now. I punch in Lana's number. She answers on the first ring. "Hey, Andi. How'd that lead go? Good, I hope?"

I play the role I need to play to handle this, whatever "this" is. "Oh gosh," I say. "No work. I can't do work right now. How about a drink? I need a break."

"Sure. I'm always up for a drink. And I'm off tomorrow. Where?"

"How about Albert's downtown? I'll text you the address."

"Perfect. I'll see you in, say, an hour?"

"That works."

We disconnect and I sit there a moment, digesting the idea of a friend being a killer, and I wish it were unfamiliar. But just last year one of the agents I'd consider a friend as well was stalking women, which escalated into murder. But Lana? I reject the idea and glance at my father. "She invited me to the party. It's not her. Why would you invite an FBI agent if you were going to kill someone?"

"When I hurt someone, dear daughter of mine, it's planned and I know when to stop." He picks up a photo of Oliver's damaged body. "This wasn't planned. This was a crime of passion."

"Unless it wasn't," I say. "Maybe that's just what I'm supposed to believe. And maybe, just maybe, the killer, or killers, were smart enough to use my automatic assumptions about a crime against me."

# Chapter Eighty-Five

I don't like Albert's.

The patio is open and the smoke floats over the bar, the menu is limited, and the barstools have no backs.

But I didn't choose it for the meeting with Lana because I enjoy visiting. I chose it because it's a slow part of downtown Denver at this time of day, the bar is always empty, and I don't want anywhere I like to be ruined by this little talk. Not that I make a habit of letting bad people ruin things for me. I am my father's daughter. But when things get rowdy, people don't tend to invite you back. Not that I plan on things getting rowdy, either, but you just never know, and I'm not unwilling to do what I have to do, should it become necessary. That's not about being my father's daughter. It's about wearing my badge and living by the pledge to protect and serve.

I arrive early, sit at the end of the bar where I can see the door, and order a light beer with a dark bottle that I can nurse slowly without impairing my mind or body. Lana appears in the doorway fifteen minutes later, still in her scrubs. She waves and I wave back, and as she rushes toward me, I pray she isn't involved in Oliver's death. I consider myself a good judge of people, and nothing about her screams killer. But then, the best of the best never do. There's a reason why people got in the car with Bundy. He was good-looking and charismatic.

Lana settles onto a seat next to me and says, "Good choice of bar. No crowd."

"It's not my favorite place, but it's a good place to actually hear each other speak."

"Points all around," she says, flagging the bartender. "A lemon drop, please. Easy on the vodka."

"Going easy, are you?" I ask.

"I have to drive home, and I've never been a big drinker, especially since I started working in the ER. I've seen too many DUI accidents."

"How is the ER going?"

"Horrible. I hate the blood and misery." The bartender sets her drink in front of her. "But I won't have to do it long. Sadly, in some ways. I'm leaving."

"Really?" I ask. "To where?"

"Nashville. When I first got married, my ex had a job there. I actually love it. The food, girl. It's so damn good. And the cowboys. Gotta love a cowboy in those tight-fitting jeans. I applied months back, and they finally have an opening that allows me to get back to a world where women only scream while delivering the new love of their lives, their new babies."

Instant red flag. *Had a job there?* I think. He's still there. He still works in Nashville. And the talk about hating blood and gore. Maybe it's true. Or maybe it's a cover. My gut is telling me she's not here to protect Oliver. "I'm sad you're leaving," I say. "We were just getting to know each other again."

"I know, but you can come visit. You'll love it. Have you ever been?"

"Once, years ago for a case, but it was a fly in and fly out the same day kind of thing. And I think I'll be working on this case for the rest of my life, the way it's going. I may never get another vacation."

"That bad, huh?"

"Carrie's in a rehab center, which is good and bad," I say. "It allows me time to build my case against her, but she's also been out of reach. She can at least have visitors now."

"I never pegged her as unstable," Lana says. "Just the opposite. She's always the calm one when the emergencies come through the door. Oh. Did you find the box?"

"We did, actually."

"Really? Well, was he cheating like she thought?"

"You know I can't tell you details," I say, tipping back my beer and pretending to drink.

"Right. Sorry." She sips her drink. "I get it. It's the law and all."

We sit and chat about random things, and I let us slip into a comfortable conversation for a good forty minutes before I sigh. "You know, I wish I knew Oliver's state of mind that night. Sorry. I just went right back into work mode."

"Well, when he was giving his speech with Carrie, they seemed happy. She certainly was."

"That's the kind of response everyone gives me. I need thoughts from someone who actually spoke to him one-on-one. You didn't, right? Please tell me you did."

"No. Sorry. I didn't see him at all—well, from afar, like I said, when he was giving that speech."

Another lie. I grab my phone and glance at my messages, pretending to read a message that doesn't exist. "Oh. Great." I glance over at her. "Interesting and unexpected good news." I set my cell aside. "A ghost-hunting group had cameras all over the place in the hotel. They caught almost every location the hotel cameras did not. Now we have blanket coverage. Maybe I'll find more of Oliver on the feed. Of course I will." I toast with my beer. "To my job just getting easier."

"Well, there you go." She cuts her gaze and downs part of her drink, her hand shaking slightly. "I need to pee," she announces, and she slides off her seat and heads for the bathroom. I text Aiden, who

I got involved right after setting up the drink meetup: She's about to leave. And she's guilty, I'm just not sure of what just yet.

I'm ready to follow, he replies.

Lana returns and doesn't sit down. "They just called me back to work. See why I want to move?" She grabs her purse.

"Oh no," I say. "That sucks. When do you move?"

"Two weeks." She calls out to the bartender, "Check, please."

"I got it," I say. "You go work, but let's have lunch before you leave."

"Yes. Great. I'd love that."

"Before you go, I just received a text message from my team, when you were in the bathroom. Did you know Carrie and your ex were at the same medical convention?"

She laughs, a choked, nervous laugh. "I didn't know my ex was on your radar."

"It's my job. I look at all links."

"Meaning me?" she challenges, a crack in her voice.

"Everyone has to be ruled out," I reply.

You think *I killed Oliver?*"

"I just want you to tell me about your ex and that medical convention. That's all."

"Those events are massive," she replies dismissively. "That really doesn't even seem strange to me."

"You aren't going to ask me what conference and in what city?"

She sips her drink through a straw rather than picking up her glass again with her trembling hand. "They're held all over the country. Actually, the world."

I wait for her to look at me, but when she refuses, I say, "Nashville."

She shrugs, flicking me a fleeting look before staring at the TV above the bar. "Nashville is a popular convention spot. But the medical community is a small world." She points to some car insurance advertisement being played. "I'm obsessed with the ostrich on those commercials now."

"Did they meet?" I ask.

"That seems highly unlikely. And it might not have even been when we were married."

"I think it was."

"I don't." She shifts the topic. "I hate this, but we're understaffed with Carrie gone. I'll call you," she says, already turning toward the door.

She walks to the exit, but I can feel her energy.

And right then, I'm fairly certain of where this is headed, and I do all I can. I turn off my emotions. She is a suspect in the crime of murder. She is no friend of mine.

A suspect who's at least thinking about running.

Now we just have to watch and see where her panic leads her. And us.

# Chapter Eighty-Six

By the time I'm in the car, Aiden is calling me. "She's driving toward the treatment facility."

"Oh my God," I say. "Could they be in on this together?"

"Seems more right than wrong right about now," he says and then adds, "Yep. We're headed to Rosewood."

"I'm on my way." I disconnect and start my engine, blown away. Lana is way more involved in this than I know, and I start playing with a variety of hypotheses. Lana might have killed Oliver. Or helped kill him? Maybe she helped Carrie clean up just enough to look like she wasn't straddling Oliver to stab him? Or maybe she and her ex are not exes at all, and there is some kind of financial plot? I need to look into Lana's finances. People who lose money can become desperate.

I come back to Carrie and Lana. The two of them working together doesn't feel right.

How would Lana or her ex know about Carrie's biological father? That answer comes quickly. Money. Lana has money. And money can buy things it sometimes shouldn't. Some people might say, If she has money, why kill for money? Because money is as addictive as a drug. Or again, full circle here, the source of money runs out.

All of the facts, or lack thereof, don't matter, though. I have a bad feeling clawing at me. And that feeling has never been wrong. Urgency builds inside me, and it feels like a lifetime before I pull into the parking lot of the center.

The instant the building is in my view, I must be in Aiden's because he calls again. "She just left. I'm following her."

"Damn it," I murmur. "I'm going in to talk to Carrie. Why can't anything be simple?" I disconnect and head inside the building.

In the lobby, I flash my badge at the receptionist. "I need to see Carrie Reynolds."

"Visiting hours just ended."

"That wasn't a question," I say. "This is urgent FBI business. Call your supervisor and do it now."

Her eyes go wide and she grabs her phone. "Dr. Thompson, I need you up front now. It's urgent."

I reach over the counter and grab the phone from the receptionist. "Dr. Thompson, this is Agent Castle. I need to talk to Carrie right now about the visitor she just had, and it's time sensitive. Have her buzz the door. *Now.*"

"I'll have to call her attorney."

That feeling I'm having tells me to push, and I do. "I need five minutes and you can sit in. I'll get Ms. Littleton on the phone."

She must hear the seriousness in my voice, because she says, "I assume she's gone back to her room. I'll get her and meet you in the room where we talked to her previously. Put the receptionist on the line."

I hand the receptionist the phone. She listens a moment and then hangs up. Without a word, she buzzes the door. I dial Ms. Littleton even as I hurry toward the room I've visited in the past. I get her voicemail and leave a message. "I need five minutes with your client in a meeting that could work in her favor. Now. I'm at the center. Call me back."

I reach the room in question and open the door. To my surprise, Carrie is standing with her back to me, facing the fireplace. Alone. She must not have ever gone back to her room. "Carrie," I say, shutting the door behind me.

She turns to face me, and her expression is emotionless, a coldness about her I don't recognize, not in her. "I need to know what Lana just said to you," I say.

She hesitates and then huffs out her confession. "She said she's the one who sent Oliver my adoption records. She wanted him to hate me and dump me."

"Why?"

"Because she says I slept with her husband at some medical convention in Nashville."

*Everything suddenly makes sense.*

"She killed him," she adds, before I can ask a question. "He found out she was the one who was trying to expose my biological father and ruin me, and therefore he was going to ruin her. So she killed him, and she says she should have killed me."

"What did you say? Why didn't you get help?"

Her eyes bottom out with nothing but darkness, cold, hard. Her voice changes, deepens. "I told her that her husband told me that I was pretty, a better fuck than her. I told her we fucked over and over and over, and he couldn't get enough of me. And I told her that he could hardly stand the sight of her. Kissing her made his skin crawl because he wanted to be kissing me."

There is a brutality to her words that sends chills down my spine. This is not the sweet, innocent Carrie I've met with before.

The door behind me opens and Dr. Thompson says, "What is happening? I told you, her attorney has to be consulted before we talk. Come with me now, Carrie."

There is a slight curve to Carrie's lips, as if she's won in some way, before she tilts her chin upward and walks toward Dr. Thompson, but she pauses next to me, lowers her voice, and says, "I have no idea who her husband is." With that, she leaves the room.

# Chapter Eighty-Seven

I exit the center just as Aiden calls. "I don't know what just happened," I say.

"What does that mean?"

"Carrie claims Lana killed Oliver because she slept with Lana's husband. But . . . it's a little more complicated than that. And strange. I'll explain. Where's Lana?"

"Talk about strange. She pulled into a McDonald's parking lot, and she's just sitting there. She hasn't gotten out of her car."

"Yes, well, if you heard what Carrie said to her, you might not think so."

"I think it's time to bring her in for questioning."

"Agreed. I want to be there. I want to use what Carrie told me. Send me your location."

"You got it."

We disconnect and my phone buzzes with his location. Fifteen minutes later, I bring the McDonald's into view and find emergency vehicles everywhere. I know what's happened even before I park and flash my badge to enter the crime scene. Aiden runs toward me, and I meet him off to the side of an ambulance.

"She killed herself," he says, confirming my assumption.

I wait for the punch of emotion that should follow, but it doesn't. I've apparently mastered the art of coldness. Perhaps a little too well, and I think that should perhaps scare me a bit. I shove aside that thought and focus on my job, on my duty to my badge and community. "How?"

"Gunshot," he says grimly.

"Any note?"

"Nothing. But I think this is closure for the family."

Except it doesn't feel like closure at all. Not after the side of Carrie I saw today.

# Chapter Eighty-Eight

Oliver's funeral is three weeks later, on a snowy, cold day, not long after Carrie checked out of the treatment center. As far as the rest of the world is concerned, Lana killed Oliver. I don't attend the funeral, but I do go to the cemetery and stand at a distance, watching as the ground swallows the casket. Watching Carrie collapse in front of it. It's a lie. She is a lie.

I leave there and head home, changing into workout gear and showing up on my father's doorstep. He knows what's going on, and he motions me forward. "Let's go spar, Sugar Bear. Come try and beat your pop's ass. You know that always makes you feel better. Or better yet," he says after I enter and he shuts the door behind me, "you can pretend you're doing what I would do—making sure Carrie can't hurt anyone else."

If only I could.

We confirmed Lana lived in Nashville before moving to Boston. Thanks to my dad, we found the dirty PI and the dirty politician who helped him get Lana the adoption records. And we talked to Lana's ex and confirmed that yes, he slept with someone at a medical convention. And yes, Carrie was at that convention. Of course, Carrie continues to deny the affair, but when our team showed a photo of Carrie to Lana's ex, he knew her. She was happily engaged to Oliver at the time.

Something tells me her denial is real. I've seen people who lied so much they literally believed their own lies. We all have a dark side, but only some of us allow it to form a life outside our minds.

Lana has her share of guilt in all that has happened, no doubt, but now that she's dead, I don't know if we will ever know if she had any part in Oliver's murder.

But I still believe Carrie held that knife and stabbed Oliver.

I'm not done with this case until I prove it, either.

# Chapter Eighty-Nine

I barely sleep that night.

For hours on end, I scour documents, researching Carrie's past and her father. The bastard wasn't just a serial killer. He raped them. The really sick part was he worked as a sexual abuse counselor. And thanks to my father, and his contacts, I'm able to find the truth behind Carrie's adoption. Her mother was raped by her serial killer father and couldn't bring herself to keep Carrie. Her father was, and is, a wolf in sheep's clothing, which rings a little too true of Carrie. I wonder if she was always one trigger from becoming her father, and that trigger was the day her brother died. Or maybe she was just born this way, and she really did push her brother into traffic.

Through all my studies, Lana's life and death are in the back of my mind. Nothing about her says killer. Perhaps it's just space and time, allowing me to feel the loss of a friend, but I still can't shake the idea that I can buy a vindictive side of Lana but not a killer. I don't believe that, which is exactly why I want to talk to her ex, but he's not taking my calls, and I send Boone to talk to him.

He's nowhere to be found.

Apparently, we aren't quite done with this case.

The hunt is on.

———

It's a full week after Oliver's funeral when Lana's body is officially cleared for release to the family. After a difficult conversation with Lana's mother, in which she cries and I feel gutted—I'm apparently not as cold as I feared—I plan to meet the family upon their local arrival.

Turns out that decision leads to an interesting development.

Derrek, the ex, shows up with them, when they told us they hadn't seen him. I meet them at the coroner's office and manage to find a moment with the ex alone without much effort. He steps out of the bathroom as I'm about to enter the ladies' room myself. He's a tall man, with dark hair and a fit physique. Today his blue eyes are bloodshot. "Agent," he greets me, his voice gravelly. "I was hoping to talk to you."

"I tried to call."

"I know. I was just not okay. I'm still not okay." His voice cracks. "I know we broke up, but I loved her."

I motion to the sitting areas just beyond where we stand.

He steps into the hallway and halts. "This won't take long. I just thought you should know a few things."

"Such as?"

He swallows hard. "I wasn't faithful to Lana. I slept with Carrie. It meant nothing, but it was a fuckup that cost me my marriage."

"How'd she find out?"

"Someone saw us together. It was stupid. I'm never going to get over how that led us here. She would never kill anyone," he adds vehemently.

"She followed Carrie here."

"I know. I'm shocked. I didn't even think she loved me. Maybe she didn't. Maybe she just hated Carrie *that* much. But not her husband. Nothing about any of this makes sense to me."

"Why wasn't Lana at the convention?"

"Her mom came into town. But she ended up coming, the morning after I was with Carrie. It was a hellish situation. I was destined to get caught and pay for my stupidity."

My mind goes to the video of Lana cozying up to Oliver. I don't think she was trying to sleep with him, but maybe warn him? She didn't kill him. As if he reads my mind, he says, "Lana didn't kill Oliver. You were friends. She talked about you. She knew how good you are at your job. She didn't come here, and connect with you, to kill someone."

"I never said she killed anyone."

"I've heard murmurs."

"From who?"

"Here. A couple ladies didn't know who I was or that I was behind them. I heard them gossiping. I heard what they said about her with her body right here in the building." He all but growls out those last words.

"That was unprofessional, and I'll handle it," I promise. "She was my friend. I'm not going to fail her or Oliver. I have a question. Did you hear anything about a woman who received a box, like a gift with a red ribbon, and then ended up dead? It was made to look like suicide, but it wasn't?"

"Not at the conference, but it was all over the news when it happened. It was a sensationalized story by the media. Why?"

"Oliver got a box," I say.

He pales. "That means nothing. Lots of people heard about that woman. Can you prove Lana sent the box?"

"No, but it held nasty secrets about Carrie's past. The kind that might have made a man leave his fiancée. Seems like that could feel like a way to punish the woman who ruined her marriage."

"Okay, well, in that case Oliver had to be alive to leave Carrie. Lana didn't want him dead. He wanted her to suffer. Speculation, of course, but that seems like what you're doing, too."

"It is right now, and now that Lana's dead, we may never know."

He draws a deep breath and exhales. "If I could change that, I would. And I can't focus on that or I won't be okay." His voice is low and raspy. I need to go to her parents. They're in a lot of pain. Let me know if I can do anything else."

"Answer your phone."

"I will." He starts to leave but pauses. "If she was going to kill someone, don't you think it would be me?" He doesn't wait for a reply. He walks away.

I think back to a night when Lana and I went to a restaurant and the waitress was rude to her. Lana called everyone and their uncle trying to get her fired. She would not let it go. But later, she found out the woman was a single mom with two kids. She called back and told everyone she'd had bad PMS that night and was the one who was wrong.

I don't think Lana would kill anyone. But seek vengeance? Maybe. Carrie was no single mom, likely to inspire guilt or sympathy. And the box and the scandal it carried don't equal murder. I hypothesize that Lana most likely heard about the box with the red ribbon with a secret inside sent to Elsa Ward by an ex on the news since the case became a headline story. Such a story would make for delicious gossip by the watercooler. Even more so lubricated by booze at a medical convention. It was, after all, a box with a secret so nasty that Elsa's ex hoped the police would believe she killed herself when he, in fact, murdered her. Perhaps Lana didn't think about it again, at least not until she arrived in Denver, when the talk of Carrie's wedding and gifts brought it to the front of her mind. What better way to serve her revenge on Carrie than in a box, delivered to her fiancé, before the wedding.

I'll be looking into Derrek with a keen eye, but my gut says he's not involved in Oliver's murder. And any member of law enforcement will tell you that gut feelings, when backed up with facts, matter.

---

I stay up most of the night reading all there is to know about Carrie's father. The medical experts refused to declare him insane. The notes from one psychiatric professional said, *"I've never experienced such evil up close and in person,"* but I think maybe I have. It's time to visit the one person who may very well know Carrie like no one else.

Her father.

# Chapter Ninety

Norman Morrow is being held in a supermax prison in Florence, Colorado, just two hours from Denver.

After a shower and change into my standard dress pants, dress shirt, and jacket, I hit a drive-thru and then pound out the miles. On the way, I confirm with my team that Carrie has never visited Norman. Of course, Carrie could have used an alias, and probably would have. She's clever and devious.

It's already sunset when I arrive, and the haze of evening on a snowy, cold day has an eerie effect. I always think about the crimes a prison represents, the violence, the pain. The devastation. Prisons are the walls of evil. And I'm about to go visit the evilest of all. I sit in my car and spend a good half hour reading the file we have on Norman, and not for the first time. But I need his history to be fresh in my mind, useful in every way possible.

I head for the door, that encounter with Carrie playing in my head. *I told her that her husband told me that I was pretty, a better fuck than her.* This from a woman who until then I couldn't even imagine using such crassness. The warden, Tom Green—a tall, stocky fiftysomething man with a bald head—greets me, even invites me into his office.

"Agent Castle," he says, once I'm seated at a small round table with him, "are you sure you want to talk to Norman Morrow? Because it's not a pleasant experience."

"Neither is much of what I do for a living. And considering he has a daughter I believe to be a chip off the ole block, it's necessary."

"A daughter?"

"Yes," I confirm. "She was put up for adoption. Her brother died when she was twelve and he was fourteen. Some believe she had something to do with his demise."

"Interesting. And now? What did she do now?"

"Her fiancé was stabbed to death. Right now, she's going to get off. I need to stop that from happening. I need to understand her and how to trigger her."

"We have yet to figure out Norman's triggers, so good luck on that one. But fair warning: One minute, he appears to be a perfectly normal person. Then the other Norman appears. And you do *not* want to know that Norman. He likes to play the whole split personality card."

"Is there a medical diagnosis associated with that behavior?"

"His legal team went down that path, but at least three mental evaluations concluded that was bull crap. He's a master manipulator who plays games with his victims, which they said is every other human he ever speaks with. The more normal he seems one moment, the more confusing the bad side is when you finally see it. The more intense the reaction. He enjoys that part. He lives for the victory it gives him. Your shock and fear are his drugs."

I can only hope the apple doesn't fall too far from the tree. If that's true, Carrie is ripe for my taking. She's due her victory dance or, if I have my way, her murder confession.

———

A few minutes later, I'm outside a cell set up for high-risk visitations.

"You sure you want to do this?" Warden Green asks.

"Very," I say, but what I don't say is that I have sat across from a serial killer; I've looked in his unshuttered eyes. That man is proud of the evil inside him. And I'm thankful we put him away for life. I need just that with Carrie. Because she, too, is evil walking, hidden behind the sweet facade of a nurse. In some ways, that makes her more dangerous than the Spider Man.

"We'll be close and watching." He motions to the guard to open the door. He turns a lock.

The door opens and I step inside to find a man sitting behind a table, his hands cuffed underneath the wooden top. A man who looks too young to be Carrie's father, with thick, dark hair and pale, chiseled features. The door slams behind me and I manage not to flinch.

"Agent Castle, is it?" he asks.

"Yes," I say, claiming the seat across from him.

Once we're face-to-face, I can see that his eyes are brown like Carrie's.

"What can I help you with, Agent?"

"Do you know why you're here?" I ask.

"I know what they say I've done."

"You don't believe them?"

"I didn't kill anyone. I would never hurt anyone."

There is an honest, believable quality about him that is so very Carrie. "Have you looked at photos of your victims?"

"Not my victims," he says. "I would never, ever." He looks up, his bottom lip trembling before he levels me with a stare. "I wouldn't do those horrid things to anyone."

"Did you know you have a daughter, Mr. Morrow?"

"I do not."

"You do," I insist. "Selma Summer gave birth to your child and put her up for adoption."

"I don't know a Selma Summer."

"She says you do."

"I don't."

"Has your daughter ever come to visit you?"

"I don't have a daughter."

"You *do* have a daughter," I push. "You raped her mother."

"I did not rape—" he begins and then reels himself in. "I would never do such a thing."

"Why do you think she says that you did?"

"I think they all have me confused with someone else. I think there must be a look-alike. But I've given up hope that anyone will ever find him. This is my life now."

"Your daughter looks like you."

"What is her name? This woman you say is my daughter."

"Carrie."

"What does this woman do for a living? How does she live her life?"

"She's a nurse."

"She helps people. *Good.* Maybe she is my daughter."

"You were a counselor at a sexual assault clinic, correct?"

"I was. And I liked helping people."

"Carrie does, too," I say, believing that as truth. "But she has another side to her. A darker side."

"What does that mean?" he asks, and I feel like I'm getting somewhere. He's engaging with me.

"She killed her fiancé, but she says she doesn't remember doing it. What do you think I can do to help her remember?"

"She's not my daughter. I can't help you."

"Try."

"She's not my daughter," he says, more firmly this time. "Just because some woman kills someone does *not* make her my daughter. I thought maybe you came to help me. You don't want to help me. You want to turn someone else into a criminal because she's like me."

*Because she's like me.* Now he's claimed the other side of himself. "She's like you. And yet, you didn't kill anyone, right?"

"Why don't you leave now."

"I don't want to leave," I reply.

"I think you should leave."

"And if I don't?" I challenge.

His response is not what I expect. "I won't say another word."

In other words, he's promised me the childish silent treatment. I don't accept that answer. I look for any sign of his humanity. "Surely you want to know if you have a daughter."

He says nothing.

"Everyone needs to know who their family is."

Again, he says nothing.

I shift gears. I try a different tactic, pushing him, not coddling him, using the information I've read about Norman over the days since finding out he's Carrie's father. "Selma says you were gentle, touching her, kissing her. She wanted to slow down and then you changed. You strangled her. You hurt her. Is that how it started? You just wanted to touch your victims, and then they made you angry? Maybe they rejected you? So you had to kill them?"

He says nothing.

For ten minutes I try to get him to speak, but he just won't let me push his buttons.

Finally, I say, "If you decide you want to talk to me, the warden knows how to reach me."

I try to stand up and suddenly his legs grab my legs. My heart leaps and I struggle to free myself. "I was never gentle. I liked to surprise them," he says, his voice this raspy, deeper baritone, his eyes darker, shifty. *Evil.*

I twist again and free one leg, ramming him in the groin. He grunts and releases me while I scramble to my feet. The door bursts open behind me and the warden joins me. "Are you okay?"

"I'm fine," I say, holding up a hand for him to stay silent.

Norman is leaning down, his face toward the table, and starts laughing. "Tell me, Agent Castle." His head lifts and he looks at me, evil barely contained in human skin. "Did she stab him? Is she *just* like me?"

"Yes," I say. "She stabbed him."

"Do you know why she stabbed him?"

"No. *Tell me.*"

"Because every time the knife goes in, you're killing them all over again." He gurgles out more laughter and his head tilts back. I don't stay to look into those eyes again. I leave.

And I leave knowing that the same cold, hard, flat stare I saw in Norman's eyes I'd seen in Carrie's eyes when she'd spoken of Lana. Evil lives in father and daughter.

# Chapter Ninety-One

I exit the prison to find my own father leaning on his muscle car, legs in front of him, ankles crossed.

"What are you doing here?" I ask.

"Aiden told me about his conversation with you. You believe Carrie is a killer, just like her father. You went to the same place I'd go. What'd you find out?"

"You know what I found."

"She's a cold-blooded killer."

"Yes, but I can't prove it."

"You know what you need to do."

He means break the rules to break her.

"I'm an FBI agent, Dad. You know how I feel about my job."

"Sworn to protect and serve. How is letting a criminal walk free to kill again doing either of those things?"

He's pushing me, and not in a good way. "I need to go home and think."

"Whit caught his killer. He said he thought the person killing people and faking suicides was a serial killer, the guy he thought was a Spider Man protégé, but you said no. You said it sounded like revenge killings. You were right. Trust yourself. You're good at what you do."

I let that sink in with appreciation for his words. "Thank you."

"Go think."

I nod, turn away from him, and walk to my car, climbing inside and grabbing the steering wheel, shaking my head with the reality of my situation. I have nothing on Carrie now. Unless I find the weapon with her prints, she'll go free.

I start my engine and my dad pulls up next to me, driver's side to driver's side, his window down. "She'll sleep easy tonight. Will you? One day you'll figure out that you're a Castle, honey. Some people say. Castles do." He winks. "Love you, kiddo." He revs his engine and drives away.

# Chapter Ninety-Two

I tell myself to go home. I don't go home. I end up in front of Carrie Reynolds's home. The home she once shared with Oliver Phoenix. A man who believed her to be the best thing that ever happened to him. Instead, she ended him. I turn on the recorder on my phone. Anything I capture may or may not be admissible in court, but it might be enough to shift the narrative of Lana killing Oliver.

One last thought has me latching my phone to my waistband and sliding out of my coat, not wanting the bulkiness to muffle the recording. Drawing a steeling breath, I exit into the bitter cold evening, but I'm hot. I'm angry. I'm ready to make this visit with Carrie count. And yet, my steps are slowed, measured. My actions calculated.

Once on the porch, I ring the bell. Carrie answers. She's in jeans and a pink sweater, her dark hair soft around her shoulders. She looks sweet, innocent, angelic. The devil in sheep's clothing. Her greeting is far from welcoming. "What are you doing here, Agent Castle?" she asks.

Undeterred I ask, "Can we talk?"

"No. No, I don't think I want to talk. I need to breathe a little. You have your killer. Lana killed Oliver."

"Part of our investigation includes wrapping up all loose ends. Can I please just come in for a minute?"

"Another time. Call Ms. Littleton. I'm sorry." Her eyes tear up. "I can't do this." She shuts the door and the lock slides into place.

My head lowers, chin to my chest. "Damn it," I whisper, hesitating before I walk back to my car and climb inside. I'm about to start the engine again when my father's words play in my head: *She'll sleep easy tonight. Will you?*

I open the door and I'm out, up the walkway, and on her doorstep in ten seconds. I ring the bell. When she doesn't answer, I knock. She cracks the door open, and I don't give myself time to second-guess my actions. I'll be suspended. I don't give a flying flip.

"Go away," she says. "I'm calling Ms. Littleton."

She tries to shut the door again. I shove it backward, ramming it into her face. She yells out and goes down. I charge over the threshold. She's on her knees, holding her face, and when she looks up at me, blood streams from her nose, down her chin, staining her teeth as she laughs, evil, deep. "I can have your badge for this, Agent Castle. Won't that be fun? No more Agent Castle. You'll be just another Andrea."

I kneel in front of her. "You killed him."

"If I did, you will never be agent enough to prove it. You're no agent at all."

"He loved you."

"I hated him," she says. "He was going to leave me over my father. Leave *me*. I deserved better."

"So you stabbed him."

She laughs again and licks blood from her lip, moaning a bit as if it tastes good. "Blood scares some people, but it doesn't me. It's the juice of life."

"Where'd you put the knife, Carrie?"

She smirks. "Wouldn't you like to know."

"Tell me."

"No. *Never.* Should we call the police now?"

I grab my phone, pull up the recording, and send it to Aiden. Then I play it for Carrie. She listens to it and then looks at me, and I watch the animal in her come to life, snarling before she launches herself at me. But I'm ready for her. I have her flat on her stomach, my foot between her shoulders, before she ever knows what's happening. Thank you, Dad. Yes, this position really works. While she shouts profanity at me, I snatch my phone from the floor and dial 911.

———

It's eight the next morning when I walk out of the police station where Carrie has been booked for the murder of Oliver Phoenix. Ms. Littleton was, of course, appalled at my actions. She demanded my suspension. And she might have gotten it if it had taken me more than three hours to break Carrie Reynolds in the interrogation room. Carrie went from whimpering, innocent angel to a demon in the blink of an eye, and when she did, she attacked Ms. Littleton. With four long scratches down her face, Ms. Littleton's asked to be removed as Carrie's counsel.

I slide into my Jeep and dial my father.

"Daughter. Why the hell are you calling me this early?"

A female voice in the background says, "Is that Susie? I thought you were done with her?"

"My daughter. Go back to sleep. Talk to me, Sugar Bear. What's happening?"

"How about a steak, Dad?"

"I thought you'd never ask. Let me guess. You've decided life as a Castle isn't such a bad road to pave?"

"I've always been a proud Castle, Dad. I'll see you tonight? Six?"

"Six it is. And bring that banana pudding you make."

"I'll bring the pudding. Right now, I'm going home to bed. I haven't slept."

"Sleep well, Andi," he says and hangs up.

I start my car. And there is no question. I will definitely be sleeping like a baby.

# ACKNOWLEDGMENTS

To my husband, Diego, who I'd say watches way too much true crime if he didn't always have a great idea on how to kill off a character. Thank you for talking me off the ledge every time I get stuck at a spot in a book and plotting murder with me. Thank you also to my assistant of over a decade, Emily, who sleeps with the lights on when I'm writing a thriller but still manages to be my cheerleader every chance she gets.

# ABOUT THE AUTHOR

*Photo © 2013 Teresa Lee*

L. R. Jones is a pseudonym for *New York Times* and *USA Today* best-selling author Lisa Renee Jones. Her dark, edgy fiction includes the novels *You Look Beautiful Tonight*, *The Poet*, *A Perfect Lie*, and the Lilah Love series. Prior to publishing, Lisa owned a multistate staffing agency recognized by the *Austin Business Journal* and was #7 in *Entrepreneur* magazine's list of growing women-owned businesses. Lisa lives in Colorado with her husband, a cat who always has something to say, and a golden retriever who's afraid of her own bark. For more information, visit www.lisareneejones.com.